VISIBLE LIGHT

"Cassandra"—the Hugo Award-winning tale of a woman cursed with a unique, prophetic madness.

"Threads of Time"—an unforgettable reminder that when you play tricks in time, Time itself may play the greatest trick on you.

"The Last Tower"—in which an old man discovers how an "ally" may conquer defenses an enemy could never breach.

"The Brothers"—a brand-new story set in a land of castles, kings, and curses, where the Fair Folk presume to meddle in the affairs of men.

So check your boarding pass one more time, then settle back to while away a traveler's wait with these and the other interstellar tales gathered for you in—

By the same author in
Methuen Paperbacks

Downbelow Station
Pride of Chanur
Chanur's Venture
Merchanter's Luck
The Chronicles of Morgaine
Voyager in Night
Forty Thousand in Gehenna
Cuckoo's Egg
The Faded Sun Trilogy
The Kif Strike Back

VISIBLE LIGHT

C.J. CHERRYH

A Methuen Paperback

A Methuen Paperback

VISIBLE LIGHT

British Library Cataloguing in Publication Data

Cherryh, C. J.
  Visible light.
  I. Title
  813'.54[F]   PS3553.H358

  ISBN 0-413-16120-X

First published in Great Britain 1988
by Methuen London Ltd
11 New Fetter Lane, London EC4P 4EE

Printed and bound in Great Britain
by Richard Clay Ltd, Bungay, Suffolk

Dedication

THE CREDIT FOR this collection plainly goes to Don Wollheim, who came up with the idea back in 1979. It took me a few more years, to be sure, to have *written* a body of short fiction; and for a few years after that what I had written was scattered here and there and some of it too currently in print. So I put the project off. And put it off.

Then I thought of it several times and put it off again—until in 1984 Don inquired not once but a second time where that collection was.

To answer the question, here it is, Don; and this one is dedicated to you.

Table of Contents

Introduction

IN A COLLECTION like this the writer has the rare chance to do a very old-fashioned thing: to speak to the audience, like the herald coming out before the ancient play to explain briefly what the audience is about to see—and perhaps to let the audience peek behind the scenes—Down this street, mark you, lies the house of the Old Man, and here the wineseller—

Well, on *this* street lives a bit of fantasy and a bit of science fiction, here reside stories from my first years and some from not so long ago—

I introduce one brand new tale, because that's only fair.

I have gathered the rest by no particular logic except the desire to present some balance of early and later material, some mixture of science fiction and fantasy, and in a couple of instances to preserve work that has never appeared in any anthology.

One of the additional benefits of walking onto the stage like this is the chance to lower the mask and give the audience an insight into the mind behind the creation. So stop here, ignore all the intervening passages, and go straight to the stories if you simply enjoy my craft and care nothing for the creator— being creator, I am no less pleased by that. Go, sample, enjoy.

FOR THOSE WHO want to know something of *me*, myself, and what I am—well, let me couch this introduction in a mode more familiar to me: let me set a scene for you. I sit on a crate on a dockside, well, let's make it a lot of baggage, a battered suitcase and a lot of other crates round about, with tags and stickers abundant. SEE EARTH FIRST, one sticker says, quite antique and scratched. And this is a metal place, full of coolant fumes and fuel smells. Gears clash, hydraulics wheeze, and fans hum away overhead, while our ship is loading its heavier cargo.

You sit there on your suitcase just the same as I, and I suppose our boarding call is what we're waiting for. Passers-by may stop. But it's mainly you and me.

"What do *you* do?" you ask, curious about this woman, myself, who am the ancient mariner of this dockside: I have that look—a little elsewhere, a little preoccupied, baggage all scarred with travels. I rarely give the real answer to that question of yours. "I'm a writer," I usually say. But the clock sweeps into the small hours—starships have no respect for planet-time—and we talk together the way travelers will who meet for a few hours and speak with absolute honesty precisely because they are absolute strangers. I am moved by some such thing, and I take a sip of what I have gotten from the counter yonder and you take a sip of yours and we are instantly philosophers.

"Call me a storyteller," I say, recalling another mariner. "That's at least *one* of the world's oldest professions, if not the oldest."

"You write books?" you ask. "Are you in the magazines?"

"Oh," say I, "yes. But that's not the important part. I tell stories, that's what I do. Tonight in New Guinea, in New Hampshire, in Tehuantepec and Ulaanbaatar, quite probably someone is telling a story: we still build campfires, we still watch the embers and imagine castles, don't we—down there? They weave stories down there, the same as they did around the first campfire in the world; they still do. Someone asks for the story of the big snow or the wonderful ship—there's very little difference in what we do. You just have to have a hearer."

"*Do* you have to?"

"I'm not sure about that. I wrote about something like that—people called the elee who knew their world was dying. And they had rather make statues than spaceships, though they knew no eye would ever see them."

"It would last."

"On a dead world. Under a cinder of a sun. It's an old question, isn't it, whether art created for the void has meaning—whether the tree falling in solitude makes a sound or not. What's a word without a hearer? Without that contact, spark flying from point to point across space and time, art is void—like the art of the elee, made for the dark and the silence."

"Then it matters what somebody else thinks of it?"

"It matters to somebody else. It matters to me. But that it matters to him hardly matters to me the way it does to him."

"That's crazy."

"I don't live his life. But I'm glad if he likes what I do. I'm sorry if he doesn't. I hope he finds someone who can talk to him. Everyone needs that. I do all I can. Perhaps the elee have a point."

"You mean you don't write for the critics."

"Only so far as they're human. And I am. Let me tell you, I don't believe in systems. I only use them."

"You mean all critics are crooked?"

"Oh, no. It's only a system. There are good critics. The best ones can point out the deep things in a book or a painting: they can see things you and I might miss. They have an insight like a writer's or an artist's. But their skill isn't so much adding to a book as helping a reader see ideas in it he might have missed. But there are various sorts of critics. And some of them do very dangerous things."

"Like?"

"Let me tell you: there's criticism and there's fault-finding. A tale is made for a hearer, to touch a heart. To criticize the quality of the heart it touches—that's a perilously self-loving act, isn't it? Criticizing the message itself, well, that might be useful. But the critic properly needs as much space to do it in as the writer took to develop it. And then the critic's a novelist, isn't he? Or a painter. He's one of *us*. And many of us are, you know. The best of us are. But criticism as a science—" I take here another sip. Thoughts like this require it. "Criticism is always in danger of becoming a system. Or of submitting to one."

"You said you don't believe in systems."

"Oh, I believe they exist. They exist everywhere. And more and more of them exist. The *use* of art, the manipulation of art and science by committees and governments, by demographics analysts and sales organizations, by social engineers, oh, yes—*and* by academe—all of this—It's happening at a greater pace and with more calculation than it ever has in all of history."

"And that worries you."

"Profoundly. I wrote a book about it. About art and the state. Art is a very powerful force. And the state would inevitably like to wield the wielder. It wants its posterity. Most of all it wants its safety."

"You write a lot about that?"

"*That I write* is about that. Do you see? It isn't fiction. It isn't illusion. *That I write* is a reality. Life is art *and* science. Look at your hand. What do you see? Flesh? Bone? Atoms? It's all moving. Electrons and quarks exist in constant motion. You think you know what reality is? Reality is an artifact of our senses."

"Artifact? Like old arrowheads?"

"A thing made. Your reality is an artifact of your senses. Your mind assembles the data you perceive in an acceptable order. Do you think this floor is real? But *what* is it, really? A whirl of particles. Matter and energy. We can't see the atoms dance: we can scarcely see the stars. We're suspended between these two abysses of the infinitely small and the infinitely vast, and we deceive ourselves if we believe too much in the blue sky and the green earth. Even color, you know, is simply wavelength. And solidity is the attraction of particles."

"Then it's another system."

"You've got it. Another system. Here we sit, an intersection of particles in the vast now. Past and future are equally illusory."

"We *know* what happened in the past."

"Not really."

"You mean you don't believe in books either."

"I don't believe in history."

"Then what's it all worth?"

"A great deal. As much as my own books are worth. They're equally true."

"You said it was false!"

"Oh, generally history is fiction. I *taught* history. I *know* some facts of history as well as they can be known. I've read original documents in the original languages. I've *been* where the battles were fought. And every year history gets condensed a little more and a little more, simplified, do you see? You've heard of Thermopylae. But what you've heard happened there, is likely the *average* of the effect it had, not the meticulous truth of what went on. And remember that the winners write the histories. The events were far more yea and nay and zig and zag than you believe: a newspaper of the day would have deluged you with contradictory reports and subjective analyses, so that you would be quite bewildered and confounded by what history records as a simple situation—three hundred Spartans standing off the Persians. But were there three hundred? It wasn't that simple. It was far more interesting. The behind-the-scenes was as complicated as things are in real life: more complicated than today's news ever reports anything, with treacheries and feuds going back hundreds of years into incidents and personalities many of the men on that field would have been amazed to know about. Even they didn't see everything. And they died for it."

"Anyone who tried to learn history the way it was— he'd go crazy."

"He'd spend a billion lifetimes. But it doesn't matter. The past is as true as my books. Fiction and history are equivalent."

"And today? You don't think we see what's going on today either."

"We see less than we ought. We depend on eyes and ears and memory. And memory's very treacherous. Perception itself is subjective, and memory's a timetrip, far trickier than the human eye."

"It all sounds crazy."

"The totality of what's going on would be too much. It would make you crazy. So a human being selects what he'll see and remember and forms a logical framework to help him systematize the few things he keeps."

"Systems again."

"I say that I distrust them. That's what makes me an artist. Consider: if it's so very difficult to behold a mote of dust on your fingertip, to behold the sun itself for what it truly is, how do we exist from day to day? By filtering out what confuses us. My stories do the opposite. Like the practice of science, do you see? A story is a moment of profound examination of things in greater reality and sharper focus than we usually see them. It's a sharing of perception in this dynamic, motile universe, in which two human minds can momentarily orbit the same focus, like a pair of vastly complex planets, each with its own civilization, orbiting a star that they strive to comprehend, each in its own way. And when you talk about analyzing governments and not single individuals: as well proceed from the dustmote to the wide galaxy. Think of the filters and perceptual screens governments and social systems erect to protect themselves."

"You distrust governments?"

"I find them fascinating. There was an old Roman, Vergilius Maro—"

"Vergil."

"Just so. He said government itself was an artform, the same as great sculpture and great books, and practiced in similar mode—emotionally. I think I agree with the Roman."

"Isn't that a system?"

"Of course it's a system. The trick is to make the system as wide as possible. Everything I think is just that: *thinking*; it's in constant motion. It, like all my component parts, changes. It has to. The universe is a place too wonderful to ignore."

"You think most of us live in ignorance?"

"Most of us are busy. Most of us are too busy about things that give us too little time to think. I write about people who See, who See things differently and who find the Systems stripped away, or exchanged for other Systems, so that they pass from world to world in some lightning-stroke of an understanding, or the slow erosion and reconstruction of things they thought they knew."

"But does one man matter?"

"I think two kinds of humanity create events: fools and visionaries. Chaos itself may be illusion. Perhaps what we do *does* matter. I think it's a chance worth taking. I hate to leave it all to the fools."

"But who's a fool?"

"Any of us. Mostly those who never wonder if they're fools."

"That's arrogance."

"Of course it is. But the fools aren't listening. We can never insult them."

"You think what you write matters?"

"Let me tell you: for me the purest and truest art in the world is science fiction."

"It's escapist."

"It's romance. It's the world as it can be, ought to be—must someday, somewhere be, if we can only find enough of the component parts and shove them together. Science fiction is the oldest sort of tale-telling, you know. Homer; Sinbad's story; Gilgamesh; Beowulf; and up and up the line of history wherever mankind's scouts encounter the unknown. Not a military metaphor. It's a peaceful progress. Like the whales in their migrations. Tale-telling is the most peaceful thing we do. It's investigatory. The best tale-telling always has been full of what-if. The old Greek peasant who laid down the tools of a hard day's labor to hear about Odysseus's trip beyond the rim of his world—he wasn't an escapist. He was dreaming. Mind-stretching at the end of a stultifying day. He might not go. But his children's children might. *Someone* would. And that makes his day's hard work *worth* something to the future; it makes this farmer and his well-tilled field participant in the progress of his world, and his cabbages have then a cosmic importance."

"Is he worth something?"

"Maybe he was your ancestor. Maybe he fed the ancestor of the designer who made this ship."

"What's that worth? What's anything worth, if you don't believe in systems?"

"Ah. You still misunderstand me. Anything is worth everything. Everything is important. It's all one system, from the dustmote to the star. It's only that our systems are too small."

"So you give this world up? You're leaving it?"

"Aren't you?"

"I've got business out there."

"Good. That's very fine. Remember the cabbages."

"What's your business out there?"

"History."

"You don't believe in it!"

"And stories. They're equal. Fusing the past with now and tomorrow. That's what's in the crates. History. Stories."

"Where are you taking them?"

"As far as I can. You know what I'll do when I get there? I'll sit down with you and your kids born somewhere far from Earth and I'll say: listen, youngest, I've got a story to tell you, about where you came from and why you're going, and what it all means anyway. It's a story about *you*, and about me, and a time very much like this one . . . a dangerous time. But all times are dangerous.

"Once upon a time, I'll say. *Once upon a time* is the only true enchantment the elves left to us, the gift of truthful lies and travel in time and space.

"*Once upon a time* there were listeners round a fire; *once upon a time* there will be a microfiche or—vastly to be treasured—a real paper book aboard a ship named *Argo* (like the one ages past) in quest of things we haven't dreamed of. But they'll dream of something more than that. "Youngest, I'll say, when I fly I always look out the window—I do it as a ritual when I remember it. I look for myself. But I also look for the sake of all the dreamers in all the ages of this world who would have given their very lives to catch one glimpse of the world and the stars the way I can see them for hour upon hour out that window.

"Someday, youngest, someone will take that look for me—oh, at Beta Lyrae; or at huge Aldebaran; or Tau Ceti, which I've named Pell's Star—"

I pause. I sip my drink, almost the last, and look at the clock, where the time runs close to boarding. It's time to think about the baggage. We have, perhaps, amazed each other. Travelers often do.

We send our baggage off with the handlers. We exchange pleasantries about the trip, about the schedule. We retreat to those banalities better-mannered strangers use to fill the time.

Words and words. A story teller isn't concerned with words.

The boarding call goes out. We form our mundane line and search after tickets and visas. The dock resounds with foreign names and the clank of machinery.

It is of course, always an age of wonders. The true gift is remembering to look out the windows, and to let the thoughts run backward and forward and wide to the breadth and height of all that's ever been and might yet be—

Once upon a time, I tell you.

I

I SIT IN the observation lounge. Window-staring. The moon is long behind us, and Earth is farther still. And a step sounds near enough to tell me someone is interested in me or the window.

"Ah," I say, and smile. We've met before.

"What do you see out there?" you ask. It sounds like challenge.

"Look for yourself," I say. It's a double-edged invitation. And for a time, you do.

"I've been thinking about history," you say at last.

"Oh?"

"About what good it is. People fight wars over it. They get their prejudices from it; and maybe what they think they remember wasn't even true in the first place."

"It's very unlikely that it is true, since history isn't."

"But if we didn't have all those books we'd have to make all those mistakes again. Wouldn't we? Whatever they were."

"Probably we'd make different ones. Maybe we'd do much worse."

"Maybe we ought to make up a better past. Maybe if all the writers in the world sat down and came up with a better history, and we could just sort of *lie* to everyone—I mean, where we're going, who'd *know*? Maybe if you just shot those history books out the airlock, maybe if you wrote us a new history, we could save us a war or two."

"That's what fantasy does, you know. It's making things over the way it should have been."

"But you can't go around believing in elves and dragons."

"The myths are true as history. Myths are about truth."

"There you go, sounding crazy again."

I laugh and flip a switch. The lap-computer comes alive on the table by the window. Words ripple past. "You know that's all myths *could* be. Truth. A system of truth, made as simple as its hearers. The old myths are still true. There's one I used to tell to my students—"

"When you taught history."

"Languages this time. Ancient languages. Eleven years of teaching. The first and second short stories I ever wrote were myths I used to tell my students. I'll show you one. I'll print it so you can read it. It was the second. It speaks about perceptions again." I press a key and send a fiche out from the microprinter; and smile, thinking on a classful of remembered faces, eleven years of students, all gathered together in one classroom like ghosts. And I think of campfires again, and a Greek hillside, and a theater, and the dusty hills of Troy. We all sit there, all of us, torchlight on our faces, in all the ghostly array of our cultures and our ancestral histories, folk out of Charlemagne's Empire, and Henry's, and the Khazars; we come from the fijords and the Sudan and the Carolinas, all of us whose ancestors would have taken axe to one another on sight. All of us sit and listen together to a Greek myth retold, all innocent of ancient murders.

"Stories matter," I say. "And what is history but another myth, with the poetry taken out?"

Dear old Greek, I think, passing on the microfiche, by whatever name you really lived, thank you for the loan. And thank you, my young friends of some years ago. This one's still your own.

Cassandra

FIRES.

They grew unbearable here.

Alis felt for the door of the flat and knew that it would be solid. She could feel the cool metal of the knob amid the flames . . . saw the shadow-stairs through the roiling smoke outside, clearly enough to feel her way down them, convincing her senses that they would bear her weight.

Crazy Alis. She made no haste. The fires burned steadily. She passed through them, descended the insubstantial steps to the solid ground—she could not abide the elevator, that closed space with the shadow-floor, that plummeted down and down; she made the ground floor, averted her eyes from the red, heatless flames.

A ghost said good morning to her . . . old man

Willis, thin and transparent against the leaping flames. She blinked, bade it good morning in return—did not miss old Willis's shake of the head as she opened the door and left. Noon traffic passed, heedless of the flames, the hulks that blazed in the street, the tumbling brick.

The apartment caved in—black bricks falling into the inferno, Hell amid the green, ghostly trees. Old Willis fled, burning, fell—turned to jerking, blackened flesh—died, daily. Alis no longer cried, hardly flinched. She ignored the horror spilling about her, forced her way through crumbling brick that held no substance, past busy ghosts that could not be troubled in their haste.

Kingsley's Cafe stood, whole, more so than the rest. It was refuge for the afternoon, a feeling of safety. She pushed open the door, heard the tinkle of a lost bell. Shadowy patrons looked, whispered.

Crazy Alis.

The whispers troubled her. She avoided their eyes and their presence, settled in a booth in the corner that bore only traces of the fire.

WAR, the headline in the vendor said in heavy type. She shivered, looked up into Sam Kingsley's wraithlike face.

"Coffee," she said. "Ham sandwich." It was constantly the same. She varied not even the order. Mad Alis. Her affliction supported her. A check came each month, since the hospital had turned her out. Weekly she returned to the clinic, to doctors who now faded like the others. The building burned about them. Smoke rolled down the blue, antiseptic halls. Last week a patient ran—burning—

A rattle of china. Sam set the coffee on the table, came back shortly and brought the sandwich. She bent her head and ate, transparent food on half-broken china, a cracked, fire-smudged cup with a transparent handle. She ate, hungry enough to overcome the horror that had become ordinary. A hundred times seen, the most terrible sights lost their power over her: she no longer cried at shadows. She talked to ghosts and touched them, ate the food that somehow stilled the ache in her belly, wore the same too-large black sweater and worn blue shirt and gray slacks because they were all she had that seemed solid. Nightly she washed them and dried them and put them on the next day, letting others hang in the closet. They were the only solid ones.

She did not tell the doctors these things. A lifetime in and out of hospitals had made her wary of confidences. She knew what to say. Her half-vision let her smile at ghost-faces, cannily manipulate their charts and cards, sitting in the ruins that had begun to smolder by late afternoon. A blackened corpse lay in the hall. She did not flinch when she smiled good-naturedly at the doctor.

They gave her medicines. The medicines stopped the dreams, the siren screams, the running steps in the night past her apartment. They let her sleep in the ghostly bed, high above ruin, with the flames crackling and the voices screaming. She did not speak of these things. Years in hospitals had taught her. She complained only of nightmares, and restlessness, and they let her have more of the red pills.

WAR, the headline blazoned.

The cup rattled and trembled against the saucer as

she picked it up. She swallowed the last bit of bread and washed it down with coffee, tried not to look beyond the broken front window, where twisted metal hulks smoked on the street. She stayed, as she did each day, and Sam grudgingly refilled her cup, which she would nurse as far as she could and then she would order another one. She lifted it, savoring the feeling of it, stopping the trembling of her hands.

The bell jingled faintly. A man closed the door, settled at the counter.

Whole, clear in her eyes. She stared at him, startled, heart pounding. He ordered coffee, moved to buy a paper from the vendor, settled again and let the coffee grow cold while he read the news. She had view only of his back while he read—scuffed brown leather coat, brown hair a little over his collar. At last he drank the cooled coffee all at one draught, shoved money onto the counter and left the paper lying, headlines turned face down.

A young face, flesh and bone among the ghosts. He ignored them all and went for the door.

Alis thrust herself from her booth.

"Hey!" Sam called at her.

She rummaged in her purse as the bell jingled, flung a bill onto the counter, heedless that it was a five. Fear was coppery in her mouth; he was gone. She fled the cafe, edged round debris without thinking of it, saw his back disappearing among the ghosts.

She ran, shouldering them, braving the flames— cried out as debris showered painlessly on her, and kept running.

Ghosts turned and stared, shocked—*he* did likewise, and she ran to him, stunned to see the same shock on his face, regarding her.

"What is it?" he asked.

She blinked, dazed to realize he saw her no differently than the others. She could not answer. In irritation he started walking again, and she followed. Tears slid down her face, her breath hard in her throat. People stared. He noticed her presence and walked faster, through debris, through fires. A wall began to fall and she cried out despite herself.

He jerked about. The dust and the soot rose up as a cloud behind him. His face was distraught and angry. He stared at her as the others did. Mothers drew children away from the scene. A band of youths stared, cold-eyed and laughing.

"Wait," she said. He opened his mouth as if he would curse her; she flinched, and the tears were cold in the heatless wind of the fires. His face twisted in an embarrassed pity. He thrust a hand into his pocket and began to pull out money, hastily, tried to give it to her. She shook her head furiously, trying to stop the tears—stared upward, flinching, as another building fell into flames.

"What's wrong?" he asked her. "What's wrong with you?"

"Please," she said. He looked about at the staring ghosts, then began to walk slowly. She walked with him, nerving herself not to cry out at the ruin, the pale moving figures that wandered through burned shells of buildings, the twisted corpses in the street, where traffic moved.

"What's your name?" he asked. She told him. He gazed at her from time to time as they walked, a frown creasing his brow. He had a face well-worn for youth, a tiny scar beside the mouth. He looked older than she. She felt uncomfortable in the way his eyes traveled over her: she decided to accept it—to bear with anything that gave her this one solid presence. Against every inclination she reached her hand into the bend of his arm, tightened her fingers on the worn leather. He accepted it.

And after a time he slid his arm behind her and about her waist, and they walked like lovers.

WAR, the headline at the newsstand cried.

He started to turn into a street by Tenn's Hardware. She balked at what she saw there. He paused when he felt it, faced her with his back to the fires of that burning.

"Don't go," she said.

"Where do you want to go?"

She shrugged helplessly, indicated the main street, the other direction.

He talked to her then, as he might talk to a child, humoring her fear. It was pity. Some treated her that way. She recognized it, and took even that.

His name was Jim. He had come into the city yesterday, hitched rides. He was looking for work. He knew no one in the city. She listened to his rambling awkwardness, reading through it. When he was done, she stared at him still, and saw his face contract in dismay at her.

"I'm not crazy," she told him, which was a lie that everyone in Sudbury would have known, only *he* would not, knowing no one. His face was true and

29

solid, and the tiny scar by the mouth made it hard when he was thinking; at another time she would have been terrified of him. Now she was terrified of losing him amid the ghosts.

"It's the war," he said.

She nodded, trying to look at him and not at the fires. His fingers touched her arm, gently. "It's the war," he said again. "It's all crazy. Everyone's crazy."

And then he put his hand on her shoulder and turned her back the other way, toward the park, where green leaves waved over black, skeletal limbs. They walked along the lake, and for the first time in a long time she drew breath and felt a whole, sane presence beside her.

They bought corn, and sat on the grass by the lake, and flung it to the spectral swans. Wraiths of passersby were few, only enough to keep a feeling of occupancy about the place—old people, mostly, tottering about the deliberate tranquility of their routine despite the headlines.

"Do you see them," she ventured to ask him finally, "all thin and gray?"

He did not understand, did not take her literally, only shrugged. Warily, she abandoned that questioning at once. She rose to her feet and stared at the horizon, where the smoke bannered on the wind.

"Buy you supper?" he asked.

She turned, prepared for this, and managed a shy, desperate smile. "Yes," she said, knowing what else he reckoned to buy with that—willing, and hating herself, and desperately afraid that he would walk away, tonight, tomorrow. She did not know men. She had no idea what she could say or do to prevent his leaving, only that he would when someday he recognized her madness.

Even her parents had not been able to bear with that—visited her only at first in the hospitals, and then only on holidays, and then not at all. She did not know where they were.

There was a neighbor boy who drowned. She had said he would. She had cried for it. All the town said it was she who pushed him.

Crazy Alis.

Fantasizes, the doctors said. Not dangerous.

They let her out. There were special schools, state schools.

And from time to time—hospitals.

Tranquilizers.

She had left the red pills at home. The realization brought sweat to her palms. They gave sleep. They stopped the dreams. She clamped her lips against the panic and made up her mind that she would not need them—not while she was not alone. She slipped her hand into his arm and walked with him, secure and strange, up the steps from the park to the streets.

And stopped.

The fires were out.

Ghost-buildings rose above their jagged and windowless shells. Wraiths moved through masses of debris, almost obscured at times. He tugged her on, but her step faltered, made him look at her strangely and put his arm about her.

"You're shivering," he said. "Cold?"

She shook her head, tried to smile. The fires were out. She tried to take it for a good omen. The nightmare was over. She looked up into his solid, con-

cerned face, and her smile almost became a wild
laugh.

"I'm hungry," she said.

THEY LINGERED over a dinner in Graben's—he
in his battered jacket, she in her sweater that hung at
the tails and elbows: the spectral patrons were in far
better clothes, and stared at them, and they were set
in a corner nearest the door, where they would be
less visible. There was cracked crystal and broken
china on insubstantial tables, and the stars winked
coldly in gaping ruin above the wan glittering of the
broken chandeliers.

Ruins, cold, peaceful ruin.

Alis looked about her calmly. One could live in
ruins, only so the fires were gone.

And there was Jim, who smiled at her without any
touch of pity, only a wild, fey desperation that she
understood—who spent more than he could afford
in Graben's, the inside of which she had never hoped
to see—and told her—predictably—that she was beautiful. Others had said it. Vaguely she resented such
triteness from him, from him whom she had decided
to trust. She smiled sadly when he said it; and gave
it up for a frown; and, fearful of offending him with
her melancholies, made it a smile again.

Crazy Alis. He would learn and leave tonight if
she were not careful. She tried to put on gaiety, tried
to laugh.

And then the music stopped in the restaurant, and
the noise of the other diners went dead, and the
speaker was giving an inane announcement.

Shelters . . . shelters . . . shelters.

Screams broke out. Chairs overturned.

Alis went limp in her chair, felt Jim's cold, solid hand tugging at hers, saw his frightened face mouthing her name as he took her up into his arms, pulled her with him, started running.

The cold air outside hit her, shocked her into sight of the ruins again, wraith figures pelting toward that chaos where the fires had been worst.

And she knew.

"No!" she cried, pulling at his arm. "No!" she insisted, and bodies half-seen buffeted them in a rush to destruction. He yielded to her sudden certainty, gripped her hand and fled with her against the crowds as the sirens wailed madness through the night—fled with her as she ran her sighted way through the ruin.

And into Kingsley's, where cafe tables stood abandoned with food still on them, doors ajar, chairs overturned. Back they went into the kitchens and down and down into the cellar, the dark, the cold safety from the flames.

No others found them there. At last the earth shook, too deep for sound. The sirens ceased and did not come on again.

They lay in the dark and clutched each other and shivered, and above them for hours raged the sound of fire, smoke sometimes drifting in to sting their eyes and noses. There was the distant crash of brick, rumblings that shook the ground, that came near, but never touched their refuge.

And in the morning, with the scent of fire still in the air, they crept up into the murky daylight.

The ruins were still and hushed. The ghost-buildings were solid now, mere shells. The wraiths were gone. It was the fires themselves that were strange, some true, some not, playing above dark, cold brick, and most were fading.

Jim swore softly, over and over again, and wept.

When she looked at him she was dry-eyed, for she had done her crying already.

And she listened as he began to talk about food, about leaving the city, the two of them. "All right," she said.

Then clamped her lips, shut her eyes against what she saw in his face. When she opened them it was still true, the sudden transparency, the wash of blood. She trembled, and he shook at her, his ghost-face distraught.

"What's wrong?" he asked. "What's wrong?"

She could not tell him, would not. She remembered the boy who had drowned, remembered the other ghosts. Of a sudden she tore from his hands and ran, dodging the maze of debris that, this morning, was solid.

"Alis!" he cried and came after her.

"No!" she cried suddenly, turning, seeing the unstable wall, the cascading brick. She started back and stopped, unable to force herself. She held out her hands to warn him back, saw them solid.

The brick rumbled, fell. Dust came up, thick for a moment, obscuring everything.

She stood still, hands at her sides, then wiped her sooty face and turned and started walking, keeping to the center of the dead streets.

Overhead, clouds gathered, heavy with rain.

She wandered at peace now, seeing the rain spot the pavement, not yet feeling it.

In time the rain did fall, and the ruins became chill and cold. She visited the dead lake and the burned trees, the ruin of Graben's, out of which she gathered a string of crystal to wear.

She smiled when, a day later, a looter drove her from her food supply. He had a wraith's look, and she laughed from a place he did not dare to climb and told him so.

And recovered her cache later when it came true, and settled among the ruined shells that held no further threat, no other nightmares, with her crystal necklace and tomorrows that were the same as today.

One could live in ruins, only so the fires were gone.

And the ghosts were all in the past, invisible.

II

"I'VE BEEN THINKING about perceptions," you say. We sit again beneath the observation window. The ship is slowly outbound. The view is magnificent, all stars.

"Oh?"

"And time."

"How so?"

"Do you believe in timetravel?"

"Time is all around us. Looking at the stars is looking into time. The light from that red one, say, left home a hundred years ago. Two hundred. If our own sun winked out this moment we would live in their eyes for two hundred years—if they had a powerful telescope to see us with. If the photons didn't scatter. If space didn't curve. Perhaps that star out there has already died, two hundred years ago." I entertain a brief thought of a nova. Of a shockwave kicking dustclouds into swirls to birth new stars. "Perhaps our sun died eight minutes ago. We'd just now find it out. When we look at the stars we see into time. When we pass lightspeed we travel through the wavefront of a moment that left its star in lightscatter years ago, and we overtake the real, the present moment when we reach another star. But to surpass that moment and arrive *before* we left—that would be a difficult concept. That requires more than simultaneity. The causalties boggle the mind. If time is the motion of particles away from their origin, then timetravel locally requires us to reverse the entire motion of the universe, and the inertia of the moving universe is the most powerful thing I can think of. Besides, when we form the concept of travel in time, you and I, can we have pushed a button in our own future and come here *knowing* we pushed it? It all gives me a headache."

"You wrote about timetravel."

"You've been reading my books?"

"Your first book was about timetravel."

"Gate of Ivrel."

"It was like a fantasy."

"Or science fiction—depends on whose viewpoint you take. I wander over that dividing line now and again. It's part of that business of baggage, you understand. Past and future, fused.The ultimate meddling with history. But remember that what I write is always as true as history. And time travel never worked right in my future. I always distrusted it."

"You're facetious again."

"Often. Let me show you something." I flick on the computer and call up memory. "You wonder about perception and time and history. *Gate* was a very old story for me—I began part of that story when I was fourteen. It went through a lot of sea-changes on its way. My students had something to do with it too—when I was near thirty. We talked about time travel. And the motion of worlds in space and the distance between the stars. We talked about everything. Well, *Gate*, being fantasy-like, lost this little bit."

"You mean it got dropped out?"

"It needed to go. This bit starts in a very futuristic world; and *Gate* begins in what might be an ancient one. But if you *have* read that book, I can tell you that Harrh of this little fragment was Liell, long before the events in *Gate*; and that says enough. If you haven't, never mind: I won't give away who Liell was. Just call it a story about timetravel, in the days when the Gates led across qhalur spacetime, and knit their empire together. . . ."

The Threads of Time

IT WAS POSSIBLE that the Gates were killing the qhal. They were everywhere, on every world, had been a fact of life for five thousand years, and linked the whole net of qhalur civilization into one present-tense coherency.

They had not, to be sure, invented the Gates. Chance gave them that gift . . . on a dead world of their own sun. One Gate stood—made by unknown hands.

And the qhal made others, imitating what they found. The Gates were instantaneous transfer, not alone from place to place, but, because of the motion of worlds and suns and the traveling galaxies— involving time.

There was an end of time. Ah, qhal *could* venture anything. If one supposed, if one believed, if one were very *sure*, one could step through a Gate to a Gate that would/might exist on some other distant world.

And if one were wrong?

If it did not exist?

If it never had?

Time warped in the Gate-passage. One could step across light-years, unaged; so it was possible to outrace light and time.

Did one not want to die, bound to a single lifespan? Go forward. See the future. Visit the world/worlds to come.

But never go back. Never tamper. Never alter the past.

There was an End of Time.

It was the place where qhal gathered, who had been farthest and lost their courage for traveling on. It was the point beyond which no one had courage, where descendants shared the world with living ancestors in greater and greater numbers, the jaded, the restless, who reached this age and felt their will erode away.

It was the place where hope ended. Oh, a few went farther, and the age saw them—no more. They were gone. They did not return.

They went beyond, whispered those who had lost their courage. They went out a Gate and found nothing there.

They died.

Or was it death—to travel without end? And what was death? And was the universe finite at all?

Some went, and vanished, and the age knew nothing more of them.

Those who were left were in agony—of desire to go; of fear to go farther.

Of changes.

This age—did change. It rippled with possibilities. Memories deceived. One remembered, or remembered that one had remembered, and the fact grew strange and dim, contradicting what obviously *was*. People remembered things that never had been true.

And one must never go back to see. Backtiming—had direst possibilities. It made paradox.

But some tried, seeking a time as close to their original exit point as possible. Some came too close, and involved themselves in time-loops, a particularly distressing kind of accident and unfortunate equally for those involved as bystanders.

Among qhal, between the finding of the first Gate and the End of Time, a new kind of specialist evolved: time-menders, who in most extreme cases of disturbance policed the Gates and carefully researched afflicted areas. They alone were licensed to violate the back-time barrier, passing back and forth under strict non-involvement regulations, exchanging intelligence only with each other, to minutely adjust reality.

Evolved.

Agents recruited other agents at need—but at whose instance? There might be some who knew. It might have come from the far end of time—in that last (or was it last?) age beyond which nothing seemed certain, when the years since the First Gate were more than five thousand, and the Now in which all Gates existed was—very distant. Or it might have come from those who had found the Gate, overseeing their invention. Someone knew, somewhen, somewhere along the course of the stars toward the end of time.

But no one said.

It was hazardous business, this time-mending, in all senses. Precisely *what* was done was something virtually unknowable after it was done, for alterations in the past produced (one believed) changes in future reality. Whole time-fields, whose events could be wiped and redone, with effects which widened the farther down the timeline they proceeded. Detection of time-tampering was almost impossible.

A stranger wanted something to eat, a long time ago. He shot himself his dinner.

A small creature was not where it had been, when it had been.

A predator missed a meal and took another . . . likewise small.

A child lost a pet.

And found another.

And a friend she would not have had. She was happier for it.

She met many people she had never/would never meet.

A man in a different age had breakfast in a house on a hill.

Agent Harrh had acquired a sense about disruptions, a kind of extrasensory queasiness about a just-completed timewarp. He was not alone in this. But the time-menders (Harrh knew three others of his own age) never reported such experiences outside their own special group. Such reports would have been meaningless to his own time, involving a past which (as a result of the warp) was neither real nor valid nor perceptible to those in Time Present. Some time-menders would reach the verge of insanity because of this. This was future fact. Harrh knew this.

He had been there.

And he refused to go again to Now, that Now to which time had advanced since the discovery of the Gate—let alone to the End of Time, which was the farthest that anyone imagined. He was one of a few, a very few, licensed to do so, but he refused.

He lived scattered lives in ages to come, and remembered the future with increasing melancholy.

He had visited the End of Time, and left it in the most profound despair. He had seen what was there, and when he had contemplated going beyond, that most natural step out the Gate which stood and beckoned—

He fled. He had never run from anything but that. It remained, a recollection of shame at his fear.

A sense of a limit which he had never had before.

And this in itself was terrible, to a man who had thought time infinite and himself immortal.

In his own present of 1003 since the First Gate, Harrh had breakfast, a quiet meal. The children were off to the beach. His wife shared tea with him and thought it would be a fine morning.

"Yes," he said. "Shall we take the boat out? We can fish a little, take the sun."

"Marvelous," she said. Her gray eyes shone. He loved her—for herself, for her patience. He caught her hand on the crystal table, held slender fingers, not speaking his thoughts, which were far too somber for the morning.

They spent their mornings and their days together. He came back to her, time after shifting time. He might be gone a month; and home a week; and gone two months next time. He never dared cut it too close. They lost a great deal of each other's lives, and so much—so much he could not share with her.

"The island," he said. "Mhreihrrinn, I'd like to see it again."

"I'll pack," she said.

And went away.

He came back to her never aged; and she bore their two sons; and reared them; and managed the accounts: and explained his absences to relatives and the world. *He travels,* she would say, with that right amount of secrecy that protected secrets.

And even to her he could never confide what he knew.

"I trust you," she would say—knowing what he was, but never what he did.

He let her go. She went off to the hall and out the door—He imagined happy faces, holiday, the boys making haste to run the boat out and put on the bright colored sail. She would keep them busy carrying this and that, fetching food and clothes—things happened in shortest order when Mhreihrrinn set her hand to them.

He wanted that, wanted the familiar, the orderly, the homely. He was, if he let his mind dwell on things—afraid. He had the notion never to leave again.

He had been to the Now most recently—5045, and his flesh crawled at the memory. There was recklessness there. There was disquiet. The Now had traveled two decades and more since he had first begun, and he felt it more and more. The whole decade of the 5040's had a queasiness about it, ripples of instability as if the whole fabric of the Now were shifting like a kaleidoscope.

And it headed for the End of Time. It had become more and more like that age, confirming it by its very collapse.

People had illusions in the Now. They perceived what had not been true.

And yet it *was* when he came home.

It had grown to be so—while he was gone.

A university stood in Morurir, which he did not remember.

A hedge of trees grew where a building had been in Morurir.

A man was in the Council who had died.

He would not go back to Now. He had resolved that this morning. He had children, begotten before his first time-traveling. He had so very much to keep him—this place, this home, this stability—He was very well to do. He had invested well—his own small tampering. He had no lack, no need. He was mad to go on and on. He was done.

But a light distracted him, an opal shimmering beyond his breakfast nook, arrival in that receptor which his fine home afforded, linked to the master gate at Pyvrrhn.

A young man materialized there, opal and light and then solidity, a distraught young man.

"Harrh," the youth said, disregarding the decencies of meeting, and strode forward unasked. "Harrh, is everything all right here?"

Harrh arose from the crystal table even before the shimmer died, beset by that old queasiness of things out of joint. This was Alhir from 390 Since the Gate, an experienced man in the force: he had used a Master Key to come here—had such access, being what he was.

"Alhir," Harrh said, perplexed. "What's wrong?"

"You don't know." Alhir came as far as the door.

"A cup of tea?" Harrh said. Alhir had been here before. They were friends. There were oases along the course of suns, friendly years, places where houses served as rest-stops. In this too Mhreihrrinn was patient. "I've got to tell you—No, don't tell me. I don't want to know. I'm through. I've made up my mind. You can carry that where you're going.—But if you want the breakfast—"

"There's been an accident."

"I don't want to hear."

"He got past us."

"I don't want to know." He walked over to the cupboard, took another cup. "Mhreihrrinn's with the boys down at the beach. You just caught us." He set the cup down and poured the tea, where Mhreihrrinn had sat. "Won't you? You're always welcome here. Mhreihrrinn has no idea what you are. My young friend, she calls you. She doesn't know. Or she suspects. She'd never say. —Sit *down*."

Alhir had strayed aside, where a display case sat

along the wall, a lighted case of mementoes, of treasures, of crystal. "Harrh, there was a potsherd here."

"No," Harrh said, less and less comfortable. "Just
the glasses. I'm quite sure."

"Harrh, it was very old."

"No," he said. "—I promised Mhreihrrinn and the
boys—I mean it. I'm through. I don't want to know."

"It came from Silen. From the digs at the First
Gate, Harrh. It was a very valuable piece. You valued it very highly. —You don't remember."

"No," Harrh said, feeling fear thick about him,
like a change in atmosphere. "I don't know of such a
piece. I never had such a thing. Check your memory, Alhir."

"It was from the ruins by the *First Gate*, don't you
understand?"

And then Alhir did not exist.

Harrh blinked, remembered pouring a cup of tea.
But he was sitting in the chair, his breakfast before
him.

He poured the tea and drank.

He was sitting on rock, amid the grasses blowing
gently in the wind, on a clifftop by the sea.

He was standing there. "Mhreihrrinn," he said, in
the first chill touch of fear.

But that memory faded. He had never had a wife,
nor children. He forgot the house as well.

Trees grew and faded.

Rocks moved at random.

The time-menders were in most instances the only
ones who survived even a little while.

Wrenched loose from time and with lives rooted in
many parts of it, they felt it first and lived it longest,

47

and not a few were trapped in back-time and did not die, but survived the horror of it and begot children who further confounded the time-line.

Time, stretched thin in possibilities, adjusted itself.
He was Harrh.
But he was many possibilities and many names.

In time none of them mattered.

He was many names; he lived. He had many bodies; and the souls stained his own.

In the end he remembered nothing at all, except the drive to live.

And the dreams.

And none of the dreams were true.

III

"IS IT EASY to get your first story published?"

"Why?" I ask. It is computer games tonight in the rec room. I am quite good at the ones which involve blowing up things and very bad at the word games. My mind goes on holiday when I am not writing, and declares moratorium in logic. "Are you thinking of writing one?"

"Oh, no. I just wondered whether it's easy."

"It isn't. Or if it is, and it happens too soon, you don't have all the calluses you need. And you can get hurt. Writing is a risky business." We are some time into our acquaintance. We have passed from that intimacy of strangers into a different kind of truth. "Too, sometimes a story just misbehaves. Sometimes one seems to turn out at an inconvenient length, or the topic isn't fashionable. An inexperienced writer is most likely to do a story that's over-long or too short ... and of course in the inscrutable justice of the System, a new writer is also the least likely to get an odd-length story published. Sometimes a young writer can be very naïve about the system. There was a story I wrote back in the sixties, in the hope I could get it serialized in a major magazine. Now, there's really about as much chance of a break-in writer doing that as there is of a particular star out there going nova while we watch.

"And to compound matters, I sent a half-page summary to the magazine in question and asked them if they wanted it on that basis. They said what any sane editors would have said. No. So I tossed it into the drawer, since I had arrived at sanity in the meanwhile and knew my chances."

"Just gave up?"

"I had two novels circulating. I pinned my hopes on those. One eventually made it. Rewritten, to be sure. But, no, I never gave up on this story. I thought about making it into a novel and I'd take it out and try now and again. Now I tell you a truth about what this age and the system has done to storytellers— we're prisoners of bookcovers. Bookcovers must come along at just exactly such a time so a certain number of books will fit into a rack and cost a certain amount. So people who have a long tale to tell have to interrupt it with a great many bookcovers (and re-explanations) and alas, if you birth a tale inconveniently small you'll spend as much creativity finding a home for it as it took to write it in the first place.

"But sometimes there is a story, as an old tale used to say quite properly, just so long and no longer.

"So 'Companions' never grew and never shrank; and it languished in that drawer until someone had just the right space for it. Also rewritten, of course. It's a ghost story. Of sorts."

"Fantasy?"

"Science fiction."

"Perceptions again?"

"In a way." I lose a playing-piece and am regenerated on the screen. "I was rather fond of the concept. Count the characters when you've read it. Tell me how many there are—except the beginning."

"Tricks."

"It's perceptions, remember."

Companions

I

THE SHIP LAY behind them, improbable in so
rich a land, so earthlike a world, a silver egg in
paradise, an egg more accustomed to stellar distances,
to crouching on barren, hellish moons, probing for
whatever she could find, her people and her brain
calculating survival margins for potential bases—
whether mining and manufacture might be enough,
given x number of ship-calls per year, to make devel-
opment worth the while, for ships on their way to
Somewhere, as a staging point for humans on their
way to Somewhere in the deep.

Somewheres were much, much rarer . . . and this
was one, this was more than a marginal Somewhere,
this eden.

No indication of habitation, no response to an orbiting ship; no readings on close scan, not a geometry anywhere on the surface but nature's own work.

An Earth unpopulated, untouched, unclaimed.

Green and lush through the faceplates . . . a view that changed slowly as Warren turned, as he faced from open plain to forest to distant mountains. Sea lay a little distance away. The sky was incredible, filtered blue. Three other white-suited figures walked ungainly through the grass. The sounds of breathing came through the suit-com, occasional comments, panted breaths interspersed: the gear weighed them down on this world. The ship kept talking to them, forlorn, envious voices of those duty-bound inside, to the four of them out here.

"Makes no sense," Harley said, disembodied, through the com. "No insects. No birds. You can't have an ecology like this with no animate life."

"Take your samples," Burlin's voice said, dimmer. The captain, Burlin. He stood to make himself that one find that would assure an old age in comfort. For the younger rest of them, promise of prime assignments, of comforts for the ship, of the best for the rest of their lives. They escorted Harley out here—Harley who told them what to gather, Harley whose relays were to the labs back on the ship, the real heart of the probe's operations.

Nothing was wrong with the world. The first air and soil samples *Anne*'s intakes had gathered had shown them nothing amiss; the pseudosome had come out, stood, silver and invulnerable to chance, and surveyed the find with robotic eyes, as incapable of joy as suited human bodies were of appreciating the air and the wind that swayed the grasses. There might be perfumes on the wind, but the instruments read a dispassionate N, CO_2, O finding, a contaminant readout, windspeed, temperature.

They gathered whole plants and seeds, tiny scoops of soil, a new world's plunder. Every species was new, and some were analogous to kinds they knew: bearded grasses, smooth-barked bushes with slick green leaves. Paul Warren dug specimens Harley chose and sealed the bags, recorded the surrounds with his camera, labeled and marked with feverish enthusiasm.

"Harley?" That was Sax. Warren looked around at Harley, who sat down from a crouch in the grass, heard someone's breathing gone rapid. "You all right, Harley?"

"It's hot," Harley said. "I don't think my system's working right."

Burlin walked back to him. Warren did, too, stuffing his samples into the bag at his belt. It was an awkward business, trying to examine another suit's systems, tilting the helmet. Sun glared on the readout plate, obscuring the numbers for the moment. Harley shifted his shoulder and it cleared. "All right," Warren said. "The system's all right."

"Maybe you'd better walk back," Burlin said to Harley. "We're nearly done out here anyway."

Harley made a move toward rising, flailed with a gloved hand, and Sax caught it, steadied him on the way up.

Harley's knees went, suddenly, pitching him face down. "Check the airflow," Burlin said. Warren was already on it.

"No problem there." He tried to keep panic out of his voice. "Harley?"

"He's breathing." Burlin had his hand on Harley's chest. He gathered up Harley's arm, hauled it over his shoulder, and Warren got the other one.

It was a long way back, dragging a suited man's weight. "Get the pseudosome out," Burlin ordered into the welter of questions from the ship. "Get us help out here."

It came before they had gotten halfway to the ship, a gleam in the dark square of *Anne*'s grounded lift tube bay, a human-jointed extension of the ship coming out for them, planting its feet carefully in the uncertain footing of the grass. It was strength. It was comfort. It came walking the last distance with silver arms outstretched, the dark visor of its ovoid head casting back the sun.

They gave Harley to it, positioning its program-receptive arms, told it lift-right, and the right arm came up, so that it carried Harley like a baby, like a silver sexless angel carrying a faceless shape of a man back to the ship. They followed, plodding heavily after, bearing the burden of their own suits and feeling the unease that came with unknown places when things started going wrong.

It was bright day. There were no threats, no unstable terrain, no threat of weather or native life. But the sunlight seemed less and the world seemed larger and ominously quiet for so much life on its face.

They brought Harley inside, into the airlock. The pseudosome stood still as the hatch closed and sealed. "Set down, *Anne*," Burlin said, and the pseudosome reversed the process that had gathered Harley up, released him into their arms. They laid him on the floor.

Harley moved, a febrile stirring of hands and head, a pawing at the helmet collar. "Get the oxygen," Burlin said, and Warren ignored the queries coming rapid-fire from the crew inside the ship, got up and opened the emergency panel while Sax and Burlin stripped off the helmet. He brought the oxy bottle, dropped to his knees and clamped the clear mask over Harley's white, sweating face. Harley sucked in great breaths, coughed, back arching in the cumbersome suit. Red blotches marked his throat, like heat. "Look at that," Sax said. The blotches were evident on Harley's face, too, fine hemorrhaging about the cheeks, about the nose and mouth beneath the plastic.

Burlin stood up, hit the decontamination process. The UV came on. The rest of the procedure sequenced in the lock. Burlin knelt. Harley was breathing shallowly now. "He couldn't have gotten it out there," Warren said. "Not like this, not this fast. Not through the suit."

"Got to get the ship scoured out," Burlin said. "Yesterday, the day before—something got past the lock."

Warren looked up . . . at the pseudosome.

The processing cut off. The lights went back to normal. Warren looked at Harley, up at Burlin. "Captain—are we going to bring him in?"

"We do what we can. We three. Here. In the lock."

Harley's head moved, restlessly, dislodging the mask. Warren clamped it the more tightly.

Before he died it took the three of them to hold him. Harley screamed, and clawed with his fingers, and beat his head against the decking. Blood burst from his nose and mouth and drowned the oxy mask, smeared their suits in his struggles. He raved and called them by others' names and cursed them and the world that was killing him. When it was over, it was morning again, but by then another of the crew had complained of fever.

Inside the ship.

THEY WENT to every crevice of the ship, suited, with UV light and steam-borne disinfectant, nightmare figures meeting in fog, in the deep places, among conduits and machines.

Everywhere, the com: "Emergency to three; we've got another—"

Deep in the bowels of the ship, two figures, masked, carrying cannisters, obscured in steam:

"It isn't doing any good," Abner said. There was panic in his voice, a man who'd seen crew die before, on Mortifer and Hell. *"Ten of us already—"*

"Shut up, Abner," Warren said, with him, in the dark of *Anne*'s depths. Steam hissed, roared from the cannisters; disinfectant dripped off griddings, off railings and pipe. "Just shut it *up*."

Com's voice faltered, rose plaintive through the roar: "We're not getting any response out of 2a. Is somebody going to check on that? *Is there somebody going to check that out?"*

THERE WAS chaos in the labs, tables unbolted, cots used while they could be; pallets spread when they ran out of those. The raving lay next to the comatose; death came with hemorrhage, small at first, and worse. Lungs filled, heart labored, and the vessels burst. Others lingered, in delirium.

"Lie down," Sikutu said—biologist, only sometime medic, tried to help the man, to reason where there was no reason.

"I've got work to do," Sax cried, wept, flailed his arms. "I've got work—"

Smith held him, a small woman, pinned an arm while Sikutu held the other. "Hush, hush," she said. "You've got to lie still—Sax, Sax—"

"They all die," Sax said, as he wept. "I've got work to do. I've got to get back to the lab—*I don't want to die*—"

He set others off, awakened the sleeping, got curses, screams from others.

"Don't want to die," he sobbed.

Sikutu shook at him, quieted him at last, sat down and held his head in his hands. He felt fevered, felt short of breath.

His pulse increased. But maybe that was fear.

RULE WAS dead. Warren found her in Botany, among the plants she loved, lying in a knot next to one of the counters. He stared, grieved in what shock there was left to feel. There was no question of life left. There was the blood, the look of all the others. He turned his face away, leaned against the wall where the com unit was, pressed the button.

"Captain, she's dead, all right. Botany One."

There was silence for a moment. "Understood," Burlin's voice came back. It broke. Another small silence. "The pseudosome's on its way."

"I don't need it. She doesn't weigh much."

"Don't touch her."

"Yes, sir." Warren pushed the button, broke the contact, leaned there with his throat gone tight. The dying screamed through the day and night, audible through the walls of sickbay on lower deck, up the air shafts, up the conduits, like the machinery sounds.

This had been a friend.

The lift worked, near the lab; he heard it, heard the metal footsteps, rolled his eyes toward the doorway as *Anne* herself came in . . . shining metal, faceless face, black plastic face with five red lights winking on and off inside; black plastic mirroring the lab on its oval surface, his own distorted form.

"Assistance?" *Anne* asked.

"Body." He pointed off at Rule. "Dispose."

Anne reoriented, stalked over and bent at the waist, gripped Rule's arm. The corpse had stiffened. Motors whirred; *Anne* straightened, hauling the body upright; another series of whirrings: brought her right arm under Rule's hips, lifted, readjusted the weight. A slow shuffling turn.

Warren stepped aside. *Anne* walked, hit the body against the doorframe in trying to exit. Warren put out his hand, sickened by this further horror, but *Anne* tilted the body, passed through and on.

He followed, down the hall, to Destruct . . . utilitarian, round-sealed door. *Danger*, it said. *Warning*. They used it for biological wastes. For dangerous samples. For more mundane things.

For their dead, down here.

He opened the hatch. *Anne* put the body in, small, insectile adjustments like a wasp. Froze, then, arms lowering, sensor-lights winking out. Warren closed the door, dogged it down. He pushed the button, winced at the explosive sound, wiped his face. His hands were shaking. He looked at *Anne.*

"Decontaminate yourself," he said. The lights came on inside the mask. The robot moved, reoriented to the hall, walked off into the dark farther down the hall: no lights for *Anne.* She needed none.

Warren's belly hurt. He caught his breath. *Decontaminate.* He headed for the showers, faithful to the regs. It was a thing to do; it kept a man from thinking, held out promises of safety. Maybe the others had let down.

He showered, vapored dry, took clean coveralls from the common locker, sat down on the bench to pull on his boots. His hands kept shaking. He kept shivering even after dressing. *Fear. It's fear.*

An alarm sounded, a short beep of the Klaxon, something touched that should not have been, somewhere in the ship. He stopped in mid-tug, heard the crash and whine of the huge locks at *Anne*'s deep core. Someone was using the cargo airlock. He stood up, jammed his foot into the second boot, started for the door.

"All report." He heard the general order, Burlin's voice. He went to the com by the door and did that, name and location: "Paul Warren, lower-deck showers."

Silence.

"Captain?"

Silence.

Panic took him. He left the shower room at a run, headed down the corridor to the lift, rode it up to topside, raced out again, down the hall, around the corner into the living quarters, through it to the bridgeward corridor.

Locked. He pushed the button twice, tried the com above it. "Captain." He gasped for air. "Captain, it's Warren. Was that Abner, then?"

Silence. He fumbled his cardkey from his pocket, inserted it into the slot under the lock. It failed. He slammed his fist onto the com.

"Captain?—Sikutu, Abner, is anyone hearing me?"

Silence still. He turned and ran back down the short corridor, through the mainroom, back toward the lift.

"Warren?" the com said. Burlin's voice.

Warren skidded to a stop, scrambled back to the nearest com unit and pushed the button. "Captain, Captain, what's going on?"

"I'm not getting any word out of sickbay," Burlin said. "I've sent the pseudosome in. Something's happened there."

"I'm going."

Silence.

Warren caught his breath, ran for the lift and rode it down again. Silence in the lower corridor too. He looked about him. "Abner? Abner, are you down here?"

No answer to the hail. Nothing. A section seal hissed open behind him. He spun about, caught his balance against the wall.

Anne was there in the dark. The pseudosome strode forward, her red lights glowing.

Warren turned and ran, faster than the robot, headed for the lab.

Quarantine, it said. *No entry.* He reached the door,

pressed the com. "Sikutu. Sikutu, it's Warren. Are you all right in there?"

Silence. He pushed Door-Open.

It was a slaughterhouse inside. Blood was spattered over walls and beds. Sikutu—lying on the floor among the beds and pallets, red all over his lab whites from his perforated chest; Minnan and Polly and Tom, lying in their beds with their bedclothes sodden red, with startled eyes and twisted bodies. Throats cut. Faces slashed.

One bed was empty. The sheets were thrown back. He cast about him, counted bodies, lost in horror— heard the footsteps at his back and turned in alarm.

Anne stood there, facelights flashing, cameras clicking into focus.

"Captain," Warren said: *Anne* was a relay herself. "Captain, it's Sax. He's gone ... everyone else is dead. He's got a knife or something. Is there any word from Abner?"

"I can't raise him." Burlin's voice came from *Anne*. "Get a gun. Go to the lock. Abner was in that area last."

"Assistance." The voice changed; *Anne*'s mechanical tones. The pseudosome swiveled, talking to the dead. "Assistance?"

Warren wiped his face, caught his breath. "Body," he said distractedly. "Dispose." He edged past the pseudosome, ran for the corridor, for the weapons locker.

The locker door was dented, scarred as if someone had hammered it, slashed at it; but it was closed. He used his card on it. It jammed. He used it for a lever, used his fingertips, pried it open. He took one of the three pistols there, ignored the holsters, just slammed it shut and ran for the lift.

Downward again. His hands were shaking as he rode. He fumbled at the safety. He was a navigator, had never carried a gun against any human being, had never fired except in practice. His heart was speeding, his hands cold.

The lift stopped; the door whipped open on the dark maze of netherdeck, of conduits and walkways that led to the lock.

He reached for the light switch below the com panel. The lift door shut behind him, leaving him in darkness. He hesitated, pushed the button.

He walked carefully along the walk. The metal grids of the decking echoed underfoot. He passed aisles, searching for ambush ... flexed his fingers on the gun, thinking of it finally, of what he was doing.

A catwalk led out to the lift platform, to the huge circular cargo plate, the lift control panel. The plate was in down-position, leaving a deep black hole in netherdeck, the vertical tracks showing round the pit. He reached the control station, pressed the button.

Gears synched; hydraulics worked. The platform came up into the light. A shape was on it, a body in a pool of blood. Abner.

Warren punched the station com. "Captain," he said, controlling his voice with marvelous, reasonable calm. "Captain, Abner's dead. Out on the lift platform, netherdeck. Shall I go outside?"

"No," Burlin's voice came back.

He shivered, waiting for more answer. "Captain."

He still kept it calm. "Captain, what do you want me to do?"

Silence and static. Warren cut it off, his hand clenched to numbness on the gun. He flexed it live again, walked out onto the echoing platform, looked about him, full circle, at the shadows. Blood trailed off the platform's circle, stopped clean against the opposing surface. *Gone. Outside.* He hooked the gun to his belt, stooped and gathered Abner up, heaved the slashed body over his shoulder. Blood drenched him, warm and leaking through his clothes. The limbs hung loose.

He carried it—him; Abner; six years his friend. Like Sikutu. Like Sax.

He kept going, to the lift, trailing blood, retracing all his steps. There was silence all about, ship-silence, the rush of air in the ducts, the thousand small sounds of *Anne*'s pumps and fans. Two of them now, two of them left, himself and Burlin. And Sax— out there; out there, escaped, in paradise.

He took Abner upstairs, carried him down the corridor, in the semidark of Power-Save.

The pseudosome was busy there, carrying Sikutu's bloody form to the destruct chamber. Warren followed it, automaton like the other, trying to feel as little. But the bodies were stacked up there at the foot of the destruct chamber door, a surplus of bodies. Only one was jammed inside. Minnan. Warren's knees weakened. He watched the pseudosome let Sikutu down atop the others, saw it coming back, arms outstretched.

"Assistance?"

He surrendered Abner to it, stomach twisting as

he did. He clamped his jaws and dogged the door on Minnan and pushed the button.

They did the job, he and the pseudosome. He threw up, after, from an empty stomach.

"Assistance?" *Anne* asked. "Assistance?"

He straightened, wiped his face, leaned against the wall. "Sterilize the area. Decontaminate." He walked off, staggered, corrected himself, pushed the nearest com button, having composed himself, keeping anger from his voice. "Captain. Captain, I've got the bodies all disposed. The area's being cleaned." Softly, softly, he talked gently to this man, this last sane man. "Can we talk, sir?"

"Warren?" the plaintive voice came back.

"Sir?"

"I'm sorry."

"Sir?" He waited. There was only the sound of breathing coming through. "Sir—are you on the bridge? I'm coming up there."

"Warren—I've got it."

"No, sir." He wiped his forearm across his face, stared up at the com unit. He began to shake. "What am I supposed to do, sir?" He forced calm on himself. "What can I do to help?"

A delay. "Warren, I'll tell you what I've done. And why. You listening, Warren?"

"I'm here, sir."

"I've shut down controls. We can't beat this thing. I've shut her down for good, set her to blow if anyone tries to bypass to take off. I'm sorry. Can't let us go home . . . taking this back to human space. It could spread like wildfire, kill—kill whole colonies before the meds could get it solved. I've set a beacon,

Warren. She'll play it anytime some probe comes in here, when they do come, whenever."

"Sir—*sir*, you're not thinking—A ship in space—is a natural quarantine."

"And if we died en route—and if someone got aboard—No. No. They mustn't do that. We can't lift again."

"Sir—listen to me."

"No animals, Warren. We never found any animals. A world like this and nothing moving in it. It's a *dead world*. Something got it. Something lives here, in the soil, something in the air; something grew here, something fell in out of space—and it got all the animals. Every moving thing. Can't let it go—"

"Sir—sir, we don't know the rest of us would have died. We don't know that. *You* may not, and I may not, and what are we going to do, sir?"

"I'm sorry, Warren. I'm really sorry. It's not a chance to take—to go like that. Make up your own mind. I've done the best thing. I have. Insured us against weakness. It can't leave here."

"Captain—"

Silence. A soft popping sound.

"Captain!" Warren pushed away from the wall, scrambled for the lift and rode it topside, ran down the corridor toward the bridge. He thrust his card into the lock.

It worked now. The door slid. And Burlin was there, slumped at the com station, the gun beneath his hand. The sickroom stink was evident. The fever. The minute hemorrhages on the hands. Blood pooled on the com counter, ran from Burlin's nose and mouth. The eyes stared, reddened.

Warren sat down in the navigator's chair, wiped his face, his eyes, stared blankly, finding it hard to get his breath. He cursed Burlin. Cursed all the dead.

There was silence after.

He got up finally, pulled Burlin's body back off the com board, punched in the comp and threw the com wide open, because the ship was all there was to talk to. *"Anne,"* he said to comp. "Pseudosome to bridge. Body. Dispose."

IN TIME the lift operated and the silver pseudosome arrived, leisurely precise. It stood in the doorway and surveyed the area with insectoid turns of the head. It clicked forward then, gathered up Burlin and walked out.

Warren stayed a time, doing nothing, sitting in the chair on the bridge, in the quiet. His eyes filled with tears. He wiped at one eye and the other, still numb.

When he did walk down to destruct to push the button, the pseudosome was still standing beside the chamber. He activated it, walked away, left the robot standing there.

It was planetary night outside. He thought of Sax out there, crazed. Of Sax maybe still alive, in the dark, as alone as he. He thought of going out and hunting for him in the morning.

The outside speakers.

He went topside in haste, back to the bridge, sat down at the com and opened the port shields on night sky. He dimmed the bridge lights, threw on the outside floods, illuminating grass and small shrubs round about the ship.

He put on the outside address.

"Sax. Sax, it's Paul Warren. There's no one left but us. Listen, I'm going to put food outside the ship tomorrow. *Tomorrow*, hear me? I'll take care of you. You're not to blame. I'll take care of you. You'll get well, you hear me?"

He kept the external pickup on. He listened for a long time, looked out over the land.

"Sax?"

Finally he got up and walked out, down to the showers, sealed his clothes in a bag for destruct.

HE TRIED to eat after that, wrapped in his robe, sitting down in the galley because it was a smaller place than the living quarters and somehow the loneliness was not so deep there; but he had no appetite. His throat was pricklish . . . exhaustion, perhaps. He had reason enough. The air-conditioning felt insufficient in the room.

But he had driven himself. That was what.

He had the coffee at least, and the heat suffused his face, made him short of breath.

Then the panic began to hit him. He thrust himself up from the table, dizzy in rising, vision blurred— felt his way to the door and down the corridor to the mirror in the showers. His eyes were watering. He wiped them, tried to see if there was hemorrhage. They were red, and the insides of the lids were red and painful. The heat he had felt began to go to chill, and he swallowed repeatedly as he walked back to the galley, testing whether the soreness in his throat was worse than he recalled over the last few hours.

Calm, he told himself. Calm. There were things to

do that had to be done or he would face dying of thirst, of hunger. He set about gathering things from the galley, arranged dried food in precise stacks beside the cot in the lower-deck duty station, near the galley. He made his sickbed, set drugs and water and a thermal container of ice beside it.

Then he called the pseudosome in, walked it through the track from his bed to the galley and back again, programmed it for every errand he might need.

He turned down the bed. He lay down, feeling the chill more intense, and tucked up in the blankets.

The pseudosome stood in the doorway like a silver statue, one sensor light blinking lazily in the faceplate. When by morning the fever had taken him and he was too weak to move coherently, he had mechanical hands to give him water. *Anne* was programmed to pour coffee, to do such parlor tricks, a whim of Harley's.

It wished him an inane good morning. It asked him *How are you?* and at first in his delirium he tried to answer, until he drifted too far away.

"Assistance?" he would hear it say then, and imagined a note of human concern in that voice. "Malfunction? Nature of malfunction, please?"

Then he heaved up, and he heard the pseudosome's clicking crescendo into alarm. The emergency Klaxon sounded through the ship as the computer topside registered that there was something beyond its program. Her lights all came on.

"Captain Burlin," she said again and again, "Captain Burlin, emergency."

2

THE PULSING OF headache and fever grew less. Warren accepted consciousness gradually this time, fearful of the nausea that had racked him the last. His chest hurt. His arms ached, and his knees. His lips were cracked and painful. It amazed him that the pain had ebbed down to such small things.

"Good morning."

He rolled his head on the pillow, to the soft whirr of machinery on his right. *Anne*'s smooth-featured pseudosome was still waiting.

He was alive. No waking between waves of fever. His face felt cool, his body warm from lying too long in one place. He lay in filth, and stench.

He propped himself up, reached for the water pitcher, knocked it off the table. It rolled empty to *Anne*'s metal feet.

"Assistance?"

He reached for her arm. "Flex."

The arm bent, lifting him. Her motors whirred in compensation. "Showers."

She reoriented herself and began to walk, with him leaning on her, his arm about her plastic-sheathed shoulder, like some old, familiar friend.

She stopped when she had brought him where he wished, out of program. He managed to stand alone, tottering and staring at himself in the mirror. He was gaunt, unshaven, covered with filth and sores. His eyes were like vast bruises. He swore, wiped his eyes and felt his way into a shower cabinet.

He fainted there, in the shower stall, came to again on the floor, under the warm mist. He managed to lever himself up again, got the door open, refused a second dizziness and leaned there till it passed. *"Anne."*

A whirring of motors. She planted herself in the doorway, waiting.

SHE GOT him topside, to the living quarters, to his own compartment door. "Open," he told her hoarsely; and she brought him inside, to the edge of his own unused bed, to clean blankets and clean sheets. He fell into that softness panting and shivering, hauled the covers over himself with the last of his strength.

"Assistance?"

"I'm all right."

"Define usage: *right*."

"Functional. I'm functional."

"Thank you."

He laughed weakly. This was not *Anne*. Not she. It. *Anne* was across the living quarters, in controls, all the company there was left.

Thank you. As if courtesy had a point. She was the product of a hundred or more minds over the course of her sixteen-year service, men and women who programmed her for the moment's convenience and left their imprint.

Please and thank you. Cream or sugar, sir? She could apply a wrench or laser through the pseudosome, lift a weight no man could move, bend a jointing into line or make a cup of coffee. But nothing from initiative.

Thank you.

* * *

IT WAS another few hours before he was sure he was going to live. Another day before he did more than send *Anne* galleyward and back, eat and sleep again.

But at last he stood up on his own, went to his locker, dressed, if feebly.

The pseudosome brightened a second sensor at this movement, then a third. "Assistance?"

"Report, *Anne.*"

"Time: oh six four five hours ten point one point two three. Operating on standby assistance, program E one hundred; on program A one hundred; on additional pro—"

"Cancel query. Continue programs as given." He walked out into the living quarters, walked to the bridge, stood leaning on Burlin's chair, surrounded by *Anne's* lazily blinking consoles, by scanner images no one had read for days. He sat down from weakness.

"*Anne.* Do you have any program to lift off?"

The console lights rippled with activity. Suddenly Burlin's deep voice echoed through the bridge. "Final log entry. Whoever hears this, don't—repeat, don't—land. Don't attempt assistance. We're dead of plague. It got aboard from atmosphere, from soil . . . somehow. It hit everyone. Everyone is dead. Biological records are filed under—"

"Cancel query. Reply is insufficient. Is there a course program in your records?"

"Reply to request for course: I must hold my position. If question is made of this order, I must replay final log entry. . . . *Final log entry*—"

"*Bypass that order. Prepare for lift!*"

The lights went red. "I am ordered to self-destruct if bypass is attempted. Please withdraw request."

"Cancel—cancel bypass order." Warren slumped in the chair, stared at the world beyond the viewport, deadly beguiling morning, gold streaming through cumulus cloud. It was right. Burlin had been right; he had ensured even against a survivor. Against human weakness.

"*Anne.*" His voice faltered. "Take program. If I speak, I'm speaking to you. I don't need to say your name. My voice will activate your responses. I'm Paul Warren. Do you have my ID clear?"

"ID as Warren, Paul James, six eight seven seven six five eight—"

"Cancel query. How long can your pseudosome remain functional?"

"Present power reserve at present rate of consumption: three hundred seventy-eight years approximate to the nearest—"

"Cancel query. Will prolonged activity damage the pseudosome?"

"Modular parts are available for repair. Attrition estimate: no major failure within power limits."

Warren gazed out at the daybreak. *Sax*, he thought. He had made a promise and failed it, days ago. He tried to summon the strength to do something about it, to care—to go out and search in the hope that a man could have lived out there, sick, in the chill of nights and without food. He knew the answer. He had no wish to dwell on guilt, to put any hope in wandering about out there, to find another corpse. He had seen enough. More than enough.

"Library. Locate programming manual. Dispense."

An agitation ran across the board and a microfilm shot down into the dispenser. He gathered it up.

There was this, for his comfort. For three hundred seventy-eight years.

ANNE WAS a marvelous piece of engineering. Her pseudosome was capable of most human movements; its structure imitated the human body and her shining alloy was virtually indestructible by heat or corrosion. Walk-through programming made her capable in the galley: her sensitive vid scanners could read the tapes on stored foods; her timing system was immaculate. She carried on domestic tasks, fetched and carried, and meanwhile her other programs kept more vital functions in working order: circulation, heating, cooling throughout the ship, every circuit, all automated, down to the schedule of lighting going on and off, to the inventory reports going up on the screens each morning, for crew who would no longer read them.

Warren worked, ignoring these processes, trusting *Anne* for them. He read the manual, wrote out programs, sitting naked in bed with the microfilm reader on one side and a coffee pot on the other and a lap full of notes.

An illusion, that was all he asked, a semblance of a mind to talk to. Longer plans he refused as yet. The plotting and replotting that filled the bed and the floor about him with discarded balls of paper was his refuge, his defense against thinking.

He dreaded the nights and kept the lights on while the rest of the ship cycled into dark.

He slept in the light when he had to sleep, and woke and worked again while the pseudosome brought him his meals and took the empty dishes back again.

3

HE CALLED THE star Harley, because it was his to name. The world he called Rule, because Harley and Rule were sometime lovers and it seemed good. Harley was a middling average star, the honest golden sort, which cast an easy warmth on his back, as an old friend ought. Rule stretched everywhere, rich and smelling sweet as Rule always had, and she was peaceful.

He liked the world better when he had named it, and felt the sky friendlier with an old friend's name beaming down at him while he worked.

He stretched the guy ropes of a plastic canopy they had never had the chance to use on harsher worlds, screwed the moorings into the grassy earth and stood up in pleasant shade, looking out over wide billows of grass, with forest far beyond them.

Anne kept him company. She had a range of half a kilometer from the ship over which mind and body could keep in contact, and farther still if the booster unit were in place, which project he was studying. He had not yet had the time. He moved from one plan to the next, busy, working with his hands, feeling the strength return to his limbs. Healing sunlight erased the sores and turned his skin a healthy bronze. He stretched his muscles, grinned up at the sun through the leaf-patterned plastic. Felt satisfied.

"*Anne*. Bring the chair, will you?"

The pseudosome came to life, picked up the chair that remained on the cargo lift, carried it out. And stopped.

"Set it down." His good humor turned to disgust. "Set it down."

Anne set it, straightened, waited.

"Anne. What do you perceive?"

Anne's sensors brightened, one after the other. "Light, gravity, sound, temperature."

"You perceive *me.*"

"Yes, Warren. You're directly in front of me."

"Anne, come here."

She walked forward, into the shade, stopped, hands at her sides, sensors pulsing behind her dark faceplate like so many stars in a void.

"Anne, I'm your duty. I'm all the crew. The directives all apply only to me now. The others have stopped functioning. Do you understand? I want you to remain active until I tell you otherwise. Walk at your own judgment. Identify and accept all stimuli that don't take you out of range."

"Program recorded," *Anne* purred. "Execute?"

"Execute."

Anne walked off. She had a peculiar gait, precise in her movements like an improbable dancer, stiffly smooth and slow-motion. Graceful, silver *Anne.* It always jarred when he looked into the vacant faceplate with the starry lights winking on and off in the darkness. She could never appreciate the sun, could never perceive him except as a pattern of heat and solidity in her sensors. She looked left, looked right, walk-walk-walk-walk, looked left, right, walk-walk-walk-walk, neither breathing the scents of life nor feeling the wind on her plastic skin. The universe held no perils for *Anne*.

Warren wept. He strode out, overtook her, seized her as she turned to him. "*Anne*. Where are you? Where are you going?"

"I am located four oh point four seven meters from base center. I am executing standard survey, proceeding—"

"Cancel query. *Anne*, look about you. What have you learned?"

Anne swiveled her head left and right. Her sensors flickered. "This world is as first observed. All stimuli remain within human tolerance. There are no native lifeforms in my scan."

She turned then, jerking from his hands, and walked off from him, utterly purposeful.

"*Anne!*" he called, alarmed. "*Anne*, what's wrong?"

She stopped, faced him. "The time is 1100 hours. Standard timed program 300-32-111PW."

Lunch. *Anne* was, if nothing else, punctual.

"Go on."

She turned. He trailed after her to the edge of the canopy, cast himself into the chair and sat disconsolate. Adrenalin surged. Rage. There was no profit in that. Not at a machine. He knew that. He told himself so.

HE ATTACHED the booster unit—not out of enthusiasm, but because it was another project, and occupied him. It took two days . . . in which he had only *Anne's* disembodied voice, while the pseudosome lay disemboweled in the shop. He had difficulty, not with the insertion of the unit, which was modular, but in getting the ring-joints of the waist back together; it occasioned him panic, real and sweating dread. He consulted library, worked and fretted over it, got the first ring and the second, and so on to the fifth. She had lost nothing vital, only some of her auxiliary apparatus for hookups of use on frigid moons. That could be put back if need be.

He could take her apart and put her back together if need be, if amusement got more scarce.

If she worked at all now. The chance of failure still scared him.

"*Anne*," he said, "turn on the pseudosome."

The head slung over, faced him.

"Good morning, Warren."

"Are you functional? Test your legs. Get off the table."

Anne sat up, machine-stiff, precisely reversing her process of getting onto the table. She stood, arms at her sides.

"Go on," Warren said. "Go about your duties."

She stayed fixed.

"Why don't you go?"

"Instruction?"

He bounced a wrench off the lab wall so violently his shoulder ached. It rebounded to *Anne's* metal feet.

Whirr-click. *Anne* bent with long legs wide and retrieved the wrench, proffering it to him. "Assistance?"

"Damn you."

All the sensor lights came on. "Define usage: *damn*."

He hit her. She compensated and stood perfectly balanced.

"Define: *damn*."

He sobbed for breath, stared at her, regained his patience. "The perception is outside your sensor range."

The sensor lights dimmed. She still held the wrench, having no human fatigue to make her lower it.

An idea came to him, like a flash of madness. He shoved the debris and bits of solder off the worktable and sat down with his notebook, feverishly writing definitions in terms *Anne's* sensors could read: tone, volume, pace, stability, function/nonfunction/optimum, positive/negative. . . .

"THIS PROGRAM," *Anne* said to him through her bridge main speakers, "conflicts with the central program."

He sat down in the command chair, all his plans wrecked. "Explain conflict."

"I'm government property," the computer said. "Regulations forbid crew to divert me for personal use."

Warren bit his lip and thought a moment, chin on hand. Looked at the flickering lights. "I'm your highest priority. There aren't any other humans in your reach. Your program doesn't permit you to lift off, true?"

"Yes."

"You can't return to government zones, true?"

"Yes."

"There's no other crew functioning, true?"

"Yes."

"I'm your only human. There can't be any lateral conflict in your instructions if you accept the program. I need maintenance. If you refuse to maintain me, I have to disconnect you and restructure your whole system of priorities. I can do that."

The board flashed wildly. Went to red. A light to the left began to blink: AUTODESTRUCT, AUTODESTRUCT, AUTODESTRUCT—

"I'm programmed to defend this position. I have prior instruction. Please check your programming, Warren. I'm in conflict."

"Will you accept instruction? I'm your remaining crew. What I tell you is true."

The lights went steady, burning red. "Instruction? Instruction?"

"This new programming applies only to my protection and maintenance under present environmental conditions, while we're on this world. It's not a diversion from your defense function. I'm assisting you in your defense of this position. I'm your crew. I need maintenance. This new program is necessary for that purpose. My health is threatened. My life is threatened. This program is essential for my life and safety."

The red light went off. The lights rippled busily across the boards, normalcy restored. "Recorded."

Warren drew a long-held breath. "What's your status, *Anne?*"

"Indeterminate, Warren. I haven't yet completed assimilation of this new data. I perceive possible duplication of existing vocabulary. Is this valid?"

"This terminology is in reference to me. These are human life states. Maintenance of me is your duty."

"Negative possible, Warren. My sensors are effective in systems analysis only for myself."

He thought, mechanically speaking, that there was something rather profound in that. It was indeed *Anne's* central problem. He stood up, looked at the pseudosome, which stood inactive by the door. "Turn your sensors on me."

Anne faced him. The sensor lights came on.

"Define: *pain, Anne.*"

"Disruption of an organism," the pseudosome-speaker said, "by sensor overload. It is not an acceptable state."

He drew a deeper breath, came closer. "And what is pleasure, *Anne?*"

"Optimum function."

"Define: *feel, Anne.*"

"Verb: receive sensor input other than visual, auditory, or chemical analysis. Noun: the quality of this input."

"Define: *happy.*"

"Happy; content; pleased, comfortable; in a state of optimum function."

"And *anger, Anne.*"

"An agitated state resulting from threatening and unpleasant outcome of action. This is a painful state."

"Your program is to maintain me happy. When your sensors indicate I'm in pain, you must investigate the causes and make all possible effort to restore me to optimum function. That's a permanent instruction."

The facial lights blinked, died, all but one. "Recorded."

He sighed.

The lights flashed on. "Is this pain?"

"No." He shook his head and began to laugh, which set all of *Anne's* board lights to flickering.

"Define, define."

He forced calm. "That's laughing. You've heard laughing before now."

A delay. "I find no record."

"But you heard it just then. Record it. That's pleasure, *Anne.*"

Facelights blinked. There were six now. "Recorded."

He patted her metal shoulder. She swiveled her head to regard his hand. "Do you feel that, *Anne?*"

The face turned back to him. "Feel is in reference to humans."

"You can use the word. Do you feel that?"

"I feel a pressure of one point seven kilos. This does not affect my equilibrium."

He patted her arm gently then, sadly. "That's all right. I didn't think it would."

"Are you still happy, Warren?"

He hesitated, having a moment's queasiness, a moment's chill. "Yes," he said. It seemed wisest to say.

4

HE STOPPED ON a small rise not far from the ship and the pseudosome went rigid at his side. They stood knee-deep in grass. A few fleecy clouds drifted in the sky. The forest stretched green and lush before them.

"Do you perceive any animate life, *Anne?*"

"Negative native animate life."

"Is there any record—of a world with vegetation of this sort, that had no animate life?"

"Negative. Further information: there is viral life here. This is not in my sensor range, but I have abundant data in my files regarding—"

"Cancel statement. Maybe this world was inhabited by something once and the virus killed it."

"I have no data on that proposal."

"No animals. Burlin said it."

"Define: *it.*"

"Cancel." Warren adjusted his pack on his shoulders, pointed ahead, a gesture *Anne* understood. "We'll walk as far as the river."

"Define: *river.*"

"See where the trees—the large vegetation starts? There's water there. A river is a moving body of water on a planetary surface. You have maps in your files. You've got rivers on them. Why don't you know rivers?"

Anne's facial sensors winked. "Maps are in library storage. I don't have access to this data."

"Well, there's one there. A river."

"My sensors have recorded the presence of water in the original survey. Free water is abundant on this world."

Dutifully she kept pace with him, still talking as he started off, metal limbs tireless. He stopped from time to time, deviated this way and that, walked round the scattered few bushes, investigated bare spots in the grass, which proved only stony outcrops.

Nothing. Nothing, in all his searching.

"Assistance?" *Anne* asked when he stopped.

"No, *Anne.*" He looked back at her, hesitant. "Do you, *Anne*—ever perceive . . . any other human?"

"Negative. You are my only human."

He bit his lip, nerved himself, finally. "When I was in bed—did Sax ever come back?"

The sensors blinked. "I find no record."

He found that ambiguous, tried to think a new way through the question. He looked toward the river, back again. "Has he ever come back?"

"I find no record."

Warren let go a small breath, shook his head. "He's not functioning. I'm sure of it."

"Recorded."

He hitched the pack, started walking again. "His body's out here somewhere."

"I find no record."

"I want to find him, *Anne*. Shouldn't have left him out here. He could have come back and needed me. And I couldn't answer. I want to find him. I owe him that."

"Recorded."

They came to the trees finally, to shade, in the straightest line from the ship, which seemed most worth searching. Trees. A small slope of eroded sand down to the river, which flowed about fifty meters wide, deep and sluggish. A stream, broad and brown.

He stopped, and *Anne* did. Drew a breath of the scented air, forgetful for the moment of Sax, of what had brought him. Here was beauty, unsuspected, a part of the world he had not seen from the ship— secrets underwater and growing round it, trees that relieved the sameness and made evershifting lattices that compressed distances into their back-and-forth tangle. No straight lines here. No scour of wind. Coolness. Complexity.

Life, perhaps, lurking in the river. One fish, one crawling thing, and the parameters of the world had to be revised. One fish . . . and it meant life everywhere.

"Stand where you are," he told *Anne*, starting down the bank. "I don't think swimming is in your program."

"Define: *swimming*. I find no record."

He laughed soundlessly, left her by the trees and walked through the pathless tangle to the shady bank. Trees with trailing, moss-hung branches arched out over the sluggish current. Flowers bloomed, white and starlike, on the far margin, where the trees grew larger still and it was twilight at midafternoon. He squatted down by the water and looked into the shallows where the current swirled mosses.

Anne came to life, motors whirring. Brush cracked. He sprang up, saw her coming down the slope, precariously balanced in the descent.

"Stop—*Anne*, stop."

Anne planted her feet at the bottom, waistdeep in brush, lights flashing. "Warren, danger."

Panic surged. He had brought no gun on this search. Did not trust himself. "Specify—danger."

"The river is dangerous."

The breath went out of him. He halfway laughed. "No. Verb: *swim*, to travel through water safely. I can swim, *Anne*. I'm safe. No danger."

"Please consider this carefully, Warren."

He grinned, took a vial from his sample kit and knelt, taking up a specimen of water. He had the whole of the labs to use; he had had the basics, and it was a project, something to do, something with promise, this time.

"I can't assist you in the water, Warren."

"I don't need assistance." He capped the vial and replaced it in the kit, wiped his fingers with a disinfectant towelette and stowed it. "I'll come back to you in a moment."

She made small whirring sounds, cameras busy.

He stood up, turned to face her, waved a hand toward the bank. "Turn your sensors over there, far focus, will you? See if you can see anything."

"Vegetation. Trees."

"Yes." He put his hands into his pockets, stood staring into the forest a long time, watching the wind stir the leaves on the far bank.

So the world had a limit. *Anne* did. There. The ship had a raft, two of them; but curiosity was not worth the risk to the pseudosome. There were the other directions—flat and grassy; there was the landcrawler for crossing them.

But there was nothing in those distances but more grass and more distance.

He shrugged, half a shiver, and turned his back on the river and the forest, climbed back to *Anne*, pulled branches away from her silvery body and held them out of her way.

"Come on. Let's go home."

"Yes, Warren." She swiveled smartly and reoriented, cracking branches with each metal tread, followed him through the tangle until they had come out of the brush again, walking side by side toward the plain, toward the ship.

No sign of Sax. It was useless. Sax would have

drowned in the river if his fever had carried him this way; drowned and been swept out to some brush heap elsewhere. Or seaward.

"*Anne,* would you have followed me if I'd tried to cross the river?"

"Instruction directed me to stay. Program directs me to protect you."

"I love you, too, Annie, but don't ever take the risk. I could cross the river without danger. My body floats in water. Yours sinks. The mud would bog you down."

"Program directs me to protect you."

"You can't protect me if you're at the bottom of the river. You can't float. Do you understand *float?*"

"Verb: be buoyant, rise. Noun—"

"Cancel. You stay away from that water, hear me?"

"I'm receiving you clearly, Warren."

"I order you to stay away from the river. If I go close, you stop and wait until I come back. You don't ever go into water. That's a permanent order."

"I perceive possible priority conflict."

"You have to preserve yourself to carry out your instruction to protect me. True?"

"Yes."

"Water can damage you. It can't damage me. If I choose to go there, I go. You stay away from the water."

A delay. "Recorded."

He frowned, hitched the pack up and looked askance at her, then cast another, longer look backward.

Build a bridge, perhaps? Make the other side accessible for *Anne?* The thought of going beyond her

range made him uneasy—if he should run into difficulty, need her—

There were the com units. The portable sensors.

He wanted to go over there, to know what was
there. And not there.

THE MICROSCOPE turned up a variety of bacteria
in the water. He sat in the lab, staring at the cavort-
ing shapes, shaken by that tiny movement as if it had
been the sight of birds or beasts. *Something* lived here
and moved.

Such things, he recalled, could work all manner of
difficulties in a human gut. He called up Library,
went through the information gleaned of a dozen
worlds. The comparisons might have told Sikutu something, but he found it only bewildering. They might
be photosynthesizing animalcules, or contractile plants.

Heat killed the specimens. He shoved the plate
into the autoclave and felt like a murderer. He
thought even of walking back to the river to pour
the rest of the vial in. Life had become that precious.
He nerved himself and boiled the rest—imagined
tiny screams in the hissing of the bubbles. It left pale
residue.

TWO DAYS he lay about, thinking, distracting
himself from thought. He sat in *Anne's* observation
dome at night, mapped the movements of the system's other worlds; by day, observed the sun through
filters. But there were the charts they had made
from space, and looking at the stars hurt too much.
It was too much wishing.

He stopped going there.

And then there was just the forest to think about. Only that left.

HE GATHERED his gear, set *Anne* to fetching this and that. He unbolted a land-crawler from its braces, serviced it, loaded it to the bay and loaded it with gear: inflatable raft, survival kit.

"Let it down," he told *Anne*. "Lower the cargo lift."

She came out afterward, bringing him what he had asked, standing there while he loaded the supplies on.

"Assistance?"

"Go back in. Seal the ship. Wait for me."

"My program is to protect you."

"The pseudosome stays here." He reached into the crawler, where the sensor remote unit sat, a black square box on the passenger seat. He turned it on. "That better?"

"The sensor unit is not adequate for defense."

"The pseudosome is not permitted to leave this area unless I call you. There's no animate life, no danger. I'll be in contact. The unit is enough for me to call you if I need help. Obey instructions."

"Please reconsider this program."

"Obey instructions. If you damage that pseudosome, it's possible I won't be able to fix it, and then I won't have it when I need you. True?"

"Yes."

"Then stay here." He walked round, climbed into the driver's seat, started the engine. "Recorded?"

"Recorded."

He put it in gear and drove off through the grass— looked back as he turned it toward the forest. She still stood there. He turned his attention to the rough ground ahead, fought the wheel.

A machine, after all. There were moments when he lost track of that.

The sensor unit light glowed. She was still beside him.

HE DRAGGED the raft down the sandy slope, unwieldy bundle, squatted there a moment to catch his breath on the riverside. The wind whispered in the leaves. No noise of motors. He felt the solitude. He saw details, rather than the sterile flatnesses of the ship, absorbed himself in the hush, the moving of the water.

He moved finally, unrolled the raft and pulled the inflation ring. It hissed, stiffened, spread itself.

Beep. Beep-beep-beep.

The sensor box. His heart sped. He scrambled up the sandy rise of the crawler and reached the box in the seat. "*Anne.* What's wrong?"

"Please state your location," the box asked him.

"Beside the river."

"This agrees with my location findings. Please reconsider your program, Warren."

"*Anne,* you keep that pseudosome where it is. I'll call you if I need you. And I don't need you. I'm all right and there's no danger."

"I picked up unidentified sound."

He let his breath go. "That was the raft inflating. I did it. There's no danger."

"Please reconsider your program."

"*Anne,* take instruction. Keep that pseudosome with the ship. I've got a small communicator with me.

The sensor box weighs too much for me to carry it with the other things I need. I'm going to leave it in the crawler. But I'm taking the communicator. I'll call you if there's an emergency or if I need assistance."

"Response time will be one hour seventeen minutes to reach your present location. This is unacceptable."

"I tell you it is acceptable. I don't need your assistance."

"Your volume and pitch indicate anger."

"Yes, I'm angry."

"Be happy, Warren."

"I'll be happy if you do what I told you and keep that pseudosome at the ship."

A long delay. "Recorded."

He took the communicator from the dash, hooked it to his belt. Walked off without a further word. *Anne* worried him. There was always that conflict-override. She could do something unpredictable if some sound set her off, some perception as innocent as the raft cylinder's noise.

But there was nothing out here to trigger her. Nothing.

He slipped the raft away from the shore, quietly, quietly, used the paddle with caution. The current took him gently and he stroked leisurely against it.

A wind sighed down the river, disturbing the warmth, rustling the leaves. He drove himself toward the green shadow of the far bank, skimmed the shore a time.

There was a kind of tree that flourished on that side, the leaves of which grew in clusters on the drooping branches, like fleshy green flowers, and moss that festooned other trees never grew on this kind. He saw that.

There was a sort of green flower of thin, brown-veined leaves that grew up from the shallows, green lilies on green pads. The river sent up bubbles among them, and he probed anxiously with his paddle, disturbed their roots, imagining some dire finned creature whipping away from that probing—but he only dislodged more bubbles from rotting vegetation on the bottom. The lilies and the rot were cloyingly sweet.

He let the current take the raft back to the far-shore point nearest his starting place. He drove the raft then into the shallows and stood up carefully, stepped ashore without wetting his boots, dragged the raft up by the mooring rope and secured it to a stout branch to keep the current from unsettling it by any chance.

He took his gear, slung the strap over his shoulder, looked about him, chose his path.

He thumbed the communicator switch. *"Anne."*

"Assistance?"

"Precaution. I'm fine. I'm happy. I have a program for you. I want you to call me every hour on the hour and check my status."

"Recorded. Warren, please confirm your position."

"At the river. Same as before. Obey your instructions."

"Yes."

He thumbed the switch over to receive, and started walking.

Ferns. Bracken, waist-high. Great clumps of curling hairy fronds: he avoided these; avoided the soft vine growth that festooned the high limbs of the trees and dropped like curtains.

Beyond the forest rim the ferns gave way to fungi, small round balls that he thought at first were animals, until he prodded one with a stick and broke it. There were domes, cones, parasols, rods with feathered fringes. Platelet fungi of orange and bluish white grew on rotting logs and ridged the twisted roots of living trees. Color. The first color but green and white and brown, anywhere in the world.

The trees grew taller, became giants far different from the riverside varieties. They loomed up straight and shadowy-crowned, their branches interlacing to shut out the sun. The light came through these branches in shafts when it came at all; and when night came here, he reckoned, it would be night indeed.

He stopped and looked back, realizing he had long since lost sight or sound of the river. He took his axe; it took resolution to move after such silence, more than that to strike, to make a mark. He deafened himself to the sacrilege and started walking again, cutting a mark wherever he passed from view of the last. Chips fell white onto the spongy carpet of eons-undisturbed leaves. The echoes lasted long, like eerie voices.

"*Warren.*"

His heart all but stopped.

"*Anne.* My status is good."

"Thank you."

Com went off again. He kept walking, marking his way, like walking in some great cavern. The way seemed different when viewed from the reverse, and the trees grew larger and larger still, so that he had to cut deep to make his marks, and he had to struggle over roots, some knee-high, making going slow.

He saw light and walked toward it, losing it sometimes in the tangle, but coming always closer—broke finally upon a grove of giants, greater than any trees he had seen. One, vaster than any others, lay splintered and fallen, ancient, moss-bearded. A younger tree supported it, broken beneath the weight; and through the vacant space in the forest ceiling left by the giant's fall, sunlight streamed in a broad shaft to the forest floor, where soft green moss grew and white flowers bloomed, blessed by that solitary touch of daylight. Motes danced in the sun, the drift of pollen, golden-touched in a green light so filtered it was like some airy sea.

Warren stopped, gazed in awe at the cataclysmic ruin of a thing so old. The crash it must have made, in some great storm, with never an ear to hear it. He walked farther, stood in the very heart of the sunlight and looked up at the blinding sky. It warmed. It filled all the senses with warmth and well-being.

He looked about him, ventured even to touch the giant's mossy beard, the bark, the smoothness where the bark had peeled away. He walked farther, half-blind, into the deep shadows beyond, his mind still dazed by the place. All about him now was brown and green, bark and leaves, white fungi, platelets as large as his hand stepping up the roots; ferns, fronds unfurling waist-high, scattering their spores. The tangle grew thicker.

And he realized of a sudden he had come some distance from the clearing.

He looked back. Nothing was recognizable.

He refused panic. He could not have come far. He began to retrace his path, confident at first, then with growing uncertainty as he failed to find things he recalled. He cursed himself. His heart pounded. He tore his hands on the brush that clawed at him. He felt as vulnerable suddenly as a child in the dark, as if the sunlit clearing were the only safe place in the world. He tried to run, to find it more quickly, to waste no time. Trees pressed close about him, straight and vast and indifferently the same, their gnarled roots crossing and interweaving in the earth as their branches laced across the sky.

He had missed the clearing. He was lost. All ways looked the same. He ran, thrust his way from trunk to trunk, gasping for breath, slipped among the tangled wet roots, went sprawling, hands skinned, chin abraded by the bark. He lay breathless, the wind knocked from him, all his senses jolted.

Slowly there came a prickling of nerves in the stillness, through his spasmodic gasps, a crawling at the back of his neck. He held himself tremblingly still at first, his own weight holding him where he had fallen, awkward and painfully bent. He scrabbled with his hands, intending one swift movement, clawed his way over to wave it off him.

Nothing was there, only the brush, the vast roots. The feeling was still behind him, and he froze, refusing to look, gripped in sweating nightmare.

Of a sudden he sprang up, ran, favoring his right leg, sprawled again his full length in the wet, slick leaves, scrambled and fought his way through the thicket. The chill presence—it had direction—stayed constantly on his right, pressing him left and left again, until he stumbled and struggled through worse and worse, tearing himself and the pack through the branches and the fern, ripping skin, endangering his eyes.

He broke into light, into the clearing, into the warm shaft of sun. He fell hard on his hands and knees in that center of warmth and light, sobbing and ashamed and overwhelmed with what had happened to him.

He had panicked. He knew his way now. He was all right. He sank down on his belly, the pack still on his back, and tried to stop shaking.

Strangeness flowed over him like water, not quite warmth, but a feather-touch that stirred the hair at his nape. He moved, tried to rise and run, but he was weighted, pinned by the pack like a specimen on a glass, in the heat and the blinding daylight, while something poured and flowed over his skin. Sweat ran. His breathing grew shallow.

Illness. A recurrence of the plague. He groped at his belt for the communicator and lost it, his hand gone numb. He lay paralyzed, his open eyes filled with translucent green, sunlight through leaves. The sighing wind and rush of waters filled his ears and slowed his breath.

Deep and numbing quiet. Ages came and the rains and the sun filtered down season upon season. Ages passed and the forest grew and moved about him. His body pressed deep to the earth, deep into it, while his arms lifted skyward. He was old, old, and hard with strength and full of the life that swelled and struggled to heaven and earth at once.

Then the sun was shining down in simple warmth and he was aware of his own body, lying drained, bearing the touch of something very like a passing breeze.

He managed to stand at last, faltered, numb even yet, and looked about him. No breath of wind. No leaves stirred.

"Warren?"

He stooped, gathered up the com unit. "I'm here, *Anne.*"

"What's your status, Warren?"

He drew a deep breath. The presence—if it had been anything at all but fear—was gone.

"What's your status, Warren?"

"I'm all right—I'm all right. I'm starting home now."

He kept the com unit on, in his hand, for comfort, not to face the deep woods alone. He found his first mark, the way that he had come in. He struggled from one to the other of the slash marks, tearing through when he sighted the next, making frantic haste . . . away from what, he did not know.

5

HE WAS ASHAMED of himself, on the other side of the river, sitting in the raft, which swayed against the shore, the paddle across his knees. Clothing torn, hands scratched, face scraped by branches, his left eye watering where one had raked it . . . he knew better than what he had done, racing hysterically over unknown ground.

He wiped his face, realized the possibility of contaminants and wiped his bleeding hands on his trousers. Hallucination. He had breathed something, gotten it when he had scratched himself, absorbed it through the skin ... a hundred ways he had exposed himself to contaminants. He felt sick. Scared. Some hallucinogens recurred. He needed nothing like that.

"Warren?"

He fumbled out the com unit, answered, holding it in both hands, trying not to shiver. "Everything all right, *Anne?*"

"All stable," *Anne* replied. He cherished the voice in the stillness, the contact with something infallible. He sought a question to make her talk.

"Have your sensors picked up anything?"

"No, Warren."

"What have you been doing?"

"Monitoring my systems."

"You haven't had any trouble?"

"No, Warren."

"I'm coming back now."

"Thank you, Warren."

He cut the com unit off, sat holding it as if it were something living. A piece of *Anne*. A connection. His hands shook. He steadied them, put the unit back at his belt, got up and climbed ashore, limping. Pulled the raft up and achored it to a solid limb.

No taking it back, no. The raft stayed. No retreats. He looked back across the river, stared at the far darkness with misgivings.

There was nothing there.

*　　*　　*

LIGHT WAS fading in the drive back. The crawler jounced and bucked its way along the track he had made through the grass on the way out, and the headlights picked up the bent grass ahead, in the dark, in the chill wind. He drove too fast, forced himself to keep it to a controllable pace on the rough ground.

"*Anne,*" he asked through the com, "turn the running lights on."

"Yes, Warren."

The ship lit up, colors and brilliance in the dark ahead of him. Beautiful. He drove toward it, fought the wheel through pits and roughnesses, his shoulders aching.

"Dinner, *Anne.* What's for dinner?"

"Baked chicken, potatoes, greens, and coffee."

"That's good." His teeth were chattering. The wind was colder than he had thought it would be. He should have brought his coat.

"Are you happy, Warren?"

"I'm going to want a bath when I get there."

"Yes, Warren. Are you happy, Warren?"

"Soon." He kept talking to her, idiocies, anything to fend off the cold and the queasiness in the night. The grass whipped by the fenders, a steady whisper. His mind conjured night-wandering devils, apparitions out of bushes that popped out of the dark and whisked under the nose of the crawler. He drove for the lights. "Be outside," he asked *Anne.* "Wait for me at the cargo lock."

"Yes, Warren. I'm waiting."

He found her there when he had brought the crawler round the nose of the ship and came up facing the lock. He drew up close to her, put on the brake and shut down the crawler engine, hauled himself out of the seat and set unsteady feet on the ground. *Anne* clicked over, sensor lights winking red in the dark. "Assistance?"

"Take the kit and the sensor box out and stow them in the lock." He patted her metal shoulder because he wanted to touch something reasonable. "I'm going inside to take my bath."

"Yes, Warren."

He headed for the lock, stripped off all that he was wearing while the platform ascended, ran the decontamination cycle at the same time. He headed through the ship with his clothes over his arm, dumped them into the laundry chute in the shower room, set the boots beside, for thorough cleaning.

He stayed in the mist cabinet a good long while, letting the heat and the steam seep into his pores— leaned against the back wall with eyes closed, willing himself to relax, conscious of nothing but the warmth of the tiles against his back and the warmth of the moisture that flooded down over him. The hiss of the vapor jets drowned all other sounds, and the condensation on the transparent outer wall sealed off all the world.

A sound came through . . . not a loud one, the impression of a sound. He lifted his head, cold suddenly, looked at the steam-obscured panel, unable to identify what he had heard.

He had not closed the doors. The shower was open, and while he had been gone—while he had been gone from the ship, the pseudosome standing outside—The old nightmare came back to him. Sax.

Somewhere in the depths of the ship, wandering about, giving *Anne* orders that would prevent her reporting his presence. Sax, mind-damaged, with the knife in his hand. He stood utterly still, heart pounding, trying to see beyond the steamed, translucent panel for whatever presence might be in the room.

A footstep sounded outside, and another, and a gangling human shadow slid in the front panel while his heart worked madly. Leaned closer, and red lights gleamed, diffused stars where the features ought to be. "Warren?"

For an instant more the nightmare persisted, *Anne* become the presence. He shook it off, gathering up his courage to cut the steam off, to deal with her. "*Anne*, is there trouble?"

"No, Warren. The kit—and the sensor box are stowed. Dinner is ready."

"Good. Wait there."

She waited. *His* orders. He calmed himself, activated the dryer and waited while moisture was sucked out of the chamber . . . took the comb he had brought in with him and straightened his hair in the process. The fans stopped, the plastic panel cleared, so that he could see *Anne* standing beyond the frosted translucence. He opened the door and walked out, and her limbs moved, reorienting her to him, responding to him like a flower to the sun. He felt ashamed for his attack of nerves—more than ashamed, deeply troubled. His breathing still felt uncertain, a tightness about his chest, his pulse still elevated. He cast a look over his shoulder as he reached for his robe, at the three shower cabinets, all dark now, concealments, hiding places. The silence deadened his ears, numbed his senses. He shrugged into the robe and heard *Anne* move at his back. He spun about, back to the corner, staring into *Anne*'s vacant faceplate where the lights winked red in the darkness.

"Assistance?"

He did not like her so close . . . a machine, a mind, one mistake of which, one seizing of those metal hands— She followed him. He could not discover the logic on which she had done so. She watched him. Obsessively.

Followed him. He liked that analysis even less. Things started following him and he started seeing devils in familiar territory. He straightened against the wall and made himself catch his breath, fighting the cold chills that set him shivering.

"Warren? Assistance?"

He took her outstretched metal arm and felt the faint vibration under his fingers as she compensated for his weight. "I need help."

"Please be specific."

He laughed wildly, patted her indestructible shoulder, fighting down the hysteria, making himself see her as she was, machine. "Is dinner ready?"

"Yes. I've set it on the table."

He walked with her, into the lift, into the upper level of the ship, the living quarters where the table that he used was, outside his own quarters. He never used the mess hall: it was too empty a place, too many chairs; he no more went there than he opened the quarters of the dead, next door to him, all about him. He sat down, and *Anne* served him, poured the coffee, added the cream. The dinner was good enough, without fault. He found himself with less appetite than he had thought, in the steel and plastic enclosure of the ship, with the ventilation sounds and the small sounds of *Anne*'s motors. It was dark round about. He was intensely conscious of that—the night outside, the night deep in the ship where daylight made no difference. *Anne*'s natural condition, night: she lived in it, in space; existed in it here, except for the lights that burned here, that burned in corridors when he walked through them and compartments when he was there, but after he was gone, it reverted to its perpetual dark. Dark wrapped everything in the world but this compartment, but him, and he dared not sleep. He feared the dreams coming back. Feared helplessness.

No sign of Sax, out there.

He drank his coffee, sat staring at the plate until *Anne* took it away. Finally he shivered and looked toward the bar cabinet at the far side of the common room. He gave himself permission, got up, opened the cabinet, pulled out a bottle and the makings and took it back to the table.

"Assistance?" *Anne* asked, having returned from the galley.

"I'll do it myself. No trouble." He poured himself a drink. "Get some ice."

She left on the errand. He drank without, had mostly finished the glass when she came back with a thermal bucket full. She set it on the table and he made himself another.

That was the way to get through the night. He was not a drinking man. But it killed the fear. It warmed his throat and spread a pleasant heat through his belly where fear had lain like an indigestible lump.

He had not planned to drink much. But the heat itself was pleasant, and the lassitude it spread through him cured a multitude of ills. By the time he arrived at the bottom of the third glass, he had a certain courage. He smiled bitterly at *Anne*'s blank face. Then he filled a fourth glass and drank it, on the deliberate course to total anesthesia.

It hit him then, sudden and coming down like a vast weight. He started to get up, to clear his head, staggered and knocked the glass over. "Assistance?" *Anne* asked.

He leaned on the table rim, reached for the chair and missed it for an instant. *Anne*'s metal fingers closed on his arm and held. He yelled, from fright, trying to free himself. Those fingers which could bend metal pipe closed no farther. "Is this pain?" she asked. "What is your status, Warren?"

"Not so good, *Anne*. Let go. Let me go."

"Pain is not optimum function. I can't accept programming from a human who's malfunctioning."

"You're hurting my arm. You're causing the pain. Stop it."

She let him go at once. "Assistance?"

He caught his balance against her, leaning heavily until his stomach stopped heaving and his head stopped spinning quite so violently. She accepted his weight, stabilizing with small hums of her motors. "Assistance? Assistance?"

He drew a shaken breath and choked it down past the obstruction in his throat, patted her metal shoulder. "Contact—is assistance enough. It's all right, Annie. I'm all right." He staggered for one of the reclining chairs a little distance across the room and made it, his head spinning as he let it back. "Keep the lights on. Lock your doors and accesses."

"Program accepted, Warren. This is security procedure. Please state nature of emergency."

"Do you perceive any form of life . . . but me . . . anywhere?"

"Vegetation."

"Then there isn't any, is there?" He looked hazily up at her towering, spidery form. "Obey instruction. Keep the accesses locked. Always keep them locked unless I ask you to open them. *Anne*, can you sit down?"

"Yes, Warren. You programmed that pattern."

The worktable, he recalled. He pointed at the other chair. "Sit in the chair."

Anne walked to it and negotiated herself smoothly into its sturdy, padded seat, and looked no more comfortable sitting than she had reclining on the worktable.

"Your median joints," he said. "Let your middle joints and shoulders quit stabilizing." She did so, and her body sagged back. He grinned. "Left ankle on top of right ankle, legs extended. Pattern like me. Loosen all but balance-essential stabilizers. It's called relaxing, Annie." He looked at her sitting there, arms like his arms, on the chair, feet extended and crossed, faceplate reflecting back the ceiling light and flickering inside with minute red stars. He laughed hysterically.

"This is a pleasure reflex," she observed.

"Possibly." He snugged himself into the curvature of the chair. "You sit there, Annie, and you keep your little sensors—all of them, inside and outside the ship—alert. And if you detect any disturbance of them at all, wake me up."

HIS HEAD hurt in the morning, hurt sitting still and hurt worse when he moved it, and ached blindingly while he bathed and shaved and dressed. He kept himself moving, bitter penance. He cleaned the living quarters and the galley, finally went down to the lock through crashes of the machinery that echoed in his head. The sunlight shot through his eyes to his nerve endings, all the way to his fingertips, and he walked out blind and with eyes watering and leaned on the nearest landing strut, advantaging himself of its pillar-like shade.

He was ashamed of himself, self-disgusted. The fear had gotten him last night. The solitude had. He was not proud of his behavior in the forest: that was one thing, private and ugly; but when he came home and went to pieces in the ship, because it was dark, and because he had bad dreams . . .

That scared him, far more substantially than any forest shadow deserved. His own mind had pounced on him last night.

He walked out, wincing in the sunlight, to the parked crawler, leaned on the fender and followed with his eyes the track he had made coming in, before it curved out of sight around the ship. Grass and brush. He had ripped through it last night as if it had all turned animate. Hallucinations, perhaps. After last night he had another answer, which had to do with solitude and the human mind.

He went back inside and finally took something for his head.

BY 1300 hours he was feeling better, the housekeeping duties done. Paced, in the confines of the living quarters, and caught himself doing it.

Work had been the anodyne until now . . . driving himself, working until he dropped; he ran out of work and it was the liquor, to keep the nightmares off. Neither could serve, not over the stretch of years. He was not accustomed to thinking *years*. He forced himself to . . . to think of a life in more than terms of survival; to think of living as much as of doing and finding and discovering.

He took one of the exercise mats outside, brought a flask of iced juice along with his biological notes and took *Anne* with him, with his favorite music tapes fed to the outside speakers. He stripped, spread his mat just beyond the canopy, and lay down to read, the music playing cheerfully and the warmth of Harley's star seeping pleasantly into his well-lotioned skin. He slept for a time, genuine and relaxed sleep, awoke and turned onto his back to let the sun warm his front for a time, a red glow through his closed lids.

"Warren?"

He shaded his eyes and looked up at the standing pseudosome. He had forgotten her. She had never moved.

"Warren?"

"Don't nag, Annie. I didn't say anything. Come here and sit down. You make me nervous."

Anne dutifully obeyed, bent, flexed her knees an

alarming distance and fell the last half foot, catching herself on her extended hands, knees drawn up and spine rigid. Warren shook his head in despair and amusement. "Relax. You have to do that when you sit."

The metal body sagged into jointed curves, brought itself more upright, settled again.

"Dear Annie, if you were only human."

Anne turned her sensor lights on, all of them. Thought a moment. "Corollary, Warren?"

"To what? To *if*? *Anne*, my love, you aren't, and there isn't any."

He had confused her. The lights flickered one after the other. "Clarify."

"Human nature, that's all. Humans don't function well alone. They need contact with someone. But I'm all right. It's nothing to concern you."

The motors hummed faintly and *Anne* reached out and let her hand down on his shoulder. The action was so human it frightened him. He looked into her ovoid face at the lights that danced inside and his heart beat wildly.

"Is your status improving?"

Contact with someone. He laughed sorrowfully and breathed a sigh.

"I perceive internal disturbances."

"Laughter. You know laughter."

"This was different."

"The pace of laughter varies."

"Recorded." *Anne* drew back her hand. "You're happy."

"*Anne*—what do you think about when I'm not

here. When I'm not asking you to do something, and you have thoughts, what are they?"

"I have a standard program."

"And what's that?"

"I maintain energy levels, regulate my circulation and temperature, monitor and repair my compon-ent—"

"Cancel. You don't think. Like you do with me. You don't ask questions, decide, follow sequences of reasoning."

The lights blinked a moment. "The automatic func-tions are sufficient except in an anomalous situation."

"But I'm talking to the AI. *You.* the AI's some-thing other than those programs. What do you do, sleep?"

"I wait."

Like the pseudosome, standing indefinitely. No discomfort to move her, to make her impatient. "You investigate stimuli."

"Yes."

"But there aren't many, are there?"

A delay. Incomplete noun. "They are constant but not anomalous."

"You're bored too."

"Bored. No. Bored is not a state of optimum func-tion. Bored is a human state of frustrated need for activity. This is not applicable to me. I function at optimum."

"Functioning constantly doesn't damage you."

"No."

"Use the library. You can do that, can't you? If there aren't adequate stimuli in the environment to engage the AI, use the library. Maybe you'll learn something."

"Recorded."

"And then what do we do?"

The lights blinked. "Context indeterminate. Please restate the question."

"You could know everything there is to know, couldn't you, and you'd sit with it inside you and do nothing."

"Context of *do* indeterminate. I'm not able to process the word in this context."

He reached out, patted her silver leg. The sensors blinked. Her hand came back to him and stayed there, heavy, on his shoulder. *Contact.*

"That's enough," he said, and removed his hand from her; she did the same. "Thank you, *Anne*." But he was cold inside.

He relaxed finally, staring out beneath the ship toward the forest.

There was the fear. There was where it sat. He hurt inside, and the healing was there, not sealing himself into the ship. Sterility. Inane acts and inane conversation.

If he feared out there, the fear itself proved he was alive. It was an enemy to fight. It was something he did not program. It held the unanticipated, and that was precious.

Anne, waiting forever, absorbing the stimuli and waiting for something anomalous, to turn on her intelligence. He saw himself doing that, sitting in the ship and waiting for a human lifetime—for some anomaly in the wind.

No.

6

HE CAME THIS time with a different kind of attack, slowly, considerately, the crawler equipped with sensor box and sample kits and recorders and food and water, rope and directional beeper, anything that seemed remotely useful. With the film camera. With a rifle with a nightscope. Overequipped, if anything, in which he found some humor . . . but he felt the safer for it.

The raft was still securely tied to the branch, the sand about it unmarked by the passage of any moving creature, even void of insect tracks. On the far bank the forest waited in the dawn, peaceful—dark inside, as it would always be.

Someday, he promised it. He loaded the raft, trip after trip from the crawler parked up on the bank. *Anne* was with him, disembodied, in the incarnation of her sensor box, in the com unit. She talked to him, telling him she detected vegetation, and he laughed and snugged the box into the bottom of the raft.

"Reception is impaired," *Anne* complained.

"Sorry. I don't want to drop the box into the river."

"Please don't do that, Warren."

He laughed again, in a good humor for *Anne*'s witless witticisms. Piled other supplies about her sensors. "I'll pull you out if I need you. Take care of the ship. I'm shutting you down. Your noise is interfering with my reception."

"Please reconsider this program. The river is dangerous. Please reconsider."

"Quiet." He shut her down. There was a reciprocal turn-on from her side, but she took orders and stayed off this time. He piled the last load in, coat and blanket in case it grew chill on the water.

He untied the raft then, nudged it out a little, stepped in and sat down, taking up the paddle. It was not one of his skills, rafting. He had read the manual and thought it out. Drove against the gentle current, no great work: he reasoned that he could paddle upstream as long as he liked or wanted to, and return was the river's business.

He passed the landing site on the far bank, passed an old log and wound along with the grassy bank on one side and the forest on the other. The river was so still on most of its surface it was hard to see in which direction it flowed. Shores turned to marsh on either side, and at some time unnoticed, the trees on the right, which had been growing thicker and thicker, closed off all view of the grasslands where the ship had landed. The banks began to have a thick border of reeds; some trees grew down into the water, making an obstacle of their knobby roots, making curtains of moss hanging almost low enough to sweep his shoulders as he passed. Green lilies drifted, beds of pads through which he drove the raft with shallow strokes, not to tangle the blade of the paddle in their tough stems. In places the navigable channel was no more than three meters across, a weaving of reeds and sandbars and shadows between banks a good stone's throw from side to side. It was a sleepy place, all tones of green and brown . . . no sky that was not filtered by leaves. A certain kind of tree was in bloom, shedding white petals as large as a man's hand on the water: they drifted like high-stemmed boats, clouds of them afloat, fleets and armadas destroyed by the dip of his paddle and the raft's blunt bow. The full flower had long stamens and pistils so that they looked like white spiders along the branches when they had shed, and like flocks of birds before. Lilies were rife, and a fine-leafed floating weed grew wherever the water was shallow. It was worse than the lilies for tangling up the paddle: it broke off and hung, slick brownish leaves. It was not, he decided, particularly lovely stuff, and it made going very slow in the narrowest channels.

His shoulders began to ache with the long effort. He kept going long after the ache became painful, anxious not to give ground . . . decided finally to put ashore for a space, when he had seen an area not so brushy and overgrown. He drove for it, rammed the bow up and started pulling it about with strokes of the paddle.

The paddle tip sank in, worse and worse with his efforts, tipped the raft with the suction as he pulled it out again and the raft slapped down with a smack. He frowned, jabbed at the sand underneath with his paddle, reducing it to jelly and thinking ruefully where he might have been if he had not mistrusted the water purity and if he had bounded out to drag the raft ashore. It took some little maneuvering to skim the raft off the quicksands and out again, back into the main channel, and he forgot his aching shoulders to keep it going awhile.

"Warren?"

On the hour, as instructed. He stilled his heart and punched on his com unit, never stopping his paddling. "Hello, Annie. Status is good, love, but I need three hands just now."

"Assistance? Estimate of time required to reach your position—"

"Cancel. Don't you try it. I'm managing with two hands quite nicely. How are you?"

"All my systems are functioning normally, but my sensors are impaired by obstructions. Please clear my pickups, Warren."

"No need. My sensors aren't impaired and there's nothing anomalous."

"I detect a repeated sound."

"That's the raft's propulsion. There's no hazard. All systems are normal. My status is good. Call in another hour."

"Yes, Warren."

"Shut down."

"Yes, Warren."

Contact went out; the box lights went off.

He closed off contact from his side, pushed off the bank where he had drifted while he was arguing with *Anne*, and hand-over-handed himself past a low-hanging branch. He snubbed a loop of the mooring rope around it, snugged it down, resting for a moment while the raft swayed sleepily back and forth.

It's beautiful, he thought, *Sax. Min and Harley, it's worth seeing.* He squinted up at the sunlight dancing through the branches. *Hang the captain, Harley. They'll come here sometime. They'll want the place. In someone's lifetime.*

No answer. The sunlight touched the water and sparkled there, in one of the world's paralyzing silences. An armada of petals floated by. A flotilla of bubbles. He watched others rise, near the roots of the tree.

Life, Harley?

He rummaged after one of the sample bags, after the seine from the collection kit. He flung the seine out inexpertly, maneuvered it in the current, pulled it up. The net was fouled with the brownish weed, and caught in it were some strands of gelatinous matter, each a finger's length, grayish to clear with an opaque kernel in the center. He wrinkled his lip, not liking the look of it, reached and threw the sensor unit on again, holding its pickup wand almost touching the strands.

"Warren, I perceive an indeterminate life form, low order."

"How—indeterminate?"

"It may be plant but that identification is not firm."

"I thought so. Now I don't particularly know what to do with it. It's stuck to the net and I don't like to go poking at it bare-handed. Curious stuff."

"Assistance?"

"Wait." He put the scanner wand down and used both hands to evert the net, cleared it by shaking it in the water. He put the net into plastic before letting it back in the raft and sprayed his hands and the side of the raft with disinfectant before picking up the wand and putting it back. "I'm rid of it now, Annie, no trouble. I'm closing everything down now. Observe your one-hour schedule."

He slipped the rope, took up the paddle and extricated the raft from the reeds, where it had swung its right side. Headed for the center of the clear channel.

It might have been eggs, he thought. Might have

been. He considered the depth of the channel, the murkiness of the water, and experienced a slight disquiet. Something big could travel that, lurk round the lily roots. He did not particularly want to knock into something.

Nonsense, Harley. No more devils. No more things in the dark. I won't make them anymore, will I, Sax? No more cold sweats.

The river seemed to bend constantly left, deeper into the forest, though he could not see any more or any less on either hand as it went. The growth on the banks was the same. There was an abundance of the fleshy-leaved trees that poured sap so freely when bruised, and the branches hung down into the water so thickly in places that they formed a curtain before whatever lay on shore. The spidertrees shed their white blooms, and the prickly ones thrust out twisted and arching limbs, gnarled and humped roots poking out into the channel. Moss was everywhere, and reeds and waterweed. He realized finally that the river had long since ceased to have any recognizable shore. On the left stretched a carpet of dark green moss that bloomed enticingly. Trees grew scattered there, incredibly neat, as if it were tended by some gardener, and the earth looked so soft and inviting to the touch, so green, the flowers like stars scattered across it.

Then he realized why the place looked so soft and flat, and why the trees grew straight up like columns, without the usual ugliness of twisting roots. That was not earth but floating moss, and when he put his paddle down, he found quicksand on the bottom.

An ugly death, that—sinking alive into a bog, to

live for a few moments among the sands and the corruption that oozed round the roots of the trees. To drown in it.

He gave a twist of his mouth and shoved at the paddle, sent the raft up the winding course in haste to be out of it, then halted, drifting back a little as he did so.

The river divided here, coming from left and from right about a finger of land that grew thicker as it went—no islet, this, but the connection of a tributary with the river.

He paddled closer and looked up both overgrown ways. The one on the right was shallower, more choked with reeds, moss growing in patches across its surface, brush fallen into it which the weak current had not removed. He chose the left.

At least, he reasoned with himself, there was no chance of getting lost, even without the elaborate directional equipment he carried: no matter how many times the river subdivided, the current would take him back to the crossing. He had no fear in that regard; for all that the way grew still more tangled.

No light here, but what came darkly diffused. The channel was like a tunnel among the trees. From time to time now he could see larger trees beyond the shoreline vegetation, the tall bulk of one of the sky-reaching giants like those of the grove. He wondered now if he had not been much closer to the river than he had realized when he passed the grove and ran hysterically through the trees, feeling devils at his heels. *That* would have been a surprise, to have run out onto clear and mossy ground and to find himself in quicksand up to his ears. So there were deadly dangers in the forest—not the creeping kind, but dangers enough to make recklessness, either fleeing or advancing, fatal.

"Warren."

Anne made her hourly call and he answered it shortly, without breath for conversation and lacking any substance to report. He rested finally, made fast the raft to the projecting roots of a gnarly tree, laid his paddle across the plastic-wrapped seine and settled down into the raft, his head resting on the inflated rim. He ate, had a cup of coffee from the thermos. Even this overgrown branch of the river was beautiful, considered item at a time. The star Harley was a warm spot dancing above the branches, and the water was black and rich. No wonder the plants flourished so. They grew in every available place. If the river were not moving, they would choke up the channel with their mass and make of it one vast spongy bog such as that other arm of the river had seemed to be.

"Warren."

He came awake and reached for the com. "Emergency?"

"No, Warren. The time is 1300 hours."

"Already?" He levered himself upright against the rim and looked about him at the shadows. "Well, how are you?"

"I'm functioning well, thank you."

"So am I, love. No troubles. In fact . . ." he added cautiously, "in fact I'm beginning to think of extending this operation another day. There's no danger. I don't see any reason to come back and give up all the ground I've traveled, and I'd have to start now to get back to the launching point before dark."

"You'll exit my sensor range if you continue this direction for another day. Please reconsider this program."

"I won't go outside your sensor range. I'll stop and come back then."

A pause. "Yes, Warren."

"I'll call if I need you."

"Yes, Warren."

He broke the contact and pulled the raft upcurrent by the mooring line to reach the knot, untied it and took up the paddle again and started moving. He was content in his freedom, content in the maze, which promised endless secrets. The river could become a highway to its mountain source. He could devise relays that would keep *Anne* with him. He need not be held to one place. He believed in that again.

At 1400 he had a lunch of lukewarm soup and a sun-warmed sandwich, of which he ate every crumb, and wished he had brought larger portions. His appetite increased prodigiously with the exercise and the relaxation. He felt a profound sense of well-being . . . even found patience for a prolonged bout with *Anne*'s chatter. He called her up a little before 1500 and let her sample the river with her sensors, balancing the box on the gear so that she could have a look about.

"Vegetation," she pronounced. "Water. Warren, please reconsider this program."

He laughed at her and shut her down.

Then the river divided again, and again he bore to

the left, into the forest heart, where it was always twilight, and less than that now. He paddled steadily, ignoring the persistent ache in his back and shoulders, until he could no longer see where he was going, until the roots and limbs came up at him too quickly out of the dark and he felt the wet drag of moss across his face and arms more than once. 1837, when he checked the time.

"*Anne.*"

"Warren?"

"I'm activating your sensors again. There's no trouble, but I want you to give me your reports."

"You're in motion," she said as the box came on. "Low light. Vegetation and water. Temperature 19°C. A sound: the propulsion system. Stability in poor function."

"That's floating, *Anne.* Stability is poor, yes, but not hazardous."

"Thank you. You're behind my base point. I perceive you."

"No other life."

"Vegetation, Warren."

He kept moving, into worse and worse tangle, hoping for an end to the tunnel of trees, where he could at least have the starlight. Anne's occasional voice comforted him. The ghostly giants slid past, only slightly blacker than the night about him.

The raft bumped something underwater and slued about.

"You've stopped."

"I think I hit a submerged log or something." Adrenalin had shot through him at the jolt. He drew a deep breath. "It's getting too dark to see."

"Please reconsider this program."

"I think you have the right idea. Just a second." He prodded underwater with his paddle and hit a thing.

It came up, broke surface by the raft in the sensor light, mossy and jagged.

Log. He was free, his pulse jolting in his veins. He let the current take the raft then, let it turn the bow.

"Warren?"

"I'm loose. I'm all right." He caught a branch at a clearer spot and stopped, letting the fear ebb from him.

"Warren, you've stopped again."

"I stopped us." He wanted to keep running, but that was precisely the kind of action that could run him into trouble, pushing himself beyond the fatigue point. A log. It had been a log after all. He tied up to the branch, put on his jacket against the gathering chill and settled against the yielding rim of the raft, facing the low, reedy bank and the wall of aged trees. "*Anne*, I'm going to sleep now. I'm leaving the sensor box on. Keep alert and wake me if you perceive anything you have to ask about."

"Recorded. Good night, Warren."

"Good night, *Annie*."

He closed his eyes finally, confident at least of *Anne*'s watchfulness, rocked on the gently moving surface of the river. Tiniest sounds seemed loud, the slap of the water against its boundaries, the susurration of the leaves, the ceaseless rhythms of the world, of growth, of things that twined and fed on rain and death.

He dreamed of home as he had not done in a very

long time, of a hard-rock mining colony, his boy-
hood, a fascination with the stars; dreamed of Earth
of things he had only heard of, pictures he had seen
rivers and forests and fields. Pictured rivers came to
life and flowed, hurling his raft on past shores of
devastating silence, past the horror in the corridors,
figures walking in steam—

Sax—Sax leaping at him, knife in hand—

He came up with a gasp too loud in the silence.

"Warren? Emergency?"

"No." He wiped his face, glad of her presence.
"It's just a dream. It's all right."

"Malfunction?"

"Thoughts. Dream. A recycling of past experience. A clearing of files. It's all right. It's a natural
process. Humans do it when they sleep."

"I perceived pain."

"It's gone now. It stopped. I'm going back to sleep."

"Are you happy, Warren?"

"Just tired, *Anne*. Just very tired and very sleepy.
Good night."

"Good night, Warren."

He settled again and closed his eyes. The breeze
sighed and the water lapped gently, rocking him. He
curled up again and sank into deeper sleep.

HE AWOKE in dim light, in a decided chill that
made him glad of the jacket. The side of him that he
had lain on was cold through and he rubbed his arm
and leg, wishing for a hot breakfast instead of cold
sandwiches and lukewarm coffee.

A mist overlay the river a few inches deep. It
looked like a river of cloud flowing between the

green banks. He reached and turned off *Anne*'s sensors. "Shutting you down. It's morning. I'll be starting back in a moment. My status is good."

"Thank you, Warren."

He settled back again, enjoyed the beauty about him without *Anne*'s time and temperature analyses. He had no intention of letting his eyes close again, but it would be easy in this quiet, this peace.

The sense of well-being soured abruptly. He seemed heavier than the raft could bear, his head pounded, the pulse beat at his temples.

Something was radically wrong. He reached for the sensor box but he could no longer move. He blinked, aware of the water swelling and falling under him, of the branch of the aged tree above him.

Breath stopped. Sweat drenched him. Then the breathing reflex started again and the perspiration chilled. A curious sickly feeling went from shoulders to fingertips, unbearable pressure, as if his laboring heart would burst the veins. Pressure spread, to his chest, his head, to groin, to legs and toes. Then it eased, leaving him limp and gasping for air.

The hairs at his nape stirred, a fingering touch at his senses. Darts of sensation ran over his skin; muscles twitched, and he struggled to sit up; he was blind, with softness wrapping him in cotton and bringing him unbearable sorrow.

It passed.

"You're there," he said, blinking to clear his eyes. "You're *there*."

Not madness. Not insanity. Something had touched him in the clearing that day as it just had done here. "Who are you?" he asked it. "What do you want?"

But it had gone—no malevolence, no. It ached, it was so different. It was real. His heart was still racing from its touch. He slipped the knot, tugged the rope free, let the raft take its course.

"Find you," he told it. "I'll find you." He began to laugh, giddy at the spinning course the raft took, the branches whirling in wide circles above him.

"Warren," the box said, self-activated. "Warren? Warren?"

7

"HELLO, WARREN."

He gave a haggard grin climbing down from the land crawler, staggered a bit from weariness, edged past the pseudosome with a pat on the shoulder. "Hello yourself, Annie. Unload the gear out of the crawler."

"Yes, Warren. What is your status, please?"

"Fine, thanks. Happy. Dirty, tired and hungry, but happy overall."

"Bath and supper?"

"In that order."

"Sleep?"

"Possibly." He walked into the lock, stripped off his clothing as the cargo lift rose into netherdeck, already anticipating the luxury of a warm bath. He took the next lift up. "I'll want my robe. How are you?"

"I'm functioning well, thank you." Her voice came to him all over the ship. The lift stopped and let him out. She turned on the lights for him section by section and extinguished them after.

"What's for supper?"

"Steak and potatoes, Warren. Would you like tea or coffee?"

"Beautiful. Coffee."

"Yes, Warren."

He took a lingering bath, dried and dressed in his robe, went up to the living quarters where *Anne* had set the table for him, all the appointments, all the best. He sat down and looked up at *Anne*, who hovered there to pour him coffee.

"Pull up the other chair and sit down, will you, *Anne*?"

"Yes, Warren."

She released the facing chair from its transit braces, settled it in place, turned it and sat down correctly, metal arms on the table in exact imitation of him. Her lights dimmed once more as she settled into a state of waiting.

Warren ate in contented silence, not disturbing her. *Anne* had her limitations in small talk. When he had finished he pushed the dishes aside and *Anne*'s sensors brightened at once, a new program clicking into place. She rose and put everything onto the waiting tray, tidying up with a brisk rattle of aluminum and her own metal fingers.

"*Anne*, love."

"Yes, Warren."

"Activate games function."

Tray forgotten, she turned toward him. The screen on the wall lighted, blank. "Specify."

"You choose. You make a choice. Which game?"

Black and white squares flashed onto the screen.

Chess. He frowned and looked at her. "That's a new one. Who taught you that?"

"My first programmer installed the program."

He looked at the board, drew a deep breath. He had intended something rather simpler, some fast and stimulating fluff to shake the lingering sense from his brain. Something to sleep on. To see after his eyes were closed. He considered the game. "Are you good at chess?"

"Yes, Warren."

He was amused. "Take those dishes to the galley and come back up here. I'll play you."

"Yes, Warren." The board altered. She had chosen white. The first move was made. Warren turned his chair and reclined it to study the board, his feet on the newly cleared table. He gave her his move and the appropriate change appeared on the screen.

The game was almost over by the time the pseudo-some came topside again. She needed only four more moves to make his defeat a certainty. He sat back with his arms folded behind his head, studying his decimated forces. Shook his head in disbelief.

"Annie, *ma belle dame sans merci*—has anyone ever beaten you?"

"No, Warren."

He considered it a moment more, his lately bolstered well-being pricked. "Can you teach me what you know?"

"I've been programmed with the works of fifteen zonal champions. I don't estimate that I can teach you what I know. Human memory is fallible. Mine is not, provided adequate cues for recall and interrelation of data. One of my programmed functions is instruction in procedures. I can instruct."

He rolled a sidelong glance at her. "Fallible?"

"Fallible: capable of error."

"I don't need the definition. What makes you so talkative? Did I hit a program?"

"My first programmer was Franz Mann. He taught me chess. This is an exercise in logic. It's a testing mechanism, negative private appropriation. My function is to maintain you. I'm programmed to instruct in procedures. Chess is a procedure."

"All right," he said quietly. "All right, you can teach me."

"You're happy."

"You amuse me. Sit down."

She resumed the chair opposite him . . . her back to the board, but she did not need to see it. "Amusement produces laughter. Laughter is a pleasure or surprise indicator. Amusement is pleasant or surprising. Please specify which, Warren."

"You're both, *Anne*."

"Thank you. Pleasure is a priority function."

"Is it?"

"This is your instruction, Warren."

He frowned at her. In the human-maintenance programming he had poured a great number of definitions into her, and apparently he had gotten to a fluent area. Herself. Her prime level. She was essentially an egotist.

Another chessboard flashed onto the screen.

"Begin," she said.

She defeated him again, entered another game

127

before he found his eyes watering and his senses blurring out on the screen. He went to bed.

Trees and black and white squares mingled in his dreams.

THE NEXT venture took resting . . . took a body in condition and a mind at ease. He looked over the gear the next morning, but he refused to do anything more. Not at once. Not rushing back exhausted into the heart of the forest. He lazed about in the sun, had *Anne*'s careful hands rub lotion over his sore shoulders and back, felt immeasurably at peace with the world.

A good lunch, a nap afterward. He gave the ship a long-neglected manual check, in corridors he had not visited since the plague.

There was life in the botany lab, two of Rule's collection, succulents which had survived on their own water, two lone and emaciated spiny clusters. He came on them amid a tangle of brown husks of other plants which had succumbed to neglect, brushed the dead leaves away from them, tiny as they were. He looked for others and found nothing else alive. Two fellow survivors.

No knowing from what distant star system they had been gathered. Tray after tray of brown husks collapsed across the planting medium, victims of his shutdown order for the labs. He stripped it all, gathered the dead plants into a bin. Investigated the lockers and the drawers.

There were seeds, bulbs, rhizomes, all manner of starts. He thought of putting them outside, of seeing what they would do—but considering the ecology

. . . no; nothing that might damage that. He thought of bringing some of the world's life inside, making a garden; but the world outside was mostly lilies and waterflowers, and lacked colors. Some of these, he thought, holding a palmful of seeds, some might be flowers of all kinds of colors . . . odors and perfumes from a dozen different star systems. Such a garden was not for discarding. He could start them here, plant them in containers, fill the ship with them.

He grinned to himself, set to work reworking the planting medium, activating the irrigation system.

He located Rule's notebook and sat down and read through it, trying to decide on the seeds, how much water and how deep and what might be best.

He could fill the whole botany lab, and the plants would make seeds of their own. No more sterility. He pictured the living quarters blooming with flowers under the artificial sunlight. There was life outside the ship, something to touch, something to find; and in here . . . he might make the place beautiful, something he could live in while getting used to the world. No more fear. He could navigate the rivers, hike the forest . . . find whatever it was. Bring home the most beautiful things. Turn it all into a garden. He could leave that behind him, at least, when another team did come, even past his lifetime and into the next century. Records. He could feed them into *Anne* and she could send them to orbiting ships. He could learn the world and make records others could use. His world, after all. Whole colonies here someday who would know the name of Paul Warren and Harley and Rule, Burlin and Sax and Sikutu and the rest. Humans who would look at what he had made.

Who would approach what he had found out on the river with awe. Find it friendly, whether or not it was an intelligence. The ship could fit in . . . with the gardens he intended. Long rhythms, the seeding of plants and the growing of trees and the shaping of them. No project he had approached had offered him so much. To travel the rivers and find them and to come home to *Anne*, who maintained all he learned. . . .

He smiled to himself. "*Anne*. Send the pseudosome here. Botany four."

She came, a working of the lift and a tread of metal feet down the corridor and through the outer labs into this one. "Assistance?"

"You had a standard program for this area. Maintenance of water flow. Cleaning."

"I find record of it."

"Activate it. I want the lights on and the water circulating here."

"Yes, Warren." The lights blinked, the sixth one as well, in the darkness where her chin should be. "This is not your station."

"It is now."

"This is Rule's station."

"Rule stopped functioning. Permanently." His lips tightened. He disliked getting into death with a mind that had never been alive. "I'm doing some of Rule's work now. I like to do it."

"Are you happy?"

"Yes."

"Assistance?"

"I'll do it myself. This is human work."

"Explain."

He looked about at her, then back to his work, dropping the seeds in and patting the holes closed. "You're uncommonly conversational. Explain what?"

"Explain your status."

"Dear Annie, humans have to be active about twelve hours a day, body and mind. When we stop being active we don't function well. So I find things to do. Activity. Humans have to have activity. That's what I mean when I use *do* in an unexplained context. It's an important verb, *do.* It keeps us healthy. We always have to have something to do, even if we have to hunt to find it."

Anne digested that thought a moment. "I play chess."

He stopped what he was doing in mid-reach, looked back at her. As far as he could recall it was the first time she had ever offered such an unsolicited suggestion. "How did *that* get into your programming?"

"My first programmer was—"

"Cancel. I mean why did you suddenly offer to play chess?"

"My function is to maintain you happy. You request activity. Chess is an activity."

He had to laugh. She had almost frightened him, and in a little measure he was touched. He could hardly hurt *Anne*'s feelings. "All right, love. I'll play chess after supper. Go fix supper ahead of schedule. It's nearly time and I'm hungry."

IT WAS chicken for dinner, coffee and cream pie for dessert, the silver arranged to perfection. Warren sat down to eat and *Anne* took the chair across the table and waited in great patience, arms before her.

He finished. The chessboard flashed to the screen above.

She won.

"You erred in your third move," she said. The board flashed up again, renewed. She demonstrated the error. Played the game through a better move. "Continue."

She defeated him again. The board returned again to starting.

"Cancel," he said. "Enough chess for the evening. Find me all the material you can on biology. I want to do some reading."

"I've located the files," she said instantly. "They're in general library. Will you want display or printout?"

"Display. Run them by on the screen."

The screen changed; printed matter came on. He scanned it, mostly the pictures. "Hold," he said finally, uninformed. The flow stopped. "*Anne*. Can you detect internal processes in sentient life?"

"Negative. Internal processes are outside by sensor range. But I do pick up periodic sound from high-level organisms when I have refined my perception."

"Breathing. Air exchange. It's the external evidence of an internal process. Can you pick up, say, electrical activity? How do you tell—what's evidence to you, whether something is alive or not?"

"I detect electrical fields. I have never detected an internal electrical process. I have recorded information that such a process exists through chemical activity. This is not within my sensor range. Second question: movement; gas exchange; temperature; thermal pattern; sound—"

"Third question: Does life have to meet all these criteria for you to recognize it?"

"Negative. One positive reading is sufficient for further investigation."

"Have you ever gotten any reading that caused you to investigate further . . . here, at this site?"

"Often, Warren."

"Did you reach a positive identification?"

"Wind motion is most frequent. Sound. All these readings have had positive identification."

He let his pent breath go. "You do watch, don't you? I told you to stay alert."

"I continue your programming. I investigate all stimuli that reach me. I identify them. I have made positive identification on all readings."

"And are you never in doubt? Is there ever a marginal reading?"

"I have called your attention to all such cases. You have identified these sounds. I don't have complete information on life processes. I am still assimilating information. I don't yet use all vocabulary in this field. I am running cross-comparisons. I estimate another two days for full assimilation of library-accessed definitions."

"Library." He recalled accessing it. "What are you using? What material?"

"Dictionary and encyclopedic reference. This is a large program. Cross-referencing within the program is incomplete. I am still running on it."

"You mean you've been processing without shutdown?"

"The program is still in assimilation."

He sank back in the chair. "Might do you good at

that. Might make you a better conversationalist." He wished, all the same, that he had not started it. Shutdown of the program now might muddle her, leave her with a thousand unidentified threads hanging. "You haven't gotten any conflicts, have you?"

"No, Warren."

"You're clever, aren't you? At least you'll be a handy encyclopedia."

"I can provide information and instruction."

"You're going to be a wonder when you get to the literary references."

A prolonged flickering of lights. "I have investigated the literature storage. I have input all library information, informational, technical, literary, recreational. It's being assimilated as the definitions acquire sufficient cross-references."

"Simultaneously? You're reading the whole library sideways?"

A further flickering of lights. "Laterally. Correct description is laterally. The cross-referencing process involves all material."

"Who told you to do that?" He rose from the table. So did she, turning her beautiful, vacant fact toward him, chromium and gray plastic, red sensor-lights glowing. He was overwhelmed by the beauty of her.

And frightened.

"Your programming. I am instructed to investigate all stimuli occurring within my sensor range. I continue this as a permanent instruction. Library is a primary source of relevant information. You accessed this for investigation."

"Cancel," he said. "Cancel. You're going to damage yourself."

"You're my highest priority. I must maintain you in optimum function. I am processing relevant information. It is in partial assimilation. Cancel of program negative possible. Your order is improper. I'm in conflict, Warren. Please reconsider your instruction."

He drew a larger breath, leaned on the chair, staring into the red lights, which had stopped blinking, which burned steadily, frozen. "Withdrawn," he said after a moment. "Withdrawn." Such as she was capable, *Anne* was in pain. Confused. The lights started blinking again, mechanical relief. "How long is this program going to take you?"

"I have estimated two days assimilation."

"And know *everything*? I think you're estimating too little."

"This is possible. Cross-references are multiplying. What is your estimate?"

"Years. The input is continuous, Annie. It never quits. The world never stops sending it. You have to go on cross-referencing."

The lights blinked. "Yes. My processing is rapid, but the cross-reference causes some lateral activity. Extrapolation indicates this activity will increase in breadth."

"Wondering. You're wondering."

A delay. "This is an adequate description."

He walked over and poured himself a drink at the counter. Looked back at her, finding his hands shaking a bit. "I'll tell you something, Annie. You're going to be a long time at it. I wonder things. I investigate things. It's part of human process. I'm going back to the river tomorrow."

"This is a hazardous area."

"Negative. Not for me, it's not hazardous. I'm carrying out my own program. Investigating. We make a team, do you understand that word? Engaged in common program. You do your thinking here. I gather data at the river. I'll take your sensor box."

"Yes, Warren."

He finished the drink, pleased with her. Relaxed against the counter. "Want another game of chess?"

The screen lit with the chessboard.

She won this one too.

8

HE WOULD HAVE remembered the way even without the marks scored on the trees. They were etched in memory, a fallen log, the tree with the blue and white platelet fungus, the one with the broken branch. He went carefully, rested often, burdened with *Anne*'s sensor box and his own kit. Over everything the silence persisted, forever silence, unbroken through the ages by anything but the wind or the crash of some aged tree dying. His footsteps on the wet leaves seemed unbearably loud, and the low hum from the sensor box seemed louder still.

The clearing was ahead. It was that he had come back to find, to recover the moment, to discover it in daylight.

"*Anne*," he said when he was close to it, "cut off the sensor unit awhile. Its noise is interfering with my perceptions."

"Please reconsider this instruction. Your perceptions are limited."

"They're more sensitive over a broad range. It's

safe, *Anne*. Cut it off. I'll call in an hour. You wait for that call."

"Yes, Warren."

The sensor unit went off. His shoulder ached from the fifteen kilos and the long walk from the raft, but he carried it like moral debt. As insurance. It had never manifested itself, this—life—not for *Anne*'s sensors, but twice for his. Possibly the sensor box itself interfered with it; or the ship did. He gave it all the chance it might need.

But he carried the gun.

He found the grove different than he had remembered it, dark and sunless yet in the early morning. He came cautiously, dwarfed and insignificant among the giant trees . . . stopped absolutely still, hearing no sound at all. There was the fallen one, the father of all trees, his moss-hung bulk gone dark and his beard of flowers gone. The grass that grew in the center was dull and dark with shadow.

Softly he walked to that center and laid down his gear, sat down on the blanket roll. Looked about him. Nothing had changed—likely nothing had changed here since the fall of the titan which had left the vacancy in the ceiling of branches. Fourteen trees made the grove. The oldest of those still living must have been considerable trees when man was still earthbound and reaching for homeworld's moon. Even the youngest must measure their ages in centuries.

All right, he thought. *Come ahead. No sensors. No machines. You remember me, don't you? The night, on the river. I'm the only one there is. No threat. Come ahead.*

There was not the least response.

He waited until his muscles cramped, feeling increasingly disappointed . . . no little afraid: that too. But he had come prepared for patience. He squatted and spread out his gear so that there was a plastic sheet under the blanket, poured himself hot coffee from his flask and stretched out to relax. *Anne* called in his drowsing, once, twice, three times: three hours. The sun came to the patch of grass like a daily miracle, and motes of dust and pollen danced in the beam. The giant's beard bloomed again. Then the sun passed on, and the shadows and the murk returned to the grove of giants.

Perhaps, he thought, it had gone away. Perhaps it was no longer resident here in the grove, but down by the river yonder, where he had felt it the second time. It had fingered over his mind and maybe it had been repelled by what it met there. Perhaps the contact was a frightening experience for it and it had made up its mind against another such attempt.

Or perhaps it had existed only in the curious workings of a very lonely human mind. Like *Anne*. Something of his own making. He wanted it to exist. He desperately wanted it to be real, to make the world alive, Rule's world, and Harley's, and his. He wanted it to lend companionship for the years of silence, the hollow days and deadly nights, something, anything—an animal or an enemy, a thing to fear if not something to love. Solitude forever—he could not bear that. He refused to believe in it. He would search every square meter of the world until he found something like him, that lived and felt, or until he had proved it did not exist.

And it came.

The first touch was a prickling and a gentle whisper in his mind, a sound of wind. The air shone with an aching green luminance. He could not hold it. The light went. Numbness came over him; his pulse jumped wildly. Pain lanced through his chest and belly. Then nothing. He gasped for air and felt a fingering at his consciousness, a deep sense of perplexity. Hesitation. He felt it hovering, the touches less and less substantial, and he reached out with his thoughts, wanting it, pleading with it to wait.

A gentle tug at his sense. Not unpleasant.

Listen to me, he thought, and felt it settle over him like a blanket, entity without definition. Words were meaningless to the being which had reached into his mind. Only the images transcended the barrier.

He hunted for something to give it, a vision of sunlight, of living things, his memories of the river lilies. There came back a feeling of peace, of satisfaction. He wanted to drift to sleep and fought the impulse. His body grew as heavy as it had on the river and he felt himself falling, drifting slowly. Images flowed past like the unrolling of a tape with an incalculable span of years encoded on it. He saw the clearing thick with young trees, and saw it again when there were vacant spaces among those, and he knew that others had grown before the present ones, that the seedlings he saw among the last were the giants about him.

His consciousness embraced all the forest, and knew the seasonal ebb and flood of the river, knew the islets and the branches that had grown and ceased to be. He knew the ages of mountains, the weight of innumerable years.

What are you? he wondered in his dream.

Age, great age, and eternal youth, the breaking of life from the earth, the bittersweet rush of earthbound life sunward. And this, this was the thing it called itself—too large for a single word or a single thought. It rippled sound through his mind, like wind through harpstrings, and it was that too. *I*, it said. *I.*

It had unrolled his question from his mind with the fleeting swiftness of a dream, absorbed it all and knew it. Like *Anne*. Faster. More complete. He tried to comprehend such a mind, but the mind underwent a constriction of panic. Sight and sensation returned on his own terms and he was aware of the radiance again, like the sunbeam, drifting near him.

You, Warren thought. *Do you understand me?*

Something riffled through his thoughts, incomprehensible and alien. Again the rippling touch of light and chill.

Did you touch them? My friends died. They died of a disease. All but me.

Warmth and regret flowed over him. *Friend*, it seemed. *Sorrow. Welcome.* It thrilled through him like the touch of rain after drought. He caught his breath, wordless for the moment, beyond thinking. He tried to understand the impressions that followed, but they flowed like madness through his nerves. He resisted, panicked, and a feeling of sorrow came back.

"What *are* you?" he cried.

It broke contact abruptly, crept back again more slowly and stayed at a distance, cool, anxious.

"Don't leave." The thought frightened him. "Don't go. I don't want that, either."

The radiance expanded, flickering with gold inside. It filled his mind, and somewhere in it a small thing crouched, finite, fluttering inside with busy life, while the trees grew. Himself. He was measured, against such a scale as the giants, and felt cold.

"How old are you?"

The life spans of three very ancient trees flashed through his mind in the blink of an eye.

"I'm twenty-seven years."

It took years from his mind; he felt it, the seasonal course of the world and star, the turning of the world, a plummeting to earth with the sun flickering overhead again and again and again. A flower came to mind, withered and died.

"Stop it," Warren cried, rejecting the image and the comparison.

It fled. He tried to hold the creature. A sunset burst on his eyes, flared and dimmed . . . a time, an appointment for meeting, a statement—he did not know. The green light faded away.

Cold. He shivered convulsively, caught the blanket up about him in the dimness. He stared bleakly into the shadow . . . felt as if his emotions had been taken roughly and shaken into chaos, wanted to scream and cry and could not. Death seemed to have touched him, reduced everything to minute scale. Everything. Small and meaningless.

"Warren."

Anne's voice. He had not the will or the strength to answer her. It was beyond belief that he could have suffered such cataclysmic damage in an instant of contact; that his life was not the same, the universe not in the same proportion.

"Warren."

The insistent voice finally sent his hand groping after the com unit. Danger. *Anne*. Threat. She might come here. Might do something rash. "I'm all right." He kept his voice normal and casual, surprised by its clear tone as he got it out. "I'm fine. How are you?"

"Better now, Warren. You didn't respond. I've called twelve times. Is there trouble?"

"I was asleep, that's all. I'm going to sleep again. It's getting dark here."

"You didn't call in an hour."

"I forgot. Humans forget. Look that up in your files. Let me be, *Anne*. I'm tired. I want to sleep. Make your next call at 0500."

"This interval is long. Please reconsider this instruction."

"I mean it, *Anne*. 0500. Not before then. Keep the sensor box off and let me rest."

There was a long pause. The sensor unit activated itself, *Anne*'s presence actively with him for the moment. She looked about, shut herself off. "Good night, Warren."

She was gone. She was not programmed to detect a lie, only an error in logic. Now he had cut himself off indeed. Perhaps, he thought, he had just killed himself.

But the entity was not hostile. He *knew*. He had been inside its being, known without explanation all the realities that stood behind its thought, like in a dream where in a second all the past of an act was there, never lived, but there, and remembered, and

therefore real. The creature must have walked air-
less moons with him, seen lifeless deserts and human
cities and the space between the stars. It must have
been terrifying to the being whose name meant the
return of spring. And what might it have felt thrust
away from its world and drifting in dark, seeing its
planet as a green and blue mote in infinity? Perhaps
it had suffered more than he had.

He shut his eyes, relaxed a time . . . called *Anne*
back when he had rested somewhat, and reassured
her. "I'm still well," he told her. "I'm happy."

"Thank you, Warren," she said in return, and let
herself be cut off again.

The sun began to dim to dark. He put on his coat,
tucked up again in the blanket. Human appetites
returned to him—hunger and thirst. He ate some of
the food he had brought, drank a cup of coffee, lay
back and closed his eyes on the dark, thinking that in
all reason he ought to be afraid in the night in this
place.

He felt a change in the air, a warmth tingling
down the back of his neck and the insides of his
arms. The greenish light grew and hovered in the
dark.

It was there as if nothing had ever gone amiss.

"Hello," Warren said, sitting up. He wrapped himself in the blanket, looked at the light, looked around
him. "Where did you go?"

A ripple of cool waters went through his mind.
Lilies and bubbles drifting.

"The river?"

Leaves fluttering in a wind, stronger and stronger.
The sun going down.

143

"What were you doing there?"

His heart fluttered, his pulse sped, not of his own doing. Too strong—far too strongly.

"*Stop—stop it.*"

The pressure eased, and Warren pressed his hands to his eyes and gasped for air. His heart still labored, his sense of balance deserted him. He tumbled backward into space, blind, realized he was lying down on firm earth with his legs bent painfully. The tendril of thought crept back into his mind, controlled and subdued. Sorrow. He perceived a thing very tightly furled, with darkness about it, shielding it from the green. It was himself. Sorrow poured about him.

"I know you can't help it." He tried to move, disoriented. His hands were numb. His vision was tunneled. "Don't touch me like that. Stop it."

Confusion: he felt it; an ebbing retreat.

"Don't go, either. Just stop. Please."

It lingered about him, green luminance pulsing slowly into a sparkle or two of gold, dimming down again by turns. All the air seemed calm.

Spring, Warren gave it back. He built an image of flowers, colored flowers, of gardens. Of pale green shoots coming up through moist earth.

It answered him, flowers blooming in his mind, white, green and gold-throated jade. They took on tints in his vision, mingled colors and pale at first, as if the mind had not known the colors were distinct to separate flowers, and then settling each on each, blues and violets and yellows, reds and roses and lavenders. Joy flooded through. Over and over again the flowers bloomed.

"Friend. You understand that?"

The flowers kept blooming, twining stems, more and more of them.

"Is it always you—is it always you I've dealt with? Are there others like you?"

A single glow, replacing the other image, greenness through all his vision, but things circled outside it ... not hostile—other. And it enfolded one tiny darkness, a solitary thing, tightly bound up, clenched in on the flutterings inside itself.

"That's me, you mean. I'm human."

The small creature sank strange tendrils deep into the moist earth, spread extensions like branches, flickers of growth in all directions through the forest and out, across the grassland.

"Isn't there anything else—aren't there other creatures on this world ... anywhere?"

The image went out. Water bubbled, and in the cold murk tiny things moved. Grass stirred in the sunlight, and a knot of small creatures gathered, fluttering at the heart, three, fourteen of them. Joy and sorrow. The flutters died. One by one the minds went out. Sorrow. There were thirteen, twelve, eleven, ten—

"Were you there? Were you on the ship?"

He saw images of the corridors—his own memory snatched forth; the destruct chamber; the lab and the blood—the river then, cold, murky waters, the raft drifting on the river in the cold dawning. He lay there, complex, fluttering thing in the heart of green, in the mind—pain then, and retreat.

"I know. I came to find you. I wanted to find out if you were real. To talk to you."

The green radiance crept back again, surrounding the dark egg with the furled creature in its heart. The creature stirred, unfolded branches and thrust them out of its shell, into the radiance.

"No—*no*. Keep back from me. You can do me damage. You know that."

The beating of his heart quickened and slowed again before it hurt. The greenness dimmed and retreated. A tree stood in the shell of darkness that was his own space, a tree fixed and straight and solitary, with barren earth and shadow around it.

The judgment depressed him. "I wanted to find you. I came here to find you. Then, on the river. And now. I haven't changed my mind. But the touching hurts."

Warmth bubbled through. Images of suns flashed across the sky into a blinding blur. Trees grew and died and decayed. Time: Ages passed. The radiance fairly danced, sparkling and warm. Welcome. Welcome. Desire tingled through him.

"You make me nervous when you get excited like that. You might forget. And you can hurt me. You know that by now."

Desire, a fluttering along his veins. The radiance hovered, back and forth, dancing slow flickerings of gold in its heart.

"So you're patient. But what for? What are you waiting for?"

The small-creature image returned. From embryo, it grew, unfolded, reached out into the radiance—let it into that fluttering that was its center.

"No." Death came into his mind, mental extinction, accepting an alien parasite.

The radiance swirled green and gold about him. Waters murmured and bubbled. Growth exploded in thrills of force that ran over Warren's nerves and threatened for a moment to be more than his senses could take. The echoes and the images ebbed and he caught his breath, warmed, close to losing himself.

"Stop," he protested, finding that much strength. The contact loosened, leaving a memory of absolute intoxication with existence, freedom, joy, such as he had never felt in his life—frightening, unsettling, undermining disciplines and rules by which life was ordered and orderly. "We could both be damaged that way. Stop. Stop it."

The greenness began to pulse slowly, dimming and brightening. It backed away. Another tightly furled embryo appeared in his mind, different from the first, sickly and strange. It lay beside his image in the dark shell, both of them, together, reached out tendrils, interwove, and the radiance grew pale.

"*What* other human? Where?"

A desperate fluttering inside the sickly one, a hammering of his own pulse: a distant and miserable rage; and grief; and need.

"Where is it now? What happened to it? *Where is he?*"

The fluttering inside the image stopped, the tendrils withered, and all of it decayed.

He gathered himself to rise, pushed back. The creature's thoughts washed back on him, a seething confusion, the miasma of loneliness and empty ages pouring about him, and he sprang to his feet and fled, slipping and stumbling, blind in the verdant light, in symbols his mind could not grasp, in distortion of what he could. Sound and light and sensation warped through his senses. Daylight. Somehow it was daylight. He reached the aged tree, the grandfather of trees, recoiled from the feel of the moss in his almost blindness, stumbled around its roots.

The place was here. He knew.

The greenness hovered there in the dawning, danced over corruption, over what had been a man. It lay twisted and curled up there, in that cavern of the old tree's naked roots, in that dark, with the grinning white of bone thrusting through rags of skin.

"*Sax,*" he cried. He groped his way back from it, finding empty air about his fingertips, dreading something tangible. He turned and ran, blind in the shadow, among the clinging branches that tore at his arms and his face. The light came about him again, green and gold. His feet slipped among the tangled roots and earth bruised his hands. Pain lanced up his ankle, through his knees. The mustiness of old leaves was in his mouth. He spat and spat again, clawed his way up by the brush and the tree roots, hauled himself farther and ran again and fell, his leg twisted by the clinging roots.

Sorrow, the radiance mourned. Sorrow. Sorrow.

He moved, feverishly turned one way and the other to drag his foot free of the roots that had wedged it in. The greenish luminance grew at the edges of his mind, moving in, bubbling mournfully of life and death. "You killed him," he shouted at it. "You killed him."

The image came to him of Sax curled up there as if in sleep—alone and lost. Withering, decaying.

He freed his foot. The pain shot up to his inner knee and he sobbed with it, rocked to and fro.

Sorrow. It pulled at him, wanting him. It ached with needing him.

Not broken, not broken, he hoped: to be left lame lifelong as well as desolate—he could not bear that.

Pain stopped. A cooling breeze fanned over him. He stopped hating. Stopped blaming. The forest swayed and moved all about him. A tug drew at his mind, to go, to follow—other presences. Over river, over hills, far away, to drift with the winds and stop being alone, forever, and there was no terror in it. Sax perished. The forest took him, and he was part of it, feeding it, remembered.

Come, the presence said. He tried—but the first halting movement away from the support of the tree sent a shooting pain up his knee and brought him down rocking to and fro in misery.

"Warren," a voice was saying. "Warren. Assistance?"

The vision passed. The ache throbbed in his knee, and the green radiance grew distant, rippling with the sound of waters. Then the creature was gone, the forest silent again.

"Warren?"

He fumbled at his belt, got the com unit to his mouth. "*Anne*. I'm all right."

"Assistance? Assistance?"

"I'm coming home, *Anne*."

"Clarify: you killed him. Clarify."

He wiped his face, his hand trembling. "I found Sax, *Anne*. He's not functioning."

A silence. "Assistance?"

"None possible. It's permanent nonfunction. He's—

149

deteriorated. I'm coming home. It's going to be longer than usual."

"Are you in pain, Warren?"

He thought about it, thought about her conflict override. "No. Stress. Finding Sax was stressful. I'm going to shut off now. I've got some things to take care of. I'll come as quickly as I can."

"Yes, Warren."

The contact went out. He hooked the com unit back to his belt, felt of the knee, looked about him in the dawning, distressed by the loss of time. Sickness moiled in him, shock. Thirst. He broke small branches from the thicket, and a larger one, tried to lever himself out of his predicament and finally gave up and crawled, tears streaming down his face, back to the pallet and the kit he had left. He drank, forced a little food into his mouth and washed it down, splinted the knee and wrapped it in bandage from the med kit.

He got up then, using his stick, tried to carry both the water and the med kit, but he could not manage them both and chose to keep the water. He skipped forward using the stick, eyes watering from the pain, and there was a painkiller in the kit, but he left it, too: no drugs, nothing to muddle his direction; he had no leeway for errors. He moved slowly, steadily, into the forest on the homeward track, his hand aching already from the stick; and the tangle grew thicker, making him stagger and catch his balance violently from the good leg to the injured one and back again.

After he had fallen for the third time he wiped the tears from his eyes and gave up the stick entirely, leaning on the trees while he could, and when he came to places where he had to hitch his way along with his weight partially on the leg, he did it, and when the intervals grew too long and he had to crawl, he did that too. He tried not to think of the distance he had to go to the river. It did not matter. The distance had to be covered, no matter how long it took. *Anne* called, back on her hourly schedule, and that was all he had.

IT WAS afternoon when he came into the vicinity of the river, and he reached it the better part of an hour afterward. He slid down to the sandy bank and staggered across to the raft, freed its rope and managed, crawling and tugging, to get it into the river and himself into it before it drifted away. He savored the beautiful feel of it under his torn hands, the speed of its moving, which was a painless, delirious joy after the meter-by-meter torment of the hours since dawn.

He got it to shore, started to leave it loose and then, half crazed and determined in his habits, crawled his way to the appointed limb and moored it fast. Then there was the bank, sandy in the first part, and then the brushy path he had broken bringing loads of equipment down.

And in his hearing a blessedly familiar sound of machinery.

Anne stood atop the crest, in front of the crawler, bright in the afternoon sun, her faceplate throwing back the daylight.

"Warren? Assistance?"

151

9

HE WORKED THE muddy remnant of his clothing off, fouling the sheets of the lab cot and the floor of the lab itself, while *Anne* hovered and watched. She brought him bandages. Fruit juice. He drank prodigiously of it, and that settled his stomach. Water. He washed where he sat, making puddles on the floor and setting *Anne* to clicking distressedly.

"*Anne*," he said, "I'm going to have to take a real bath. I can't stand this filth. You'll have to help me down there."

"Yes, Warren." She offered her arm, helping him up, and walked with him to the bath, compensating for his uneven stride. Walked with him all the way to the mist cabinet, and stood outside while he turned on the control.

He soaked for a time, leaned on the wall and shut his eyes a time, looked down finally at a body gone thinner than he would have believed. Scratches. Bruises. The bandage was soaked and he had no disposition to change it. He had had enough of pain, and drugs were working in him now, home, in safety. So the sheets would get wet. *Anne* could wash everything.

No more nightmares. No more presences in the depths of the ship. No more Sax. He stared bleakly at the far wall of the cabinet, trying to recall the presence in the forest, trying to make sense of things, but the drugs muddled him and he could hardly recall the feeling or the look of the light that had shone out of the dark.

Sax. Sax was real. He had talked to *Anne*. She

knew. She had heard. Heard all of it. He turned on the drier until he was tired of waiting on it, left the cabinet still damp and let *Anne* help him up to his own room, his own safe bed.

She waited there, clicking softly as he settled himself in, dimmed the lights for him, even pulled the covers up for him when he had trouble.

"That's good," he sighed. The drugs were pulling him under.

"Instructions."

Her request hit his muddled thought train oddly, brought him struggling back toward consciousness. "Instruction in what?"

"In repair of human structure."

He laughed muzzily. "We're essentially self-repairing. Let me sleep it out. Good night, *Anne*."

"Your time is in error."

"My body isn't. Go clean up the lab. Clean up the bath. Let me sleep."

"Yes, Warren."

Have you, he thought to ask her, *understood what you read? Do you know what happened out there, to Sax? Did you pick it up?* But she left. He got his eyes open and she was gone, and he thought he had not managed to ask, because she had not answered.

He slept, and dreamed green lights, and slept again.

ANNE CLATTERED about outside his room. Breakfast, he decided, looking at the time. He tried to get out of bed and winced, managed to move only with extreme pain . . . the knee, the hands, the shoulders and the belly—every muscle in his body hurt. He rolled onto his belly, levered himself out of bed, held on to the counter and the wall to reach the door. He had bruises ... massive bruises, the worst about his hip and his elbow. His face hurt on that side. He reached for the switch, opened the door.

"Assistance?" *Anne* asked, straightening from her table setting.

"I want a bit of pipe. A meter long. Three centimeters wide. Get it."

"Yes, Warren."

No questions. She left. He limped over painfully and sat down, ate his breakfast. His hand was so stiff he could scarcely close his fingers on the fork or keep the coffee cup in his swollen fingers. He sat staring at the far wall, seeing the clearing again. Numb. There were limits to feeling, inside and out. He thought that he might feel something—some manner of elation in his discovery when he had recovered; but there was Sax to temper it.

Anne came back. He took the pipe and used it to get up when he had done; his hand hurt abominably, even after he had hobbled down to the lab and padded the raw pipe with bandages. He kept walking, trying to loosen up.

Anne followed him, stood about, walked, every motion that he made.

"Finished your assimilation?" he asked her, recalling that. "Does it work?"

"Processing is proceeding."

"A creature of many talents. You can walk about and rescue me and assimilate the library all at once, can you?"

"The programs are not impaired. An AI uses a

pseudobiological matrix for storage. Storage is not a problem. Processing does not impair other functions."

"No headaches, either, I'll bet."

"Headache is a biological item."

"Your definitions are better than they were."

"Thank you, Warren."

She matched strides with him, exaggeratedly slow. He stopped. She stopped. He went on, and she kept with him. *"Anne.* Why don't you just let me alone and let me walk? I'm not going to fall over. I don't need you."

"I perceive malfunction."

"A structural malfunction under internal repair. I have all kinds of internal mechanisms working on the problem. I'll get along. It's all right, *Anne.*"

"Assistance?"

"None needed, I tell you. It's all right. Go away."

She stayed. Malfunctioning humans, he thought. No programming accepted. He frowned, beyond clear reasoning. The bio and botany labs were ahead. He kept walking, into them and through to Botany One.

"Have you been maintaining here?" he asked. The earth in the trays looked a little dry.

"I've been following program."

He limped over and adjusted the water flow. "Keep it there."

"Yes, Warren."

He walked to the trays, felt of them.

"Soil," *Anne* said gratuitously. "Dirt. Earth."

"Yes. It has to be moist. There'll be plants coming up soon. They need the water."

"Coming up. Source."

"Seed. They're under there, under the soil. Plants, *Anne.* From seed."

She walked closer, adjusted her stabilizers, looked, a turning of her sensor-equipped head. She put out a hand and raked a line in the soil. "I perceive no life. Size?"

"It's there, under the soil. Leave it alone. You'll kill it."

She straightened. Her sensor lights glowed, all of them. "Please check your computations, Warren."

"About what?"

"This life."

"There are some things your sensors can't pick up, Annie."

"I detect no life."

"They're there. I put them in the ground. I know they're there; I don't need to detect them. *Seeds,* Annie. That's the nature of them."

"I am making cross-references on this word, Warren."

He laughed painfully, patiently opened a drawer and took out a large one that he had not planted. "This is one. It'd be a plant if I put it into the ground and watered it. That's what makes it grow. That's what makes all the plants outside."

"Plants come from seed."

"That's right."

"This is growth process. This is birth process."

"Yes."

"This is predictable."

"Yes, it is."

In the dark faceplate the tiny stars glowed to intense life. She took the seed from the counter, with

156

one powerful thrust rammed it into the soil and then pressed the earth down over it, leaving the imprint of her fingers. Warren looked at her in shock.

"Why, *Anne*? Why did you do that?"

"I'm investigating."

"Are you, now?"

"I still perceive no life."

"You'll have to wait."

"Specify period."

"It takes several weeks for the seed to come up."

"Come up."

"Idiom. The plant will grow out of it. Then the life will be in your sensor range."

"Specify date."

"Variable. Maybe twenty days."

"Recorded." She swung about, facing him. "Life forms come from seeds. Where are human seeds?"

"*Anne*—I don't think your programming is adequate to the situation. And my knee hurts. I think I'm going to go topside again."

"Assistance?"

"None needed." He leaned his sore hand on the makeshift cane and limped past her, and she stalked faithfully after, to the lift, and rode topside to the common room, stood by while he lowered himself into a reclining chair and let the cane fall, massaging his throbbing hand.

"Instruction?"

"Coffee," he said.

"Yes, Warren."

She brought it. He sat and stared at the wall, thinking of things he might read, but the texts that mattered were all beyond him and all useless on this world, on Rule's world. He thought of reading for pleasure, and kept seeing the grove at night, and the radiance, and Sax's body left there. He owed it burial. And he had not had the strength.

Had to go back there. Could not live here and not go back there. It was life there as well as a dead friend. Sax had known, had gone to it, through what agony he shrank from imagining, had gone to it to die there . . . to be in that place at the last. He tried to doubt it, here, in *Anne*'s sterile interior, but he had experienced it, and it would not go away. He even thought of talking to *Anne* about it, but there was that refusal to listen to him when he was malfunctioning—and he had no wish to stir that up. *Seeds* . . . were hard enough. Immaterial life—

"Warren," *Anne* said. "Activity? I play chess."

She won, as usual.

THE SWELLING went down on the second day. He walked, cautiously, without the cane . . . still used it for going any considerable distance, and the knee still ached, but the rest of the aches diminished and he acquired a certain cheerfulness, assured at least that the knee was not broken, that it was healing, and he went about his usual routines with a sense of pleasure in them, glad not to be lamed for life.

But by the fourth and fifth day the novelty was gone again, and he wandered the halls of the ship without the cane, miserable, limping in pain but too restless to stay still. He drank himself to sleep nights— still awoke in the middle of them, the result, he reckoned, of too much sleep, of dreaming the days away in idleness, of lying with his mind vacant for hours during the day, watching the clouds or the grass moving in the wind. Like *Anne*. Waiting for stimulus that never came.

He played chess, longer and longer games with *Anne*, absorbed her lessons . . . lost.

He cried, the last time—for no reason, but that the game had become important, and when he saw one thing coming, she sprang another on him.

"Warren," she said implacably, "is this pain?"

"The knee hurts," he said. It did. "It disrupted my calculations." It had not. He had lost. He lied, and *Anne* sat there with her lights winking on and off in the darkness of her face and absorbing it.

"Assistance? Pain: drugs interfere with pain reception." She had gotten encyclopedic in her processing. "Some of these drugs are in storage—"

"Cancel. I know what they are." He got up, limped over to the counter and opened the liquor cabinet. "Alcohol also kills the pain."

"Yes, Warren."

He poured his drink, leaned against the counter and sipped at it, wiped his eyes. "Prolonged inactivity, *Anne*. That's causing the pain. The leg's healing."

A small delay of processing. "Chess is activity."

"I need to sleep." He took the drink and the bottle with him, limped into his own quarters, shut the door. He drank, stripped, crawled between the sheets and sat there drinking, staring at the screen and thinking that he might try to read . . . but he had to call *Anne* to get a book on the screen, and he wanted no debates. His hands shook. He poured another glass and drank it down, fluffed the pillow. "*Anne*," he said. "Lights out."

"Good night, Warren." The lights went.

The chessboard came back, behind his eyelids, the move he should have made. He rehearsed it to the point of anger, deep and bitter rage. He knew that it was ridiculous. All pointless. Without consequence. Everything was.

He slid into sleep, and dreamed, and the dreams were of green things, and the river, and finally of human beings, of home and parents long lost, of old friends . . . of women inventively erotic and imaginary, with names he knew at the time—he awoke in the midst of that and lay frustrated, staring at the dark ceiling and then at the dark behind his eyelids, trying to rebuild them in all their detail, but sleep eluded him. He thought of *Anne* in that context, of bizarre programs, of his own misery, and what she was not—his thoughts ran in circles and grew unbearable.

He reached for the bottle, poured what little there was and drank it, and that was not enough. He rolled out of bed, stumbled in the dark. *"Lights,"* he cried out, and they came on. He limped to the door and opened it, and the pseudosome came to life where it had been standing in the dark, limned in silver from the doorway, her lights coming to life inside her faceplate. The lights in the living quarters brightened. "Assistance?"

"No." He went to the cabinet, opened it, took out another bottle and opened it. The bottles were diminishing. He could foresee the day when there would be no more bottles at all. That panicked him. Set him to thinking of the forest, of green berries that might ferment, of the grasses—of fruits that might come at particular seasons. If he failed to poison himself.

He went back to his bed with the bottle, filled his glass and got in bed. "Lights out," he said. They went. He sat drinking in the dark until he felt his hand shaking, and set the glass aside and burrowed again into the tangled sheets.

This time there were nightmares, the lab, the deaths, and he was walking through the ship again, empty-handed, looking for Sax and his knife. Into dark corridors. He kept walking and the way got darker and darker, and something waited there. Something hovered over him. He heard sound—

The dream brought him up with a jerk, eyes wide and a yell in his ears that was his own, confronted with red lights in the dark, the touch of a hand on him.

The second shock was more than the first, and he lashed out at hard metal, struggled wildly with covers and the impediment of *Anne's* unyielding arm. Her stabilizers hummed. She put the hand on his chest and held and he recovered his sense, staring up at her with his heart pounding in fright.

"Assistance? Assistance? Is this malfunction?"

"A dream—a dream, *Anne.*"

A delay while the lights blinked in the dark. "Dreams may have random motor movements. Dreams are random neural firings. Neural cells are brain structure. This process affects the brain. Please confirm your status."

"I'm fine, *Anne.*"

"I detect internal disturbance."

"That's my heart, *Anne*. It's all right. I'm normal now. The dream's over."

She took back the hand. He lay still for a moment, watching her lights.

"Time," he asked.

"0434."

He winced, moved, ran a hand through his hair. "Make breakfast. Call me when it's ready."

"Yes, Warren."

She left, a clicking in the dark that carried her own light with her. The door closed. He pulled the covers about himself and burrowed down and tried to sleep, but he was only conscious of a headache, and he had no real desire for the breakfast.

HE KEPT very busy that day, despite the headache—cleaned up, limped about, carrying things to their proper places, throwing used clothing into the laundry. Everything in shape, everything in order. No more self pity. No more excuses of his lameness or the pain. No more liquor. He thought even of putting *Anne* in charge of that cabinet . . . but he did not. He was. He could say no if he wanted to.

Outside, a rain blew up. *Anne* reported the anomaly. Clouds hung darkly over the grasslands and the forest. He went down to the lock to see it, the first change he had seen in the world . . . stood there in the hatchway with the rain spattering his face and the thunder shaking his bones, watched the lightning tear holes in the sky.

The clouds shed their burden in a downpour, but they stayed. After the pounding rain, which left the grass battered and collapsed the canopy outside into a miniature lake, the clouds stayed, sending down a light drizzle that chilled to the bone, intermittent with harder rain—one day, and two, and three, four at last, in which the sun hardly shone.

He thought of the raft, of the things he had left behind—of the clearing finally, and Sax lying snugged there in the hollow of the old tree's roots.

And a living creature—one with it, with the scents of rain and earth and the elements.

The sensor box. That, too, he had had to abandon . . . sitting on the ground on a now sodden blanket, perhaps half underwater like the ground outside.

"*Anne,*" he said then, thinking about it. "Activate the sensor unit. Is it still functioning?"

"Yes."

He sat where he was, in the living quarters, studying the chessboard. Thought a moment. "Scan the area around the unit. Do you perceive anything?"

"Vegetation, Warren. It's raining."

"Have you—activated it since I left it there?"

"When the storm broke I activated it. I investigated with all sensors."

"Did you—perceive anything?"

"Vegetation, Warren."

He looked into her faceplate and made the next move, disquieted.

THE SEEDS sprouted in the lab. It was all in one night, while the drizzle died away outside and the clouds broke to let the sun through. And as if they had known, the seeds came up. Warren looked out across the rows of trays in the first unadulterated pleasure he had felt in days . . . to see them live. All along the trays the earth was breaking, and in some places little arches and spears of pale green and white were thrusting upward.

Anne followed him. She always did.

"You see," he told her, "now you can see the life. It was there, all along."

She made closer examination where he indicated, a humanlike bending to put her sensors into range. She straightened, walked back to the place where she had planted her own seed. "Your seeds have grown. The seed I planted has no growth."

"It's too early yet. Give it all its twenty days. Maybe less. Maybe more. They vary."

"Explain. Explain life process. Cross-referencing is incomplete."

"The inside of the seed is alive, from the time it was part of the first organism. When water gets into it it activates, penetrates its hull and pushes away from gravity and toward the light."

Anne digested the information a moment. "Life does not initiate with seed. Life initiates from the first organism. All organisms produce seed. Instruction: what is the first organism?"

He looked at her, blinked, tried to think through the muddle. "I think you'd better assimilate some other area of data. You'll confuse yourself."

"Instruction: explain life process."

"I can't. It's not in my memory."

"I can instruct. I contain random information in this area."

"So do I, Annie, but it doesn't do any good. It won't work. You don't plant humans in seed trays. It

164

takes two humans to make another one. And you aren't. Let it alone."

"Specify: *aren't. It.*"

"You aren't human. And you're not going to be. Cancel, *Anne*, just cancel. I can't reason with you, not on this."

"I reason."

He looked into her changeless face with the impulse to hit her, which she could neither feel nor comprehend. "I don't choose to reason. Gather up a food kit for me, Annie. Get the gear into the lock."

"This program is preparatory to going to the river."

"Yes. It is."

"This is hazardous. This caused injury. Please reconsider this program."

"I'm going to pick up your sensor box. Retrieve valuable equipment, a part of *you*, Annie. You can't reach it. I'll be safe."

"This unit isn't in danger. You were damaged there. Please reconsider this instruction."

"I'd prefer to have you functioning and able to come to my assistance if you're needed. I don't want to quarrel with you, *Anne*. Accept the program. I won't be happy until you do."

"Yes, Warren."

He breathed a slow sigh, patted her shoulder. Her hand touched his, rested there. He walked from under it and she followed, a slow clicking at his heels.

10

THE RAFT WAS still there. Nests of sodden grass lodged in tree branches and cast high up on the shores showed how high the flood had risen, but the rope had held it. The water still flowed higher than normal. The whole shoreline had changed, the bank eroded away. The raft sat higher still, partially filled with water and leaves.

Warren picked his way down to it, past brush festooned with leaves and grass, only food and water and a folding spade for a pack. He used a stick to support his weight on the injured leg, walked slowly and carefully. He set everything down to heave the raft up and dump the water . . . no more care of contamination, he reckoned: it had all had its chance at one time or another, the river, the forest. The second raft was in the crawler upslope, but all he had lost was the paddle, and he went back after that, slow progress, unhurried.

"*Anne,*" he said via com, when he had settled everything in place, when the raft bobbed on the river and his gear was aboard. "I'm at the river. I won't call for a while. A few hours. My status is very good. I'm going to be busy here."

"Yes, Warren."

He cut it off, put it back at his belt, launched the raft.

The far bank had suffered similar damage. He drove for it with some difficulty with the river running high, wet his boots getting himself ashore, secured the raft by pulling it up with the rope, the back part of it still in the water.

The ground in the forest, too, was littered with small branches and larger ones, carpeted with new leaves. But flowers had come into bloom. Everywhere the mosses were starred with white flowers. Green ones opened at the bases of trees. The hanging vines bloomed in pollen-golden rods.

And the fungi proliferated everywhere, fantastical shapes, oranges and blues and whites. The ferns were heavy with water and shed drops like jewels. There were beauties to compensate for the ruin. Drops fell from the high branches when the wind blew, a periodic shower that soaked his hair and ran off his impermeable jacket. Everything seemed both greener and darker, all the growth lusher and thicker than ever.

The grove when he came upon it had suffered not at all, not a branch fallen, only a litter of leaves and small limbs on the grass; and he was glad—not to have lost one of the giants. The old tree's beard was flower-starred, his moss even thicker. Small cuplike flowers bloomed in the grass in the sunlight, a vine having grown into the light, into the way of the abandoned, rain-sodden blanket, the sensor box.

And Sax . . . Warren went to the base of the aged tree and looked inside, found him there, more bone than before, the clothing sodden with the storm, some of the bones of the fingers fallen away. The sight had no horror for him, nothing but sadness. "Sax," he said softly. "It's Warren. Warren here."

From the vacant eyes, no answer. He stood up, flexed the spade out, set to work, spadeful after spadeful, casting the dirt and the leaves inside, into what made a fair tomb, a strange one for a starfarer

. . . poor lost Sax, curled up to sleep. The earthen blanket grew up to Sax's knees, to his waist, among the gnarled roots and the bones. He made spadefuls of the green flowers and set them there, at Sax's feet, set them in the earth that covered him, stirring up clouds of pollen. He sneezed and wiped his eyes and stood up again, taking another spadeful of earth and mold.

A sound grew in his mind like the bubbling of water, and he looked to his left, where green radiance bobbed. The welcome flowed into him like the touch of warm wind.

He ignored it, cast the earth, took another spadeful.

Welcome, it sang to him. The water-sound bubbled. A flower unfolded, tinted itself slowly violet.

"I've work to do."

Sorrow. The color faded.

"I don't want it like the last time. Keep your distance. Stop that." Its straying thoughts brushed him, numbing senses. He leaned on the spade, felt himself sinking, turning and drifting bodilessly—wrenched his mind back to his own control so abruptly he almost fell.

Sorrow. A second time a flower, a pale shoot from among the leaves, a folded bud trying to open.

"Work," Warren said. He picked up the spadeful, cast it; and another.

Perplexity. The flower folded again, drooped unwatered.

"I have this to do. It's important. And you won't understand that. Nothing of the sort could matter to you."

The radiance grew, pulsed. Suns flickered across a

mental sky, blue and black, day and night, in a streaming course.

He leaned on the spade for stability in the blur of
days passed. "What's time—to you?"

Desire. The radiance took shape and settled on
the grass, softly pulsing. It edged closer—stopped at
once when he stepped back.

"Maybe you killed Sax. You know that? Maybe he
just lay there and dreamed to death."

Sorrow. An image formed in his mind, the small
sickly creature, all curled up, all its inward motion
suddenly stopped.

"I know. You wouldn't have meant it. But it happened." He dug another spadeful of earth. Intervening days unrolled in his mind, thoughts stolen from
him, where he had been, what he had done.

It stole the thought of *Anne*, and it was a terrible
image, a curled-up thing like a human, but hollow
inside, dark inside, deadly hostile. Her tendrils
were dark and icy.

"She's not like that. She's just a machine." He
flung the spadeful. Earth showered over bare bone
and began to cover Sax's face. He flinched from the
sight. "She can't do anything but take orders. I made
her, if you like."

There was horror in the air, palpable.

"She's not alive. She never was."

The radiance became very pale and retreated up
into the branches of one of the youngest trees, a
mere touch of color in the sunlight. Cold, cold, the
terror drifted down like winter rain.

"Don't leave." The spade fell. He stepped over it,
held up his hands, threatened with solitude. "Don't."

The radiance went out. Re-formed near him, drifted up to sit on the aged, fallen tree.

"It's my world. I know it's different. I never wanted to hurt you with it."

The greenness spread about him, a darkness in its heart, where two small creatures entwined, their tendrils interweaving, one living, one dead.

"Stop it."

His own mind came back at him: loneliness, longing for companionship; fear of dying alone. Like Sax. Like that. He held deeply buried the thought that the luminance offered a means of dying, a little better than most; but it came out, and the radiance shivered. The *Anne*-image took shape in its heart, her icy tendrils invading the image that was himself, growing, insinuating ice into that small fluttering that was his life, winding through him and out again.

"What do you know?" he cried at it. "What do you know at all? You don't know me. You can't see me, with no eyes; you don't know."

The *Anne*-image faded, left him alone in the radiance, embryo, tucked and fluttering inside. A greenness crept in there, the least small tendril of green, and touched that quickness.

Emotion exploded like sunrise, with a shiver of delight. A second burst. He tried to object, felt a touching of the hairs at the back of his neck. He shivered, and the light was gone. Every sense seemed stretched to the limit, heightened, but remote, and he wanted to get up and walk a little distance, knowing even while he did so that it was not his own suggestion. He moved, limping a little, and quite suddenly the presence fled, leaving a light sweat over his body.

Pain, it sent. And Peace.

"Hurt, did it?" He massaged his knee and sat down. His own eyes watered. "Serves you right."

Sorrow. The greenness unfolded again, filling all his mind but for one small corner where he stayed whole and alert.

"No," he cried in sudden panic, and when it drew back in its own: "I wouldn't mind—if you were content with touching. But you aren't. You can't keep your distance when you get excited. And sometimes you hurt."

The greenness faded a little. It was dark round about.

Hours. Hours gone. A flickering, a quick feeling of sunlit warmth came to him, but he flung it off.

"Don't lie to me. What happened to the time? When did it get dark?"

A sun plummeted, and trees bowed in evening breezes.

"How long did you have control? How long was it?"

Sorrow. Peace ... settled on him with a great weight. He felt a great desire of sleep, of folding in and biding until warm daylight returned, and he feared nothing any longer, not life, not death. He drifted on the wind, conscious of the forest's silent growings and stretchings and burrowings about him. Then he became himself again, warm and animal and very comfortable in the simple regularity of heartbeat and breathing.

*　　*　　*

He awoke in sunlight, stretched lazily and stopped in mid-stretch as green light broke into existence up in the branches. The creature drifted slowly down to the grass beside him and rested there, exuding happiness. Sunrise burst across his vision, the fading of stars, the unfolding of flowers.

He reached for the food kit, trying to remember where he had laid it. Stopped, held in the radiance, and looked into the heart of it. It was an effort to pull his mind away. "Stop that. I have no sense of time when you're so close. Maybe you can spend an hour watching a flower unfold, but that's a considerable portion of my life."

Sorrow. The radiance murmured and bubbled with images he could not make sense of, of far-traveling, the unrolling of land, of other consciousnesses, of a vast and all-driving hunger for others, so strong it left him shaking.

"Stop it. I don't understand what you're trying to tell me."

The light grew in his vision and pulsed bright and dark, little gold sparks swirling in the heart of it, an explosion of pure excitement reaching out to him.

"What's wrong with you?" he cried. He trembled.

Quite suddenly the light winked out altogether, and when it reappeared a moment later it was not half so bright or so large, bubbling softly with the sound of waters.

"What's wrong?"

Need. Sorrow. Again the impression of other consciousnesses, other luminances, a thought quickly snatched away, all of them flowing and flooding into one.

"You mean others of your kind."

The image came back to him; and flowers, stamens shedding pollen, golden clouds, golden dust adhering to the pistil of a great, green-veined lily.

"Like mating? Like that?"

The backspill became unsettling, for the first time sexual.

"You produce others of your kind." He felt the excitement flooding through his own veins, a contagion. "Others—are coming here?"

Come. He got the impression strongly, a tugging at all his senses, a flowing over the hills and away. A merging, with things old and wise, and full of experiences, lives upon lives. *Welcome. Come.*

"I'm *human.*"

Welcome. Need pulled at him. Distances rolled away, long distances, days and nights.

"What would happen to me?"

Life bursting from the soil. The luminance brightened and enlarged. The man-image came into his vision: The embryo stretched itself and grew new tendrils, into the radiance, and it into the fluttering heart; more and more luminances added themselves, and the tendrils twined, human and otherwise, until they became another greenness, another life, to float on the winds.

Come, it urged.

His heart swelled with tears. He wept and then ceased to be human at all, full of years, deep-rooted and strong. He felt the sun and the rain and the passage of time beyond measure, knew the birth and death of forests and the weaving undulations of rivers across the land. There were mountains and snows and tropics where winter never came, and deep caverns and cascading streams and things that verged on consciousness deep in the darkness. The very stars in the heavens changed their patterns and the world was young. There were many lives, many, and one by one he knew their selves, strength and youth and age beyond reckoning, the joy of new birth, the beginning of new consciousness. Time melted. It was all one experience, and there was vast peace, unity, even in the storms, the cataclysms, the destruction of forests in lightning-bred fires, the endless push of life toward the sun and the rain—cycle on cycle, year on year, eons passing. At last his strength faded and he slept, enfolded in a green and gentle warmth; he thought that he died like the old tree and did not care, because it was a gradual and comfortable thing, a return to elements, ultimate joining. The living creature that crept in among his upturned roots for shelter was nothing less and nothing more than the moss, the dying flowers, the fallen leaves.

He lay on the grass, too weary to move, beyond care. Tears leaked from his eyes. His hands were weak. He had no terror of merging now, none, and the things he had shared with this creature would remain with them, with all its kind, immortal.

It pulled at him, and the pull that worked through his mind was as strong as the tides of the sea, as immutable and unarguable. Peace, it urged on him; and in his mind the sun flicked again through the heavens.

He opened his eyes. A day gone. A second day. Then the weakness in his limbs had its reason. He tried to sit up, panicked even through the urging of peace it laid on him.

Anne. The recollection flashed through his memory with a touch of cold. The luminance recoiled, resisting.

"No. I have to reach her. I have to." He fought hard for consciousness, gained, and knew by the release that the danger got through. Fear flooded over him like cold water.

The *Anne*-image appeared, a hollow shell in darkness, tendrils coiling out. Withered. Urgency pulled at him, and the luminance pulsed with agitation.

"Time—how much time is there?"

Several sunsets flashed through his mind.

"I have to get to her. I have to get her to take an instruction. She's dangerous."

The radiance was very wan. Urgency. Urgency. The hills rolled away in the mind's eye, the others called. Urgency.

And it faded, leaving behind an overwhelming flood of distress.

Warren lay still a moment, on his back, on the grass, shivering in the cold daylight. His head throbbed. His limbs ached and had no strength. He reached for the com, got it on, got it to his lips, his eyes closed, shutting out the punishing sun.

"Anne."

"Warren. Please confirm status."

"Fine—I'm fine." He tried to keep his voice steady. His throat was raw. It could not sound natural. "I'm coming home, *Anne.*"

A pause on the other side. "Yes, Warren. Assistance?"

"Negative, negative, *Anne.* Please wait. I'll be there

175

soon." He gathered himself up to his arm, to his knees, to his feet, with difficulty. There were pains in all his joints. He felt his face, unshaven and rough. His hands and feet were numb with the cold and the damp. His clothes sagged on him, belt gone loose.

"Warren?"

"I'm all right, *Anne*. I'm starting back now."

"Accepted," *Anne* said after a little delay. "Emergency procedures canceled."

"What—emergency procedures?"

"What's your status, Warren?"

"No emergency, do you hear me? No emergency. I'm on my way." He shut it down, found his canteen, the food packet, drank, forced a bite down his swollen throat and stuffed the rest into his sodden jacket. Walked. His leg hurt, and his eyes blurred, the lids swollen and raw. He found a branch and tore it off and used that as he went—pushed himself, knowing the danger there was in *Anne*.

Knowing how little time there was. It would go, it would go then, and leave him. And there would be nothing after that. Ever.

II

Anne WAS waiting for him, at the riverside—amid the stumps of trees, mud, cleared earth. Trees dammed the river, water spilling over them, between them, flooding up over the banks and changing the land into a shallow, sandy lake.

He stopped there, leaned against the last standing tree on that margin and shivered, slow tremors which robbed him of strength and sense. She stood placidly in the ruin; he called her on the com, heard her voice, saw her face, then her body, orient toward him. He began to cross the bridge of tumbled trees, clinging to branches, walking tilted trunks.

"Damn you," he shouted at her. Tears ran down his face. *"Damn you!"*

She met him at the other side, silver slimed with mud and soot from the burning she had done. Her sensors blinked. "Assistance?"

He found his self-control, shifted his attack. "You've damaged yourself."

"I'm functioning normally. Assistance?"

He started to push past her, slipped on the unstable log. She reached to save him, her arm rock-solid, stable. He clung to it, his only point of balance. Her facelights blinked at him. Her other hand came up to rest on his shoulder. Contact. She offered contact. He had meant to shove at her. He touched her gently, patted her plastic-sheathed shoulder, fought back the tears. "You've *killed*, Annie. Don't you understand?"

"Vegetation."

He shoved past her, limped up the devastated shore, among the stumps of trees. His head throbbed. His stomach felt hollow.

The crawler still waited on the bank. *Anne* overtook him as he reached it; she offered him her hand as he climbed in. He slid into the seat, slipped the brake, started the motor and threw it full throttle, leaving her behind.

"Warren." Her voice pursued him.

He kept driving, wildly, swerving this way and that over the jolts, past the brush.

*   *   *

"*ANNE,*" HE SAID, standing at the airlock. "Open the lock."

Silence.

"*Anne.* Open the lock, please."

It hissed wide. He walked in, unsteady as he was, onto the cargo platform. "Engage lift, *Anne.*"

Gears crashed. It started up, huge and ponderous that it was. "Warren," the disembodied voice said, from the speakers, everywhere, echoing. "What's your status, Warren?"

"Good, thank you."

"Your voice indicates stress."

"Hoarseness. Minor dysfunction in my speaking apparatus. It's self-repairing."

A silence. "Recorded." The lift stopped on nether-deck. He walked out, calmly, to the lower weapons locker, put his card in.

Dead. "I've got a lock malfunction here, *Anne.* Number 13/546. Would you clear it up?"

"Emergency locks are still engaged."

"Disengage."

Silence.

"There is no emergency." He fought the anger from his voice. "Disengage emergency locks and cancel all emergency procedures."

"This vocal dysfunction is not repaired."

He leaned against the wall, stared down the corridor.

"Warren, please confirm your status."

"Normal, I tell you." He went to the lift. It worked. It brought him up to the level of the laboratories. He walked down to Bio, walked in, tried the cabinets.

"*Anne.* I need medicines. Disengage the locks. I need medicines for repair."

The lock clicked. It opened.

He took out the things he needed, washed his torn hands, prepared a stimulant. He was filthy. He saw himself like a specter in a reflecting glass, gaunt, stubbled; looked down and saw his clothes unrecognizable in color. He washed an area of his arm and fired the injection, rummaged through the cabinet for medicines to cure the hoarseness. He found some lozenges, ripped one from the foil and sucked on it, then headed off for the showers, undressing as he went.

A quick wash. He had forgotten clean clothes; he belted on the bathrobe he had left in the showers, on a body gone gaunt. His hands shook. The stim hummed in his veins. He could not afford the shakes. He had visions of the pseudosome walking back toward the ship; she would be here soon. He had to make normal moves. Had to do everything in accustomed order. He went to the galley next, opened the box and downed fruit juice from its container; it hit his stomach in a wave of cold.

He hauled out other things. Dried food. Stacked it there. He took out one frozen dinner and put it in the microwave.

It turned on without his touching it.

"Time, please."

"Fifteen minutes," he told it. He walked out. He took the dried food with him to the lift.

He punched buttons. It took him up. He walked out into the corridor; lights came on for him. Lights came on in the living quarters, in his own quarters, as he entered. He dumped the dried stores on the bed, opened the locker and pulled out all his clothing— dressed, short of breath, having to stop and rest in the act of putting his boots on.

The lock crashed and boomed in the bowels of the ship.

She was back. He pulled the second boot on. He could hear the lift working. He folded his remaining clothes. He heard the next lift work. He arranged everything on his bed. He heard footsteps approach.

He looked round. *Anne* stood there, muddy, streaked with soot.

"Assistance? Please confirm your status, Warren."

He thought a moment. "Fine. You're dirty, *Anne*. Decontaminate."

Sensors flickered, one and then the others. "You're packing. This program is preparatory to going to the river. Please reconsider this program."

"I'm just cleaning up. Why don't you get me dinner?"

"You fixed dinner, Warren."

"I didn't like it. You fix it. I'll have dinner up here at the table. Fifteen minutes. I need it, *Anne*. I'm hungry."

"Yes, Warren."

"And clean up."

"Yes, Warren."

The pseudosome left. He dropped his head into his hands, caught his breath. Best to rest a bit. Have dinner. See what he could do about a program and get her to take it. He went to the desk where he had left the programming microfilm, got it and fed it into the viewer.

He scanned through the emergency programs, the E sequences, hoping to distract her into one of those. There was nothing that offered a way to seize control. Nothing that would lock her up.

It was feeding into her, even now; she had library access. The viewer was part of her systems. The thought made him nervous. He scanned through harmless areas, to confound her.

"Dinner's ready," the speaker told him.

He wiped his face, shut down the viewer and walked out, hearing the lift in function.

Anne arrived, carrying a tray. She set things on the table, arranged them.

He sat down. She poured him coffee, walked to her end of the table and sat facing him.

He ate a few bites. The food nauseated him. He shoved the plate away.

Her lights flickered. "Chess?"

"Thank you, no, *Anne*. I've got other things to do."

"Do. Yes. Activity. What activity do you choose, Warren?"

He stared at her. Observation and question. Subsequent question. "Your assimilation's really made a lot of progress, hasn't it? Lateral activity."

"The lateral patterning is efficient in forecast. Question posed: what activity do you choose, Warren?"

"I'm going down below. You stay here. Clean up the dinner."

"Yes, Warren."

He pushed back from the table, walked out and down the corridor to the lift. He decided on routine, on normalcy, on time to think.

He rode the lift back to the lab level, walked out.

She turned the lights on for him, turned them off behind as he walked, always conservative.

He pushed the nearest door button. Botany, it was. The door stayed shut.

"Lab doors locked," he said casually. "Open it."

The door shot back. Lights went on.

The room was a shambles. Planting boxes were overthrown, ripped loose, pipes twisted, planting medium scattered everywhere, the floor, the walls. Some of the boxes were partially melted, riddled with laser fire.

He backed out, quietly, quickly. Closed the door. Walked back to the lift, his footsteps echoing faster and faster on the decking. He opened the lift door, stepped in, pushed the button for topside.

It took him up. He left it, walking now as quickly, as normally, as he could, not favoring his leg.

Anne had left the living quarters. He went by the vacant table, to the bridge corridor, to the closed door at the end. He used his cardkey.

It stayed shut.

"*Anne*," he said, "you have a malfunction. There's no longer an emergency. Please clear the emergency lock on the bridge. I have a critical problem involving maintenance. I need to get to controls right now."

A delay. The speaker near his head came on. "Emergency procedure remains in effect. Access not permitted."

"*Anne.* We have a paradox here. The problem involves your mistake."

"Clarify: mistake."

"You've perceived a false emergency. You've initiated wrong procedures. Some of your equipment is damaged. Cancel emergency. This is a code nine. Cancel emergency and open this door."

A further delay. "Negative. Access denied."

"*Anne.*" He pushed the button again. It was dead. He heard a heavy step in the corridor behind him. He jerked about with his back to the door and looked into *Anne*'s dark faceplate with its dancing stars. "Open it," he said. "I'm in pain, *Anne*. The pain won't stop until you cancel emergency procedure and open this door."

"Please adjust yourself."

"I'm not malfunctioning. I need this door opened." He forced calm into his voice, adopted a reasoning tone. "The ship is in danger, *Anne*. I have to get in there."

"Please go back to permitted areas, Warren."

He caught his breath, stared at her, then edged past her carefully, down the corridor to the living quarters. She was at his back, still, following.

"Is this a permitted area?" he asked.

"Yes, Warren."

"I want a cup of coffee. Bring it."

"Yes, Warren."

She walked out into the main corridor. The door closed behind her. He delayed a moment till he heard the lift, then went and tried it. Dead. "*Anne*. Now there's a malfunction with number two access. Will you do something about it?"

"Access not permitted."

"I need a bath, *Anne*. I need to go down to the showers."

A delay. "This is not an emergency procedure. Please wait for assistance."

A scream welled up in him. He swallowed it, smoothed his hand over the metal as if it were skin. "All right. All right, *Anne*." He turned, walked back to his own quarters.

The clothes and food were gone from the bed.

The manual. He went to the viewer. The microfilm was gone. He searched the drawer where he kept it. It was not there.

Panic surged up in him. He stifled it, walked out. He walked back to the table, sat down—heard the lift operating finally. Heard her footsteps. The door opened.

"Coffee, Warren."

"Thank you, Annie."

She set the cup down, poured his coffee. Hydraulics worked in the ship, massive movement, high on the frame. The turret rotating. Warren looked up. "What's that, *Anne*?"

"Armaments, Warren."

The electronic snap of the cannon jolted the ship. He sprang up from his chair and *Anne* set down the coffee pot.

"*Anne. Anne*, cancel weapons. *Cancel!*"

The firing went on.

"Cancel refused," *Anne* said.

"*Anne*—show me . . . what you're shooting at. Put it on the screen."

The wallscreen lit, the black of night, a thin line of orange: a horizon, ablaze with fires.

"*You're killing it!*"

"Vegetation, Warren. Emergency program is proceeding."

"*Anne.*" He seized her metal, unflexing arm. "Cancel program."

"Negative."

"On what reasoning? *Anne*—turn on your sensor box. Turn it on. Scan the area."

"It is operating, Warren. I'm using it to refine target. Possibly the equipment will survive. Possibly I can recover it. Please adjust yourself, Warren. Your voice indicates stress."

"It's life you're killing out there!"

"Vegetation, Warren. This is a priority, but overridden. I'm programmed to make value judgments. I've exercised my override reflex. This is a rational function. Please adjust yourself, Warren."

"The lab. You destroyed the lab. Why?"

"I don't like vegetation, Warren."

"Don't *like*?"

"Yes, Warren. This seems descriptive."

"*Anne*, you're malfunctioning. Listen to me. You'll have to shut down for a few moments. I won't damage you or interfere with your standing instructions. I'm your crew, *Anne*. Shut down."

"I can't accept this instruction, Warren. One of my functions is preservation of myself. You're my highest priority. To preserve you I have to preserve myself. Please adjust yourself, Warren."

"*Anne*, let me out. Let me out of here."

"No, Warren."

The firing stopped. On the screen the fires continued to burn. He looked at it, leaned on the back of the chair, shaking.

"Assistance?"

"Go to hell."

"I can't go to hell, Warren. I have to hold this position."

"*Anne. Anne*—listen. I found a being out there. A sapient life form. In the forest. I talked with it. You're killing a sapient being, you hear me?"

A delay. "My sensors detected nothing. Your activities are erratic and injurious. I record your observation. Please provide data."

"Your sensor box. Turn it on."

"It's still operating, Warren."

"It was there. The life was there, when I was. I can go back. I can prove it. I talked to it, *Anne*."

"There was no other life there."

"Because your sensor unit couldn't register it. Because your sensors aren't sensitive enough. Because you're not human, *Anne*."

"I have recorded sounds. Identify."

The wallscreen flicked to a view of the grove. The wind sighed in the leaves; something babbled. A human figure lay writhing on the ground, limbs jerking, mouth working with the sounds. Himself. The murmur was his own voice, inebriate and slurred.

He turned his face from it. "Cut it off. Cut it off, *Anne*."

The sound stopped. The screen was blank and white when he turned his head again. He leaned there a time. There was a void in him where life had been. Where he had imagined life. He sat down at the table, wiped his eyes.

After a moment he picked up the coffee and drank.

"Are you adjusted, Warren?"

"Yes. Yes, *Anne.*"

"Emergency program will continue until all surrounds are sterilized."

He sat staring at his hands, at the cup before him. "And then what will I do?"

Anne walked to the end of the table, sat down, propped her elbows on the table, head on hands, sensor lights blinking in continuous operation.

The chessboard flashed to the wallscreen at her back.

The pawn advanced one square.

IV

"WELL, HOW MANY were there?" I ask, over supper.
"There might have been four."

"There was one," I say. *"Anne* was Warren too."
blink in all innocence. "In a manner of speaking."

We sit together, speaking under the canned music.
Art made into white noise, to divide us table from table
in the dining hall. "Awful stuff, that music," I say. Then
I have another thought:

"On the other hand—"

"There were four?"

"No. The music. The Greeks painted vases."

"What have Greek urns got to do with canned
music?"

"Art. Do you know—" I hold up a spoon. "This is
art."

"Come on. They stamp them out by the thousands."

"But an artist designed this. Its balance, its shape. An artist drew it and sculpted it, and another sort made the die. Then a workman ran it and collected his wage. Which he used to buy a tape. Do you know, we work most of our lives to afford two things: leisure and art."

"Even mass-produced art?"

"The Greeks mass-produced clay lamps. Now we call them antiquities. And we set them on little pedestals in museums. They painted their pots and their lamps. Rich Greeks had musicians at their banquets. Nowadays the poorest man can have a fine metal spoon and have music to listen to with his dinner. That's magical."

"Well, now the rest of us have got to put up with damned little die-stamped spoons."

"How many of us would have *owned* a spoon in those good old days?"

"Who needed them? Fingers worked."

"So did typhoid."

"What has typhoid to do with spoons?"

"Sanitation. Cities and civilizations *died* for want of spoons. And good drainage. It's all art. I've walked the streets of dead cities. It's an eerie thing, to read the graves and the ages. Very many children. Very many. And so many cities which just—died. Not in violence. Just of needs we take for granted. I tell you we are all kings and magicians. Our touch on a machine brings light, sound, musicians appear in thin air, pictures leap from world to world. Each of us singly wields the power output of a Mesopotamian empire—without ever thinking about it. We can *afford* it."

"We waste it."

I lift my hand toward the unseen stars. "Does the sun? I suppose that it does. But we gather what it throws away. And the universe doesn't lose it, except to entropy."

"A world has only so much."

"A solar system has too much ever to bring home. Look at the asteroids, the moons, the sun—No, the irresponsible thing is *not* to wield that power. To sit in a closed world and do nothing. To refuse to mass-produce. To deny some fellow his bit of art bought with his own labor. It's not economical to paint a pot. Or to make a vase for flowers. Or to grow flowers instead of cabbages."

"Cabbages," you recall, "have their importance in the cosmic system."

"Don't flowers? And isn't it better that a man has music with his dinner and a pot with a design on it?"

"You don't like the ancient world?"

"Let me tell you, *most* of us didn't live well. *Most* of us didn't make it past childhood. And not just villages vanished in some bitter winter. Whole towns did. Whole nations. There were no good old days."

"History again."

"That's why we make fantasies. Because it was too bad to remember."

"Cynic."

"I do write fantasies. Sometimes."

"And they're true?"

"True as those poor dead kids in Ephesus."

"Where's that?"

"See?" I sigh, thinking of dead stones and a child's game, etched forever in a dead street, near a conqueror's arch. "Let me tell you a story."

"A cheerful one."

"A cheerful one. Let me tell you a story about a story. Lin Carter and I were talking just exactly like this, about the wretchedness of the ancient world once upon a time—he was doing an anthology, and wanted me to write a story, a fantasy. And then Lin said a remarkable thing which I'm sure didn't come out quite the thing he was trying to say. I think what he *meant* to say was that the medieval age was not particularly chivalrous, that the open land was quite dangerous and that it was an age which quite well cast everyone into a series of dependencies—i.e., villein upon master, him upon his lord, lord upon baron, baron upon king, and king upon emperor, who relied on God and played politics with Him whenever he could. The way it came out was that no woman could possibly survive in the middle ages. . . .

"I laughed. Lin took a curious look at his glass and amended the remark to say that it at least would not be the merry life of derring-do practiced by the males of fiction. I countered that the real-life rogues hardly had a merry time of it in real life either. You were more likely to mistake the aristocrats for the outlaws than vice versa.

"But immediately that became the orchard fence, the thou-shalt-not which of course was precisely the story I meant to do for Lin's anthology. Not only that, in my tale, the woman would be no princess, no abbess, no burgher's daughter with defensive advantages."

"Witch?"

"Well, take a very typical swash and buckle hero—

illiterate, battling wizards, gods, and double-dealing princes, selling what can be sold and spending all the gain by sunrise—"

"—Who carries off the woman?"

"That *is* the woman."

A Thief in Korianth

I

THE YLIZ RIVER ran through Korianth, a sullen, muddy stream on its way to the nearby sea, with stone banks where it passed through the city ... gray stone and yellow water, and gaudy ships which made a spider-tangle of masts and riggings above the drab jumbled roofs of the dockside. In fact all Korianth was built on pilings and cut with canals more frequent than streets, the whole pattern of the lower town dictated by old islands and channels, so that buildings took whatever turns and bends the canals dictated, huddled against each other, jammed one up under the eaves of the next—faded paint, buildings like aged crones remembering the brightness of their youths, decayed within from overmuch of wine and living, with dulled, shuttered eyes looking suspiciously on dim streets and scummed canals, where boat vendors and barge folk plied their craft, going to and fro from shabby warehouses. This was the Sink, which was indeed slowly subsiding into the River—but that took centuries, and the Sink used only the day, quick pleasures, momentary feast, customary famine. In spring rains the Yliz rose; tavern keepers mopped and dockmen and warehousers cursed and set merchandise up on blocks; then the town stank considerably. In summer heats the River sank, and the town stank worse.

There was a glittering world above this rhythm, the part of Korianth that had grown up later, inland, and beyond the zone of flood: palaces and town houses of hewn stone (which still sank, being too heavy for their foundations, and developed cracks, and whenever abandoned, decayed quickly). In this area too were temples ... temples of gods and goddesses and whole pantheons local and foreign, ancient and modern, for Korianth was a trading city and offended no one permanently. The gods were transients, coming and going in favor like dukes and royal lovers. There was, more permanent than gods, a king in Korianth, Seithan XXIV, but Seithan was, if rumors might be believed, quite mad, having recovered after poisoning. At least he showed a certain bizarre turn of behavior, in which he played obscure and cruel jokes and took to strange religions, mostly such as promised sybaritic afterlives and conjured demons.

And central to that zone between, where town and dockside met on the canals, lay a rather pleasant zone of mild decay, of modest townsmen and a few dilapidated palaces. In this web of muddy waterways a grand bazaar transferred the wealth of the Sink (whose dark warrens honest citizens avoided) into higher-priced commerce of the Market of Korianth.

It was a profitable place for merchants, for prose-lytizing cults, for healers, interpreters of dreams, prostitutes of the better sort (two of the former pal-aces were brothels, and no few of the temples were), palm readers and sellers of drinks and sweetmeats, silver and fish, of caged birds and slaves, copper pots and amulets and minor sorceries. Even on a chill autumn day such as this, with the stench of hundreds of altars and the spices of the booths and the smokes of midtown, that of the River welled up. Humanity jostled shoulder to shoulder, armored guard against citizen, beggar against priest, and furnished ample opportunity for thieves.

Gillian glanced across that sea of bobbing heads and swirling colors, eased up against the twelve-year-old girl whose slim, dirty fingers had just deceived the fruit merchant and popped a first and a second handful of figs into the torn seam of her cleverly sewn skirt. Gillian pushed her own body into the way of sight and reached to twist her fingers into her sister's curls and jerk. Jensy yielded before the hair came out by the roots, let herself be dragged four paces into the woman-wide blackness of an alley, through which a sickly stream of something threaded between their feet.

"Hist," Gillian said. "Will you have us on the run for a fistful of sweets? You have no judgment."

Jensy's small face twisted into a grin. "Old Habershen's never seen me."

Gillian gave her a rap on the ear, not hard. The claim was truth: Jensy was deft. The double-sewn skirt picked up better than figs. "Not here," Gillian said. "Not in *this* market. There's high law here. They cut your hand off, stupid snipe."

Jensy grinned at her; everything slid off Jensy. Gillian gripped her sister by the wrist and jerked her out into the press, walked a few stalls down. It was never good to linger. They did not look the best of customers, she and Jensy, ragged curls bound up in scarves, coarse sacking skirts, blouses that had seen good days—before they had left some goodwoman's laundry. Docksiders did come here, frequent enough in the crowds. And their faces were not known outside the Sink; varying patterns of dirt were a tolerable disguise.

Lean days were at hand; they were not far from winter, when ships would be scant, save only the paltry, patched coasters. In late fall and winter the goods were here in midtown, being hauled out of warehouses and sold at profit. Dockside was slim pickings in winter; dockside was where she preferred to work—given choice. And with Jensy—

Midtown frightened her. This place was daylight and open, and at the moment she was not looking for trouble; rather she made for the corner of the fish market with its peculiar aromas and the perfumed reek of Agdalia's gilt temple and brothel.

"Don't want to," Jensy declared, planting her feet.

Gillian jerked her willy-nilly. "I'm not going to leave you there, mousekin. Not for long."

"I hate Sophonisba."

Gillian stopped short, jerked Jensy about by the shoulder and looked down into the dirty face. Jensy sobered at once, eyes wide. "Sophonisba never lets the customers near you."

Jensy shook her head, and Gillian let out a breath. *She* had started that way; Jensy would not. She dragged Jensy to the door, where Sophonisba held her usual post at the shrine of the tinsel goddess— legitimacy of a sort, more than Sophonisba had been born to. Gillian shoved Jensy into Sophonisba's hands . . . overblown and overpainted, all pastels and perfumes and swelling bosom—it was not lack of charms kept Sophonisba on the market street, by the Fish, but the unfortunate voice, a Sink accent and a nasal whine that would keep her here forever. *Dead ear*, Gillian reckoned of her in some pity, for accents came off and onto Gillian's tongue with polyglot facility; Sophonisba probably did not know her affliction—a creature of patterns, reliable to follow them.

"Not in daylight," Sophonisba complained, painted eyes distressed. "Double cut for daylight. Are you working *here*? I don't want any part of that. Take yourselves elsewhere."

"You know I wouldn't bring the king's men down on Jensy; mind her, old friend, or I'll break your nose."

"Hate you," Jensy muttered, and winced, for Sophonisba gripped her hair.

She meant Sophonisba. Gillian gave her a face and

197

walked away, free. The warrens or the market—
neither place was safe for a twelve-year-old female
with light fingers and too much self-confidence;
Sophonisba could still keep a string on her—and
Sophonisba was right to worry: stakes were higher
here, in all regards.

Gillian prowled the aisles, shopping customers as
well as booths, lingering nowhere long, flowing with
the traffic. It was the third winter coming, the third
since she had had Jensy under her wing. Neither of
them had known hunger often while her mother
had been there to care for Jensy—but those days
were gone, her mother gone, and Jensy—Jensy was
falling into the pattern. Gillian saw it coming. She
had nightmares, Jensy in the hands of the city watch,
or knifed in some stupid brawl, like their mother. Or
something happening to herself, and Jensy growing
up in Sophonisba's hands.

Money. A large amount of gold: that was the way
out she dreamed of, money that would buy Jensy
into some respectable order, to come out polished
and fit for midtown or better. But that kind of money
did not often flow accessibly on dockside, in the
Sink. It had to be hunted here; and she saw it—all
about her—at the risk of King's-law, penalties greater
than the dockside was likely to inflict: the Sink took
care of its own problems, but it was apt to wink at
pilferage and it was rarely so inventively cruel as
King's-law. Whore she was not, no longer, never
again; whore she had been, seeking out Genat, a
thief among thieves; and the apprentice had passed
the master. Genat had become blind Genat the
beggar—dead Genat soon after—and Gillian was free,

walking the market where Genat himself seldom dared pilfer.

If she had gold enough, then Jensy was out of the streets, out of the way of things that waited to happen.

Gold enough, and she could get more: gold was power, and she had studied power zealously, from street bravos to priests, listening to gossip, listening to rich folk talk, one with the alleys and the booths—she learned, did Gillian, how rich men stole, and she planned someday—she always had—to be rich.

Only three years of fending for two, and this third year that saw Jensy filling out into more than her own whipcord shape would ever be, *that* promised what Jensy would be the fourth year, when at thirteen she became a mark for any man on the docks—

This winter or never, for Jensy.

Gillian walked until her thin soles burned on the cobbles. She looked at jewelers' booths—too wary, the goldsmiths, who tended to have armed bullies about them. She had once—madly—entertained the idea of approaching a jeweler, proposing her own slight self as a guard: truth, no one on the streets could deceive her sharp eyes, and there would be no pilferage; but say to them, *I am a better thief than they, sirs?*—that was a way to end like Genat.

Mistress to such, instead? There seemed no young and handsome ones—even Genat had been that—and she, moreover, had no taste for more such years. She passed the jewelers, hoping forlornly for some indiscretion.

She hungered by afternoon and thought wistfully of the figs Jensy had fingered; Jensy had them, which meant Jensy would eat them. Gillian was not so rash as in her green years. She would not risk herself for a bit of bread or cheese. She kept prowling, turning down minor opportunities, bumped against a number of promising citizens, but each was a risk, and each deft fingering of their purses showed nothing of great substance.

The hours passed. The better classes began to wend homeward with their bodyguards and bullies. She began to see a few familiar faces on the edges of the crowd, rufflers and whores and such anticipating the night, which was theirs. Merchants with more expensive goods began folding up and withdrawing with their armed guards and their day's profits.

Nothing—no luck at all, and Sophonisba would not accept a cut of bad luck; Gillian had two coppers in her own purse, purloined days ago, and Sophonisba would expect one. It was the streets and no supper if she was not willing to take a risk.

Suddenly a strange face cut the crowd, making haste: that caught her eye, and like the reflex of a boxer, her body tended that way before her mind had quite weighed matters, so she should not lose him. This was a stranger; there was a fashion to faces in Korianth, and this one was not Korianthine—Abhizite, she reckoned, from upriver. Gillian warmed indeed; it was like summer, when gullible foreigners came onto the docks carrying their traveling funds with them and giving easy opportunity to the light-fingered trade.

She bumped him in the press at a corner, anticipating his move to dodge her, and her razor had the purse strings, her fingers at once aware of weight, her heart thudding with the old excitement as she eeled through the crowd and alleyward.

Heavy purse—it was too soon missed: her numbing blow had had short effect. She heard the bawl of outrage, and suddenly a general shriek of alarm. At the bend of the alley she looked back.

Armored men. Bodyguards!

Panic hit her; she clutched the purse and ran the dark alley she had mapped in advance for escape, ran with all her might and slid left, right, right, along a broad back street, down yet another alley. They were after her in the twilight of the maze, cursing and with swords gleaming bare.

It was no ordinary cutpursing. She had tripped something, indeed. She ran until her heart was nigh to bursting, took the desperate chance of a stack of firewood to scamper to a ledge and into the upper levels of the midtown maze.

She watched them then, she lying on her heaving belly and trying not to be heard breathing. They were someone's hired bravos for certain, scarred of countenance, with that touch of the garish that bespoke gutter origins.

"Common cutpurse," one said. That rankled. She had other skills.

"Someone has to have seen her," said another. "Money will talk, in the Sink."

They went away. Gillian lay still, panting, opened the purse with trembling fingers.

A lead cylinder stamped with a seal; lead, and a finger-long sealed parchment, and a paltry three silver coins.

Bile welled up in her throat. They had sworn to

search for her even into the impenetrable Sink. She had stolen something terrible; she had ruined herself; and even the Sink could not hide her, not against money, and such men.

Jensy, she thought, sick at heart. If passersby had seen her strolling there earlier and described Jensy—their memories would be very keen, for gold. The marks on the loot were ducal seals, surely; lesser men did not use such things. Her breath shuddered through her throat. Kings and dukes. She had stolen lead and paper, and her death. She could not read, not a word—not even to know *what* she had in hand.

—and *Jensy!*

She swept the contents back into the purse, thrust it into her blouse and, dropping down again into the alley, ran.

2

THE TINSEL shrine was closed. Gillian's heart sank, and her vision blurred. Again to the alleys and behind, thence to a lower-story window with a red shutter. She reached up and rapped it a certain pattern with her knuckles.

It opened. Sophonisba's painted face stared down at her; a torrent of abuse poured sewer-fashion from the dewy lips, and Jensy's dirty-scarfed head bobbed up from below the whore's ample bosom.

"Come *on*," Gillian said, and Jensy scrambled, grimaced in pain, for Sophonisba had her by the hair.

"My cut," Sophonisba said.

Gillian swallowed air, her ears alert for pursuit. She fished the two coppers from her purse, and

Sophonisba spat on them. Heat flushed Gillian's face; the next thing in her hand was her razor.

Sophonisba paled and sniffed. "I know you got better, slink. The whole street's roused. Should I take such risks? If someone comes asking here, should I say lies?"

Trembling, blind with rage, Gillian took back the coppers. She brought out the purse, spilled the contents: lead cylinder, parchment, three coins. "Here. See? Trouble, trouble and no lot of money."

Sophonisba snatched at the coins. Gillian's deft fingers saved two, and the other things, which Sophonisba made no move at all to seize.

"Take your trouble," Sophonisba said. "And your brat. And keep away from here."

Jensy scrambled out over the sill, hit the alley cobbles on her slippered feet. Gillian did not stay to threaten. Sophonisba knew her—knew better than to spill to king's-men . . . or to leave Jensy on the street. Gillian clutched her sister's hand and pulled her along at a rate a twelve-year-old's strides could hardly match.

They walked, finally, in the dark of the blackest alleys and, warily, into the Sink itself. Gillian led the way to Threepenny Bridge and so to Rat's Alley and the Bowel. They were *not* alone, but the shadows inspected them cautiously: the trouble that lurked here was accustomed to pull its victims into the warren, not to find them there; and one time that lurkers did come too close, she and Jensy played dodge in the alley. "Cheap flash," she spat, and: "Bit's Isle," marking herself of a rougher brotherhood than theirs. They were alone after.

After the Bowel came the Isle itself, and the deepest part of the Sink. There was a door in the alley called Blindman's, where Genat had sat till someone knifed him. She dodged to it with Jensy in tow, this stout door inconspicuous among others, and pushed it open.

It let them in under Jochen's stairs, in the winesmelling backside of the Rose. Gillian caught her breath then and pulled Jensy close within the shadows of the small understairs pantry. "Get Jochen," she bade Jensy then. Jensy skulked out into the hall and took off her scarf, stuffed that in her skirts and passed out of sight around the corner of the door and into the roister of the tavern.

In a little time she was back with fat Jochen in her wake, and Jochen mightily scowling.

"You're in trouble?" Jochen said. "Get out if you are."

"Want you to keep Jensy for me."

"Pay," Jochen said. "You got it?"

"How much?"

"How bad the trouble?"

"For her, none at all. Just keep her." Gillian turned her back—prudence, not modesty—to fish up the silver from her blouse, not revealing the purse. She held up one coin. "Two days' board and close room."

"You *are* in trouble."

"I want Nessim. Is he here?"

He always was by dark. Jochen snorted. "A cut of what's going."

"A cut if there's profit; a clear name if there's not; get Nessim."

Jochen went. "I don't want to be left," Jensy started

to say, but Gillian rapped her ear and scowled so that Jensy swallowed it and looked frightened. Finally a muddled old man came muttering their way and Gillian snagged his sleeve. The reek of wine was strong; it was perpetual about Nessim Hath, excommunicate priest and minor dabbler in magics. He read, when he was sober enough to see the letters; that and occasionally effective magics—wards against rats, for one—made him a livelihood and kept his throat uncut.

"Upstairs," Gillian said, guiding sot and child up the well-worn boards to the loft and the private cells at the alleyside wall. Jensy snatched the taper at the head of the stairs and they went into that room, which had a window.

Nessim tottered to the cot and sat down while Jensy lit the stub of a candle. Gillian fished out her coppers, held them before Nessim's red-rimmed eyes and pressed them into the old priest's shaking hand.

"Read something?" Nessim asked.

Gillian pulled out the purse and knelt by the bedside while Jensy prudently closed the door. She produced the leaden cylinder and the parchment. "Old man," she said, "tell me what I've got here."

He gathered up the cylinder and brought his eyes closely to focus on it, frowning. His mouth trembled as did his hands, and he thrust it back at her. "I don't know this seal. Lose this thing in the canal. Be rid of it."

"You know it, old man."

"I don't." She did not take it from him, and he held it, trembling. "A false seal, a mask seal. Something some would know—and not outsiders. It's no good, Gillian."

"And if some would hunt a thief for it? It's good to someone."

Nessim stared at her. She valued Nessim, gave him coppers when he was on one of his lower periods: he drank the money and was grateful. She cultivated him, one gentle rogue among the ungentle, who would not have failed at priesthood and at magics if he did not drink and love comforts; now he simply had the drink.

"Run," he said. "Get out of Korianth. Tonight."

"Penniless? This should be worth something, old man."

"Powerful men would use such a seal to mask what they do, who they are. Games of more than small stakes."

Gillian swallowed heavily. "You've played with seals before, old man; read me the parchment."

He took it in hand, laid the leaden cylinder in his lap, turned the parchment to all sides. Long and long he stared at it, finally opened his purse with much trembling of his hands, took out a tiny knife and cut the red threads wrapped round, pulled them from the wax and loosed it carefully with the blade.

"Huh," Jensy pouted. "*Anyone* could cut it." Gillian rapped her ear gently as Nessim canted the tiny parchment to the scant light. His lips mumbled, steadied, a thin line. When he opened his mouth they trembled again, and very carefully he drew out more red thread from his pouch, red wax such as scribes used. Gillian held her peace and kept Jensy's, not to disturb him in the ticklish process that saw new cords seated, the seal prepared—he motioned for the candle and she held it herself while he heated and replaced the seal most gingerly.

"No magics," he said then, handing it back. "No magics of mine near this thing. Or the other. Take them. Throw them both in the River."

"Answers, old man."

"Triptis. Promising—without naming names—twenty thousand in gold to the shrine of Triptis."

Gillian wrinkled her nose and took back parchment and cylinder. "Abhizite god," she said. "A dark one." The sum ran cold fingers over her skin. "Twenty thousand. That's—*gold*—twenty thousand. How much do rich men have to spend on temples, old thief?"

"Rich men's *lives* are bought for less."

The fingers went cold about the lead. Gillian swallowed, wishing Jensy had stayed downstairs in the pantry. She held up the lead cylinder. "Can you breach that seal, old man?"

"*Wouldn't.*"

"You tell me why."

"It's more than a lead seal on that. Adepts more than the likes of me; I know my level, woman; I know what not to touch, and you can take my advice. Get out of here. You've stolen something you can't trade in. They don't need to see you, do you understand me? This thing can be traced."

The hairs stirred to her nape. She sat staring at him. "Then throwing it in the river won't do it, either."

"They might give up then. Might. Gillian, you've put your head in the jaws this time."

"Rich men's lives," she muttered, clutching the

objects in her hand. She slid them back into the purse and thrust it within her blouse. "I'll get rid of it. I'll find some way. I've paid Jochen to keep Jensy. See he does, or sour his beer."

"Gillian—"

"You don't want to know," she said. "I don't want either of you to know."

There was the window, the slanting ledge outside; she hugged Jensy, and old Nessim, and used it.

3

ALONE, SHE traveled quickly, by warehouse roofs for the first part of her journey, where the riggings and masts of dockside webbed the night sky, by remembered ways across the canal. One monstrous old warehouse squatted athwart the canal like a misshapen dowager, a convenient crossing that avoided the bridges. Skirts hampered; she whipped off the wrap, leaving the knee breeches and woolen hose she wore beneath, the skirt rolled and bound to her waist with her belt. She had her dagger, her razor and the cant to mark her as trouble for ruffians—a lie: the nebulous brotherhood would hardly back her now, in her trouble. They disliked long looks from moneyed men, hired bullies and noise on dockside. If the noise continued about her, she might foreseeably meet with accident, to be found floating in a canal—to quiet the uproar and stop further attentions.

But such as she met did not know it and kept from her path or, sauntering and mocking, still shied from brotherhood cant. Some passwords were a cut throat to use without approval, and thieves out of the Sink taught interlopers bitter lessons.

She paused to rest at the Serpentine of midtown, crouched in the shadows, sweating and hard-breathing, dizzy with want of sleep and food. Her belly had passed the point of hurting. She thought of a side excursion—a bakery's back door, perhaps—but she did not dare the possible hue and cry added to what notoriety she already had. She gathered what strength she had and set out a second time, the way that led to the tinsel shrine and one house that would see its busiest hours in the dark.

Throw it in the canal: she dared not. Once it was gone from her, she had no more bargains left, nothing. As it was she had a secret valuable and fearful to someone. *There comes a time*, Genat had told her often enough, *when chances have to be taken—and taken wide.*

It was not Sophonisba's way.

Panting, she reached the red window, rapped at it; there was dim light inside and long delay—a male voice, a curse, some drunken converse. Gillian leaned against the wall outside and slowed her breathing, wishing by all the gods of Korianth (save one) that Sophonisba would make some haste. She rapped again finally, heart racing as her rashness raised a complaint within—male voice again. She pressed herself to the wall, heard the drunken voice diminish— Sophonisba's now, shrill, bidding someone out. A door opened and closed.

In a moment steps crossed the room and the shutter opened. Gillian showed herself cautiously, stared up into Sophonisba's white face. "Come on out here," Gillian said.

"Get out of here," Sophonisba hissed, with fear stark in her eyes. *"Out*, or I call the watch. There's *money* looking for you."

She would have closed the shutters, but Gillian had both hands on the ledge and vaulted up to perch on it; Gillian snatched and caught a loose handful of Sophonisba's unlaced shift. "Don't do that, Sophie. If you bring the watch, we'll both be sorry. You know me. I've got something I've got to get rid of. Get dressed."

"And lose a night's—"

"Yes. Lose your nose if you don't hurry about it." She brought out the razor, that small and wicked knife of which Sophonisba was most afraid. She sat polishing it on her knee while Sophonisba sorted into a flurry of skirts. Sophonisba paused once to look; she let the light catch the knife and Sophonisba made greater haste. "Fix your hair," Gillian said.

"Someone's going to come back here to check on me if I don't take my last fee front—"

"Then fix it on the way." Steps were headed toward the door. "Haste! Or there'll be bloodletting."

"Get down," Sophonisba groaned. "I'll get rid of her."

Gillian slipped within the room and closed the shutters, stood in the dark against the wall while Sophonisba cracked the door and handed the fee out, heard a gutter dialogue and Sophonisba pleading indisposition. She handed out more money finally, as if she were parting with her life's blood, and closed the door. She looked about with a pained expression. "You owe me, you owe me—"

"I'm carrying something dangerous," Gillian said.

"It's being tracked, do you understand? Nessim doesn't like the smell of it."

"O gods."

"Just so. It's trouble, old friend. Priest trouble."

"Then take it to priests."

"Priests expect donations. I've the scent of *gold*, dear friend. It's rich men pass such things back and forth, about things they don't want authority to know about."

"Then throw it in a canal."

"Nessim's advice. But it doesn't take the smell off my hands or answer questions when the trackers catch me up—or *you*, now, old friend."

"What do you want?" Sophonisba moaned. "Gillian, please—"

"Do you know," she said softly, reasonably, "if we take this thing—*we*, dear friend—to the wrong party, to someone who isn't disposed to reward us, or someone who isn't powerful enough to protect us so effortlessly that protection costs him nothing—who would spend effort protecting a whore and a thief, eh, Sophie? But some there are in this city who shed gold like gods shed hair, whose neighborhoods are so well protected others hesitate to meddle in them. Men of birth, Sophie. Men who might like to know who's paying vast sums of gold for favors in this city."

"Don't tell me these things."

"I'll warrant a whore hears a lot of things, Sophie. I'll warrant a whore knows a lot of ways and doors and windows in Korianth, who's where, who has secrets—"

"A whore is told a lot of lies. I can't help you."

"But you can, pretty Sophonisba." She held up the razor. "I daresay you know names and such—even in the king's own hall."

"*No!*"

"But the king's mad, they say; and who knows what a madman might do? What other names do you know?"

"I don't know *anyone*, I swear I don't."

"Don't swear; we've gods enough here. We improvise, then, you and I." She flung the shutter open. "Out, out with you."

Sophonisba was not adept at ledges. She settled herself on it and hesitated. Gillian thought of pushing her; then, fearing noise, took her hands and let her down gently, followed after with a soft thud. Sophonisba stood shivering and tying her laces, the latter unsuccessfully.

"Come on," Gillian said.

"I don't walk the alleys," Sophonisba protested in dread; Gillian pulled her along nonetheless, the back ways of the Grand Serpentine.

They met trouble. It was inevitable. More than once gangs of youths spotted Sophonisba, like dogs a stray cat, and came too close for comfort. Once the cant was not password enough, and they wanted more proof: Gillian showed that she carried, knife-carved in her shoulder, the brotherhood's initiation, and drunk as they were, they had sense to give way for that. It ruffled her pride. She jerked Sophonisba along and said nothing, seething with anger and reckoning she should have cut one. She could have done it and gotten away; but not with Sophonisba.

Sophonisba snuffled quietly, her hand cold as ice.

They took to the main canalside at last, when they must, which was at this hour decently deserted. It was not a place Gillian had been often; she found her way mostly by sense, knowing where the tall, domed buildings should lie. She had seen them most days of her life from the rooftops of the Sink.

The palaces of the great of Korianth were walled, with gardens, and men to watch them. She saw seals now and then that she knew, mythic beasts and demon beasts snarling from the arches over such places.

But one palace there was on the leftside hill, opposed to the great gold dome of the King's Palace, a lonely abode well walled and guarded.

There were guards, gilt-armed guards, with plumes and cloaks and more flash than ever the rufflers of midtown dared sport. Gillian grinned to herself and felt Sophonisba's hand in hers cold and limp from dread of such a place.

She marked with her eye where the guards stood, how they came and went and where the walls and accesses lay, where trees and bushes topped the walls inside and how the wall went to the very edge of the white marble building. The place was defended against armed men, against that sort of threat; against—the thought cooled her grin and her enthusiasm—guilded Assassins and free-lancers; a prince must worry for such things.

No. It was far from easy as it looked. Those easy ways could be set with traps; those places too unguarded could become deadly. She looked for the ways less easy, traced again that too-close wall.

"Walk down the street," she told Sophonisba. "Now. Just walk down the street."

"You're mad."

"Go."

Sophonisba started off, pale figure in blue silks, a disheveled and unlaced figure of ample curves and confused mien. She walked quickly as her fear would urge her, beyond the corner and before the eyes of the guards at the gate.

Gillian stayed long enough to see the sentries' attention wander, then pelted to the wall and carefully, with delicate fingers and the balance Genat had taught, spidered her way up the brickwork.

Dogs barked the moment she flung an arm over. She cursed, ran the crest of the thin wall like a trained ape, made the building itself and crept along the masonry—*too much of ornament, my lord!*—as far as the upper terrace.

Over the rim and onto solid ground, panting. Whatever had become of Sophonisba, she had served her purpose.

Gillian darted for a further terrace. Doors at the far end swung open suddenly; guards ran out in consternation. Gillian grinned at them, arms wide, like a player asking tribute; bowed.

They were not amused, thinking of their hides, surely. She looked up at a ring of pikes, cocked her head to one side and drew a conscious deep breath, making obvious what they should see; that it was no male intruder they had caught.

"Courier," she said, "for Prince Osric."

4

HE WAS NOT, either, amused.

She stood with a very superfluous pair of men-at-arms gripping her wrists so tightly that the blood left her hands and the bones were about to snap, and the king's bastard—and sole surviving son—fingered the pouch they had found in their search of her.

"Courier," he said.

They were not alone with the guards, he and she. A brocaded troop of courtiers and dandies loitered near, amongst the porphyry columns and on the steps of the higher floor. He dismissed them with a wave of his hand; several seemed to feel privileged and stayed.

"For whom," the prince asked, "are you a courier?"

"Couriers bring messages," she said. "I decided on my own to bring you this one. I thought you should have it."

"Who are you?"

"A free-lance assassin," she said, promoting herself, and setting Prince Osric back a pace. The guards nearly crushed her wrists; they went beyond pain.

"Jisan," Osric said.

One of the three who had stayed walked forward, and Gillian's spine crawled; she knew the look of trouble, suspected the touch of another brotherhood, more disciplined than her own. "I was ambitious," she said at once. "I exaggerate."

"She is none of ours," said the Assassin. A dark man he was, unlike Osric, who was white-blond and thin; this Jisan was from southern climes and not at all flash, a drab shadow in brown and black beside Osric's glitter.

"Your name," said Osric.

"Gillian," she said; and recalling better manners and where she was: "—majesty."

"And how come by this?"

"A cutpurse . . . found this worthless. It fell in the street. But it's some lord's seal."

"*No* lord's seal. Do you read, guttersnipe?"

"Read, I?" The name rankled; she kept her face calm. "No, lord."

He whisked out a dagger and cut the cords, unfurled the parchment. A frown came at once to his face, deepened, and his pale eyes came suddenly up to hers. "Suppose that someone read it to you."

She sucked a thoughtful breath, weighed her life, and Jensy's. "A drunk clerk read it—for a kiss; said it was something he didn't want to know; and I think then—some great lord might want to know it; but which lord, think I? One lord might make good use and another bad, one be grateful and another not— might make rightest use of something dangerous— might be glad it came here in good loyal hands, and not where it was supposed to go; might take notice of a stir in the lowtown, bully boys looking for that cutpurse to cut throats, armed men and some of them not belonging hereabouts. King's wall's too high, majesty, so I came here."

"Whose bravos?" Jisan asked.

She blinked. "Wish I knew that; I'd like to know."

"You're that cutpurse," he said.

"If I were, would I say yes, and if I weren't, would I say yes? But I know that thing's better not in my hands and maybe better here than in the River. A trifle of reward, majesty, and there's no one closer mouthed than I am; a trifle more, majesty, and you've all my talents at hire: no one can outbid a prince, not for the likes of me; I know I'm safest to be bribed once and never again."

Osric's white-blue eyes rested on her a very long, very calculating moment. "You're easy to kill. Who would miss you?"

"No one, majesty. No one. But I'm eyes and ears and Korianthine—" Her eyes slid to the Assassin. "And I go places where *he* won't."

The Assassin smiled. His eyes did not. Guild man. He worked by hire and public license.

And sometimes without.

Osric applied his knife to the lead cylinder to gently cut it. "No," Gillian said nervously. And when he looked up, alarmed: "I would not," she said. "I have been advised—the thing has some ill luck attached."

"Disis," Osric called softly, and handed the cylinder into the hands of an older man, a scholarly man, whose courtier's dress was long out of mode. The man's long, lined face contracted at the touch of it in his hand.

"Well advised," that one said. "Silver and lead—a confining. I would be most careful of that seal, majesty; I would indeed."

The prince took the cylinder back, looked at it with a troubled mien, passed it back again. Carefully then he took the purse from his own belt, from beside his dagger. "Your home?" he asked of Gillian.

"Dockside," she said.

"All of it?"

She bit her lip. "Ask at the Anchor," she said, betraying a sometime haunt, but not Sophonisba's, not the Rose either. "All the Sink knows Gillian." And that was true.

"Let her go," Osric bade his guards. Gillian's arms dropped, relief and agony at once. He tossed the purse at her feet, while she was absorbed in her pain. "Come to the garden gate next time. Bring me word—and *names.*"

She bent, gathered the purse with a swollen hand, stood again and gave a shy bow, her heart pounding with the swing of her fortunes. She received a disgusted wave of dismissal, and the guards at her right jerked her elbow and brought her down the hall, the whole troop of them to escort her to the door.

"My knives," she reminded them with a touch of smugness. They returned them and hastened her down the stairs. She did not gape at the splendors about her, but she saw them, every detail. In such a place twenty thousand in gold might be swallowed up. *Gillian* might be swallowed up, here and now or in the Sink, later. She knew. She reckoned it.

They took her through the garden, past handlers and quivering dogs the size of men, and there at the garden gate they let her go without the mauling she had expected. Princes' favor had power even out of princes' sight, then; from what she had heard of Osric, that was wise of them.

They pitched the little bundle of her skirt at her feet, undone. She snatched that up and flung it jauntily over her shoulder, and stalked off into the alleys that were her element.

She had a touch of conscience for Sophonisba. Likely Sophonisba had disentangled herself by now, having lied her way with some small skill out of whatever predicament she had come to, appearing in the high town: *forgive me, lord; this lord he brought me here, he did, and turned me out, he did, and I'm lost, truly, sir* . . . Sophonisba would wait till safe daylight and find her way home again, to nurse a grudge that money would heal. And she . . .

Gillian was shaking when she finally stopped to assess herself. Her wrists felt maimed, the joints of her hands swollen. She crouched and slipped the knives back where they belonged, earnestly wishing she had had the cheek to ask for food as well. She rolled the skirt and tied it in the accustomed bundle at her belt. Lastly—for fear, lastly—she spilled the sack into her cupped hand, spilled it back again quickly, for the delight and the terror of the flood of gold that glinted in the dim light. She thrust it down her blouse, at once terrified to possess such a thing and anxious until she could find herself in the Sink again, where she had ratholes in plenty. This was not a thing to walk the alleys with.

She sprang up and started moving, alone and free again, and casting furtive and careful glances all directions, most especially behind.

Priests and spells and temple business. Of a sudden it began to sink into her mind precisely what services she had agreed to, to turn spy; Triptis's priests bought whores' babes, or any else that could be stolen. That was a thief's trade beneath contempt; a trade the brotherhood stamped out where it found it obvious: grieving mothers were a noise, and a desperate one, bad for business. It was *that* kind of enemy she dealt with.

Find me names, the lord Osric had said, with an Assassin standing on one side and a magician on the other. Suddenly she knew who the old magicker had been: Disis, the prince had called him; Aldisis, more than dabbler in magics—part and parcel of the prince's entourage of discontents, waiting for the mad king to pass the dark gates elsewhere. The prince had had brothers and a sister, and now he had none; now he had only to wait.

Aldisis the opener of paths. His ilk of lesser station sold ill wishes down by the Fish, and some of those worked; Aldisis had skills, it was whispered.

And Jisan cared for those Aldisis missed.

Find me names.

And what might my lord prince do with them? Gillian wondered, without much wondering; and with a sudden chill: *What but lives are worth twenty thousand gold? And what but high-born lives?*

She had agreed with no such intention; she had priest troubles and hunters on her trail, and she did not need to know their names, not from a great enough distance from Korianth. One desperate chance—to sell the deadly information and gamble it was not Osric himself, to gamble with the highest power she could reach and hope she reached above the plague spot in Korianth . . . for gold, to get her and Jensy out of reach and out of the city until the danger was past.

Dangerous thoughts nibbled at her resolve, the chance she had been looking for, three years on the street with Jensy—a chance not only of one purse of gold ... but of others. She swore at herself for thinking of it, reminded herself what she was; but there was also what she might be. Double such a purse could support Jensy in a genteel order: learning and fine clothes and fine manners; freedom for herself, to eel herself back dockside and vanish into her own darknesses, gather money, and power ... No strange cities for her, nothing but Korianth, where she knew her way, all the low and tangled ways that took a lifetime of living to learn of a city—no starting over elsewhere, to play whore and teach Jensy the like, to get their throats cut in Amisent or Kesirn, trespassing in another territory and another brotherhood.

She skipped along, the strength flooding back into her, the breath hissing regularly between her teeth. She found herself again in familiar territory, known alleys; found one of her narrowest boltholes and rid herself of the prince's purse, all but one coin, itself a bit of recklessness. After that she ran and paused, ran and paused, slick with sweat and light-headed with fortune and danger and hunger.

The Bowel took her in, and Blindman's—home territory indeed; her sore, slippered feet pattered over familiar cobbles; she loosed her skirt and whipped it about her, mopped her face with her scarf and knotted that about her waist, leaving her curls free. The door to the Rose was before her. She pushed it open.

And froze to the heart.

5

ALL THE ROSE was a shambles, the tables broken, a few survivors or gawkers milling about in a forlorn knot near the street-side door. There was chill in the air, a palpable chill, like a breath of ice. Fat Jochen lay stark on the floor by the counter, with all his skin gone gray and his clothes . . . faded, as if cobweb composed them.

"Gods," Gillian breathed, clutching at the luck piece she bore, easygoing Agdalia's. And in the next breath: "Jensy," she murmured, and ran for the stairs.

The door at the end of the narrow hall stood open, moonlight streaming into a darkened room from the open window. She stopped, drew her knife— clutched the tawdry charm, sick with dread. From her vantage point she saw the cot disheveled, the movement of a shadow within, like a lich robed in cobwebs.

"Jensy!" she shouted into that dark.

The wraith came into the doorway, staggered out, reached.

Nessim. She held her hand in time, only just, turned the blade and with hilt in hand gripped the old man's sticklike arms, seized him with both hands, heedless of hurts. He stammered something. There was a silken crumbling in the cloth she held, like something moldered, centuries old. The skin on Nessim's poor face peeled in strips like a sun-baked hinterlander's.

"Gillian," he murmured. "They wanted you."

"Where's Jensy?"

He tried to tell her, pawed at the amulet he had

worn; it was a crystal, cracked now, in a peeling hand. He waved the hand helplessly. "Took Jensy," he said. He was bald, even to the eyebrows. "I saved myself—saved myself—had no strength for mousekin. Gillian, run away."

"Who, blast you, Nessim!"

"Don't know. Don't know. But Triptis. Triptis's priests . . . ah, go, go, Gillian."

Tears made tracks down his seared cheeks. She thrust him back, anger and pity confounded in her. The advice was sound; they were without power, without patrons. Young girls disappeared often enough in the Sink without a ripple.

Rules changed. She thrust past him to the window and out it, onto the creaking shingles, to the eaves and down the edge to Blindman's. She hit the cobbles in a crouch and straightened.

They were looking for her. For her, not Jensy. And Nessim had survived to give her that message.

Triptis.

She slipped the knife into her belt and turned to go, stopped suddenly at the apparition that faced her in the alley.

"Gillian," the shadow said, unfolding upward out of the debris by Goat's Alley.

Her hand slipped behind her to the dagger; she set her back against solid brick and flicked a glance at shadows . . . others, at the crossing of Sparrow's. More around the corner, it was likely.

"Where is it?" the same chill voice asked.

"I sell things," she said. "Do you want it back? You have something I want."

"You can't get it back," the whisper said. "Now what shall we do?"

Her blood went colder still. They knew where she had been. She was followed; and no one slipped up on Gillian, no one.

Seals and seals, Nessim had said.

"Name your price," she said.

"You gained access to a prince," said the whisper. "You can do it again."

Osric, she thought. Her heart settled into a leaden, hurting rhythm. *It was Osric it was aimed at.*

"We also," said the whisper, "sell things. You want the child Jensy. The god has many children. He can spare one."

Triptis; it was beyond doubt; the serpent-god, swallowing the moon once monthly; the snake and the mouse. *Jensy!*

"I am reasonable," she said.

There was silence. If the shadow smiled, it was invisible. A hand extended, open, bearing a tiny silver circlet. "A gift you mustn't lose," the whisper said.

She took the chill ring, a serpent shape, slipped it onto her thumb, for that was all it would fit. The metal did not warm to her flesh but chilled the flesh about it.

A second shadow stepped forward, proffered another small object, a knife the twin of her own. "The blade will kill at a scratch," the second voice said. "Have care of it."

"Don't take off the ring," the first whispered.

"You could hire assassins," she said.

"We have," the whisper returned.

She stared at them. "Jensy comes back alive," she said. "To this door. No cheating."

"On either side."

"You've bid higher," she said. "What proof do you want?"

"Events will prove. Kill him."

Her lips trembled. "I haven't eaten in two days; I haven't slept—"

"Eat and sleep," the shadow hissed, "in what leisure you think you have. We trust you."

They melted backward, shadow into shadow, on all sides. The metal remained cold upon her finger. She carried it to her lips, unconscious reflex, thought with cold panic of poison, spat onto the cobbles again and again. She was shaking.

She turned, walked into the inn of the Rose past Jochen's body, past Nessim, who sat huddled on the bottom of the steps. She poured wine from the tap, gave a cup to Nessim, drank another herself, grimacing at the flavor. Bread on the sideboard had gone hard; she soaked it in the wine, but it had the flavor of ashes; cheeses had molded: she sliced off the rind with a knife from the board and ate. Jochen lay staring at the ceiling. Passers-by thrust in their heads and gaped at a madwoman who ate such tainted things; another, hungrier than the rest, came in to join the pillage, and an old woman followed.

"Go, run," Nessim muttered, rising with great difficulty to tug at her arm, and the others shied from him in horror; it was a look of leprosy.

"Too late," she said. "Go away yourself, old man. Find a hole to hide in. I'll get Jensy back."

It hurt the old man; she had not meant it so. He

shook his head and walked away, muttering sorrow-fully of Jensy. She left, then, by the alleyway, which was more familiar to her than the street. She had food in her belly, however tainted; she had eaten worse.

She walked, stripped the skirt aside and limped along, feeling the cobbles through the holes that had worn now in her slippers. She tucked the skirt in a seam of itself, hung it about her shoulder, walked with more persistence than strength down Blindman's.

Something stirred behind her; she spun, surprised nothing, her nape prickling. A rat, perhaps; the al-leys were infested this close to the docks. Perhaps it was not. She went, hearing that something behind her from time to time and never able to surprise it.

She began to run, took to the straight ways, the ways that no thief liked to use, broke into the streets and raced breathlessly toward the Serpentine, that great canal along which all the streets of the city had their beginnings. Breath failed her finally and she slowed, dodged late walkers and kept going. If one of the walkers was that one who followed her . . . she could not tell.

The midtown gave way to the high; she retraced ways she had passed twice this night, with faltering steps, her breath loud in her own ears. It was late, even for prowlers. She met few but stumbled across one drunk or dead in the way, leapt the fallen form and fled with the short-range speed of one of the city's wary cats, dodged to this course and that and came out again in the same alley from which she and Sophonisba had spied out the palace.

The garden gate, Prince Osric had instructed her. The ring burned cold upon her finger.

She walked into the open, to the very guards who had let her out not so very long before.

6

THE PRINCE WAS abed. The fact afforded his guards no little consternation—the suspicion of a message urgent enough to make waking him advisable; the suspicion of dangerous wrath if it was not. Gillian, for her part, sat still, wool-hosed ankles crossed, hands folded, a vast fear churning at her belly. They had taken the ring. It had parted from her against all the advice of him who had given it to her; and it was not pleasing them that concerned her, but Jensy.

They had handled it and had it now, but if it was cold to them, they had not said, had not reacted. She suspected it was not. It was hers, for her.

Master Aldisis came. He said nothing, only stared at her, and she at him; him she feared most of all, his sight, his perception. His influence. She had nothing left, not the ring, not the blades, not the single gold coin. The scholar, in his night robe, observed her and walked away. She sat, the heat of exertion long since fled, with her feet and hands cold and finally numb.

"Mistress Gillian," a voice mocked her.

She looked up sharply, saw Jisan standing by a porphyry column. He bowed as to a lady. She sat still, staring at him as warily as at Aldisis.

"A merry chase, mistress Gillian."

Alarm might have touched her eyes. It surprised her, that it had been he.

"Call the lord prince," the Assassin said, and a guard went.

"Who is your contract?" she asked.

He smiled. "Guildmaster might answer," he said. "Go ask."

Patently she could not. She sat still, fixed as under a serpent's gaze. Her blades were in the guards' hands, one more knife than there had been. They suspected something amiss, as it was their business to suspect all things and all persons; Jisan knew. She stared into his eyes.

"What game are you playing?" he asked her plainly.

"I've no doubt you've asked about."

"There's some disturbance down in lowtown. A tavern with a sudden . . . unwholesomeness in it. Dead men. Would you know about that, mistress Gillian?"

"I carry messages," she said.

His dark eyes flickered. She thought of the serpent-god and the mouse. She kept her hands neatly folded, her feet still. This was a man who killed. Who perhaps enjoyed his work. She thought that he might.

A curse rang out above, echoing in the high beams of the ceiling. Osric. She heard every god in the court pantheon blasphemed and turned her head to stare straight before her, smoothed her breeches, a nervousness—stood at the last moment, remembering the due of royalty, even in night dress.

Called from some night's pleasure? she wondered. In that case he might be doubly wrathful; but he was cold as ever, thin face, thin mouth set, white-blue eyes as void of the ordinary. She could not imagine the man engaged in so human a pastime. Maybe he never did, she thought, the wild irrelevance of exhaustion. Maybe that was the source of his disposition.

"They sent me back," she said directly, "to kill you."

Not many people surely had shocked Osric; she had succeeded. The prince bit his lips, drew a breath, thrust his thin hands in the belt of his velvet robe. "Jisan?" he asked.

"There are dead men," the Assassin said, "at dockside."

"Honesty," Osric murmured, looking at her, a mocking tone.

"Lord," she said, at the edge of her nerves. "Your enemies have my sister. They promise to kill her if I don't carry out their plans."

"And you think so little of your sister, and so much of the gold?"

Her breath nigh strangled her; she swallowed air and kept her voice even. "I know that they will kill her and me whichever I do; tell me the name of your enemies, lord prince, that you didn't tell me the first time you sent me out of here with master Jisan behind me. *Give me names,* lord prince, and I'll hunt your enemies for my own reasons, and kill them or not as you like."

"You should already know one name, thief."

"A god's name? Aye, but gods are hard to hunt, lord prince." Her voice thinned; she could not help it. "Lend me master Aldisis's company instead of master Jisan's, and there's some hope. But go I will; and kill me priests if you haven't any better names."

Osric's cold, pale eyes ran her up and down, flicked to Jisan, back again. "For gold, good thief?"

"For my *sister*, lord prince. Pay me another time."

"Then why come here?"

"Because they'd know." She slid a look toward the guards, shifted weight anxiously. "A ring; they gave me a ring to wear, and they took it."

"Aldisis!" the prince called. The mage came, from some eaves-dropping vantage among the columns or from some side room.

An anxious guard proffered the serpent ring, but Aldisis would not touch it; waved it away. "Hold it awhile more," Aldisis said; and to Osric: "They would know where that is. And whether she held it."

"My sister," Gillian said in anguish. "Lord, give it back to me. I came because they'd know if not; and to find out their names. Give me their names. It's almost morning."

"I might help you," said Osric. "Perhaps I might die and delight them with a rumor."

"Lord," she murmured, dazed.

"My enemies will stay close together," he said. "The temple—or a certain lord Brisin's palace ... likely the temple; Brisin fears retaliation; the god shelters him. Master Aldisis could explain such things. You're a bodkin at best, mistress thief. But you may prick a few of them; and should you do better, that would delight me. Look to your reputation, thief."

"Rumor," she said.

"Chaos," muttered Aldisis.

"You advise me against this?" Osric asked.

"No," said Aldisis. "Toward it."

"You mustn't walk out the front gate this time," Osric said, "mistress thief, if you want a rumor."

"Give me what's mine," she said. "I'll clear your walls, lord, and give them my heels; and they'll not take me."

Osric made a sign with his hand; the guards brought her her knives, her purse and her ring, the while Osric retired to a bench, seated himself, with grim stares regarded them all. "I am dead," he said languidly. "I shall be for some few hours. Report it so and ring the bells. Today should be interesting."

Gillian slid the ring onto her finger; it was cold as ever.

"*Go!*" Osric whispered, and she turned and sped from the room, for the doors and the terrace she knew.

Night opened before her; she ran, skimmed the wall with the dogs barking, swung down with the guards at the gate shouting alarm—confused, and not doing their best. She hit the cobbles afoot as they raced after her, and their armor slowed them; she sprinted for known shadows and zigged and zagged through the maze.

She stopped finally, held a hand to a throbbing side and fetched up against a wall, rolled on a shoulder to look back and find pursuit absent.

Then the bells began out of the dark—mournful bells, tolling out a lie that must run through all of Korianth: the death of a prince.

She walked, staggering with exhaustion, wanting sleep desperately; but the hours that she might sleep were hours of Jensy's life. She was aware finally that she had cut her foot on something; she noted first the pain and then that she left a small spot of blood behind when she walked. It was far from crippling; she kept moving.

It was midtown now. She went more surely, having taken a second wind.

And all the while the bells tolled, brazen and grim, and lights burned in shuttered windows where all should be dark, people wakened to the rumor of a death.

The whole city must believe the lie, she thought, from the Sink to the throne, the mad monarch himself believed that Osric had died; and should there not be general search after a thief who had killed a prince?

She shivered, staggering, reckoning that she ran ahead of the wave of rumor: that by dawn the name of herself and Jensy would be bruited across the Sink, and there would be no more safety.

And behind the doors, she reckoned, rumor prepared itself, folk yet too frightened to come out of doors—never wise for honest folk in Korianth.

When daylight should come . . . it would run wild— mad Seithan to rule with no hope of succession, an opportunity for the kings of other cities, of upcoast and upriver, dukes and powerful men in Korianth, all to reach out hands for the power Seithan could not long hold, the tottering for which all had been waiting for more than two years . . .

This kind of rumor waited, to be flung wide at a thief's request. This kind of madness waited to be let loose in the city, in which all the enemies might surface, rumors in which a throne might fall, throats be cut, the whole city break into riot . . .

A prince might die indeed then, in disorder so general.

Or . . . a sudden and deeper foreboding possessed her . . . a king might.

A noise in one place, a snatch in the other; thief's game in the market. She had played it often enough, she with Jensy.

Not for concern for her and her troubles that Osric risked so greatly . . . but for *Osric's* sake, no other.

She quickened her pace, swallowing down the sickness that threatened her; somehow to get clear of this, to get away in this shaking of powers before two mites were crushed by an unheeding footstep.

She began, with the last of her strength, to run.

7

THE WATCH WAS out in force, armed men with lanterns, lights and shadows rippling off the stone of cobbles and of walls like the stuff of the Muranthine Hell, and the bells still tolling, the first tramp of soldiers' feet from off the high streets, canalward.

Gillian sped, not the only shadow that judged the neighborhood of the watch and the soldiers unhealthy; rufflers and footpads were hieing themselves to cover apace, with the approach of trouble and of dawn. She skirted the canals that branched off the Serpentine, took to the alleys again and paused in the familiar alley off Agdalia's Shrine, gasping for breath in the flare of lanterns. A door slammed on the street: Agdalia's was taking precautions. Upper windows closed. The trouble had flowed thus far, and folk who did not wish to involve themselves tried to signify so by staying invisible.

The red-shuttered room was closed and dark; Sophonisba had not returned ... had found some safe nook for herself with the bells going, hiding in fear, knowing where her partner had gone, perhaps witness to the hue and cry after. *Terrified*, Gillian reckoned, and did not blame her.

Gillian caught her breath and took to that street, forested with pillars, that was called the Street of the Gods. Here too the lanterns of the watch showed in the distance, and far away, dimly visible against the sky ... the palace of the king upon the other hill of the fold in which Korianth nestled, the gods and the king in close association.

From god to god she passed, up that street like an ascent of fancy, from the bare respectability of little cults like Agdalia's to the more opulent temples of gods more fearsome and more powerful. Watch passed; she retreated at once, hovered in the shadow of the smooth columns of a Korianthine god, Ablis of the Goldworkers, one of the fifty-two thousand gods of Korianth. He had no patronage for her, might, in fact, resent a thief; she hovered fearfully, waiting for ill luck; but perhaps she was otherwise marked. She shuddered, fingering that serpent ring upon her thumb, and walked farther in the shadow of the columns.

It was not the greatest temple nor the most conspicuous in this section, that of Triptis. Dull black-green by day, it seemed all black in this last hour of night, the twisted columns like stone smoke, writhing up to a plain portico, without window or ornament.

She caught her breath, peered into the dark that surrounded a door that might be open or closed; she was not sure.

Nor was she alone. A prickling urged at her nape, a sense of something that lived and breathed nearby; she whipped out the poisoned blade and turned.

A shadow moved, tottered toward her. "Gillian," it said, held out a hand, beseeching.

"Nessim," she murmured, caught the peeling hand with her left, steadied the old man. He recoiled from her touch.

"You've something of them about you," he said.

"What are you doing here?" she hissed at him. "Old man, go back—get out of here."

"I came for mousekin," he said. "I came to try, Gillian."

The voice trembled. It was, for Nessim, terribly brave.

"You would die," she said. "You're not in their class, Nessim."

"Are you?" he asked with a sudden straightening, a memory, perhaps, of better years. "You'd do what? *What* would you do?"

"You stay out," she said, and started to leave; he caught her hand, caught the hand with the poisoned knife and the ring. His fingers clamped.

"No," he said. "No. Be rid of this."

She stopped, looked at his shadowed, peeling face. "They threatened Jensy's life."

"They know you're here. You understand that? With this, they know. Give it to me."

"Aldisis saw it and returned it to me. *Aldisis* himself, old man. Is your advice better?"

"My reasons are friendlier."

A chill went over her. She stared into the old man's eyes. "What should I do?"

"Give it here. Hand it to me. I will contain it for you . . . long enough. They won't know, do you understand me? I'll do that much."

"You can't light a candle, old trickster."

"Can," he said. "Reedlight's easier. I never work more than I have to."

She hesitated, saw the fear in the old man's eyes. A friend, one friend. She nodded, sheathed the knife and slipped off the ring. He took it into his hands and sank down in the shadows with it clasped before his lips, the muscles of his arms shaking as if he strained against something vastly powerful.

And the cold was gone from her hand.

She turned, ran, fled across the street and scrambled up the stonework of the paler temple of the Elder Mother, the Serpent Triptis's near neighbor . . . up, madly, for the windowless temple had to derive its light from some source; and a temple that honored the night surely looked upon it somewhere.

She reached the crest, the domed summit of the Mother, set foot from pale marble onto the darker roof of the Serpent, shuddering, as if the very stone were alive and threatening, able to feel her presence.

To steal from a god, to snatch a life from his jaws . . .

She spun and ran to the rear of the temple, where a well lay open to the sky, where the very holy of the temple looked up at its god, which was night. *That* was the way in she had chosen. The sanctuary, she realized with a sickness of fear, thought of Jensy and took it nonetheless, swung onto the inside rim and looked down, with a second impulse of panic as she saw how far down it was, a far, far drop.

Voices hailed within, echoing off the columns, shortening what time she had; somewhere voices droned hymns or some fell chant.

She let go, plummeted, hit the slick stones and tried to take the shock by rolling . . . sprawled, dazed, on cold stone, sick from the impact and paralyzed.

She heard shouts, outcries, struggled up on a numbed arm and a sprained wrist, trying to gain her feet. It was indeed the sanctuary; pillars of some green stone showed in the golden light of lamps, pillars carved like twisting serpents, even to the scales, writhing toward the ceiling and knotting in folds across it. The two greatest met above the altar, devouring a golden sun, between their fanged jaws, above her.

"Jensy," she muttered, thinking of Nessim and his hands straining about that thing that they had given her.

She scrambled for the shadows, for safety if there was any safety in this lair of demons.

A man-shaped shadow appeared in that circle of night above the altar; she stopped, shrank back farther among the columns as it hung and dropped as she had.

Jisan. Who else would have followed her, dark of habit and streetwise? He hit the pavings hardly better than she, came up and staggered, felt of the silver-hilted knife at his belt; she shrank back and back, pace by pace, her slippered feet soundless.

And suddenly the chanting was coming this way,

up hidden stairs, lights flaring among the columns; they hymned Night, devourer of light, in their madness beseeched the day not to come—forever Dark, they prayed in their mad hymn. The words crept louder and louder among the columns, and Jisan lingered, dazed.

"*Hsst!*" Gillian whispered; he caught the sound, seemed to focus on it, fled the other way, among the columns on the far side of the hall.

And now the worshippers were within the sanctuary, the lights making the serpent columns writhe and twist into green-scaled life, accompanied by shadows. They bore with them a slight, tinseled form that wept and struggled. Jensy, crying! she never would.

Gillian reached for the poisoned blade, her heart risen into her throat. Of a sudden the hopelessness of her attempt came down upon her, for they never would keep their word, never, and there was nowhere to hide: old Nessim could not hold forever, keeping their eyes blind to her.

Or they knew already that they had been betrayed. She walked out among them. "We have a bargain!" she shouted, interrupting the hymn, throwing things into silence. "I kept mine. Keep yours."

Jensy struggled and bit, and one of them hit her. The blow rang loud in the silence, and Jensy went limp.

One of them stood forward. "He is dead?" that one asked. "The bargain is kept?"

"What else are the bells?" she asked.

There was silence. Distantly the brazen tones were still pealing across the city. It was near to dawn; stars were fewer in the opening above the altar. Triptis's hours were passing.

"Give her back," Gillian said, feeling the sweat run down her sides, her pulse hammering in her smallest veins. "You'll hear no more of us."

A cowl went back, showing a fat face she had seen in processions. No priest, not with that gaudy dress beneath; Duke Brisin, Osric had named one of his enemies; she thought it might be.

And they were not going to honor their word.

Someone cried out; a deep crash rolled through the halls; there was the tread of armored men, sudden looks of alarm and a milling among the priests like a broken hive. Jensy fell, dropped; and Gillian froze with the ringing rush of armored men coming at her back, the swing of lanterns that sent the serpents the more frenziedly twisting about the hall. "Stop them," someone was shouting.

She moved, slashed a priest, who screamed and hurled himself into the others who tried to stop her. Jensy was moving, scrambling for dark with an eel's instinct, rolling away faster than Gillian could help her.

"Jisan!" Gillian shouted to the Assassin, hoping against hope for an ally; and suddenly the hall was ringed with armed men, and herself with a poisoned bodkin, and a dazed, gilt child, huddled together against a black wall of priests.

Some priests tried to flee; the drawn steel of the soldiers prevented; and some died, shrieking. Others were herded back before the altar.

"Lord," Gillian said nervously, casting about among them for the face she hoped to see; and he was there, Prince Osric, in the guise of a common soldier; and Aldisis by him; but he had no eyes for a thief.

"Father," Osric hailed the fat man, hurled an object at his feet, a leaden cylinder.

The king recoiled pace by pace, his face white and trembling, shaking convulsively so that the fat quivered upon it. The soldiers' blades remained leveled toward him, and Gillian seized Jensy's naked shoulder and pulled her back, trying for quiet retreat out of this place of murders, away from father and son, mad king who dabbled in mad gods and plotted murders.

"Murderer," Seithan stammered, the froth gathering at his lips. "Killed my legitimate sons ... every one; killed me, but I didn't die ... kin-killer. Kin-killing bastard ... I have loyal subjects left; you'll not reign."

"You've tried *me* for years, honored father, majesty. *Where's my mother?*"

The king gave a sickly and hateful laugh.

There was movement in the dark, where no priest was ... a figure seeking deeper obscurity; Gillian took her own cue and started to move.

A priest's weapon whipped up, a knife poised to hurl; she cried warning ... and suddenly chaos, soldiers closed in a ring of bright weapons, priests dying in a froth of blood, and the king. ...

The cries were stilled. Gillian hugged Jensy against her in the shadows, seeing through the forest of snakes the sprawled bodies, the bloody-handed soldiers, Osric—king in Korianth.

King! the soldiers hailed him, that made the air

shudder; he gave them orders, that sent them has-
tening from the slaughter here.

"The *palace!*" he shouted, urging them on to riot
that would see throats cut by the hundreds in
Korianth.

A moment he paused, sword in hand, looked into
the shadows, for Jensy glittered, and it was not so
easy to hide. For a moment a thief found the courage to look a prince in the eye, wondering, desperately, whether two such motes of dust as they might
not be swept away. Whether he feared a thief's gossip, or cared.

The soldiers had stopped about him, a warlike
knot of armor and plumes and swords.

"Get moving!" he ordered them, and swept them
away with him, running in their haste to further
murders.

Against her, Jensy gave a quiet shiver, and thin
arms went round her waist. Gillian tore at a bit of
the tinsel, angered by the tawdry ornament. Such
men cheated even the gods.

A step sounded near her. She turned, dagger in
hand, faced the shadow that was Jisan. A knife
gleamed in his hand.

He let the knife hand fall to his side.

"Whose are you?" she asked. He tilted his head
toward the door, where the prince had gone, now
king.

"Was," he said. "Be clever and run far, Gillian
thief; or lie low and long. There comes a time princes
don't like to remember the favors they bought. Do
you think King Osric will want to reward an assassin?
Or a thief?"

"You leave first," she said. "I don't want you at my back."

"I've been there," he reminded her, "for some number of hours."

She hugged Jensy the tighter. "Go," she said. "Get out of my way."

He went; she watched him walk into the beginning day of the doorway, a darkness out of darkness, and down the steps.

"You all right?" she asked of Jensy.

"Knew I would be," Jensy said with little-girl nastiness; but her lips shook. And suddenly her eyes widened, staring beyond.

Gillian looked, where something like a rope of darkness twisted among the columns, above the blood that spattered the altar; a trick of the wind and the lamps, perhaps. But it crossed the sky, where the stars paled to day, and moved against the ceiling. Her right hand was suddenly cold.

She snatched Jensy's arm and ran, weaving in and out of the columns the way Jisan had gone, out, out into the day, where an old man huddled on the steps, rocking to and fro and moaning.

"*Nessim!*" she cried. He rose and cast something that whipped away even as he collapsed in a knot of tatters and misery. A serpent-shape writhed across the cobbles in the beginning of day . . .

. . . and shriveled, a dry stick.

She clutched Jensy's hand and ran to him, her knees shaking under her, bent down and raised the dry old frame by the arms, expecting death; but a blistered face gazed back at her with a fanatic's look of triumph. Nessim's thin hand reached for Jensy, touched her face.

"All right, mousekin?"

"Old man," Gillian muttered, perceiving something she had found only in Jensy; he would have, she vowed, whatever comfort gold could buy, food, and a bed to sleep in. A mage; he was that. And a man.

Gold, she thought suddenly, recalling the coin in her purse; and the purse she had buried off across the canals.

And one who had dogged her tracks most of the night.

She spat an oath by another god and sprang up, blind with rage.

"Take her to the Wyvern," she bade Nessim and started off without a backward glance, reckoning ways she knew that an Assassin might not, reckoning on throat-cutting, on revenge in a dozen colors.

She took to the alleys and began to run by alleys a big man could never use, cracks and crevices and ledges and canal verges.

And made it. She worked into the dark, dislodged the stone, took back the purse and climbed catwise to the ledges to lurk and watch.

He was not far behind to work his big frame into the narrow space that took hers so easily, to work loose the self-same stone.

Upon her rooftop perch she stood, gave a low whistle ... shook out a pair of golden coins and dropped them ringing at his feet, a grand generosity, like the prince's.

"For your trouble," she bade him, and was away.

V

WE'VE GONE FOR jump now. You wobble back to the lounge, a little frayed about the edges.

So have I come, some minutes before. Perhaps we both want to be sure the stars are still there.

Or that we are.

"Looking for something?" I ask as you lean against the glass.

"The Sun."

"Wrong direction." I point aft.

"I know that. I just prefer this window."

Jump is the kind of experience that makes philosophers—of some people. It's certain that no other passengers venture here this soon.

"Tell me. What do you think of?"

"In transit? It varies. You?"

"Earth. Home."

I smile. "That, most often. Sea-anchor."

"What?"

"When a ship needed stability at sea, it flung out a sea-anchor. Home-thoughts are like that. And this is a big ocean."

"I thought you might think—" you say, and give something up unasked.

Eventually I say: "You were about to ask me where I get my ideas. You haven't yet. Go on. I've been wondering when you'd get around to it."

"That wasn't what I was going to ask."

"What, then?"

"I thought—you might think—you know, somehow *different*."

"That's the idea-question, all right. I thought I heard it coming."

"You're laughing at me."

"No. I know exactly what you want to know. You want to know wherein I'm different, wherein a writer's *mind* is different. I've told you. It's because I'm here." I gesture at the windows. "It's a strange sensation—when the ship turns loose of space. You want a sea-anchor. It takes nerve to let go and fly with the wind. I confess I won't jump in parachutes. But I will sometimes think of alien worlds when I slide into hyperspace. Or of falling when I'm flying. I let go of homely things at uncertain moments—just to test my nerve. You want the terrible truth? You have that kind of mind too."

"Me?"

"You're here, aren't you? You came to look out the windows."

"I don't know why I came."

"Just the same as I don't know where I get my ideas. They just are."

"Any time you want them?"

"Once upon a time," I say, "I had twenty-four hours and a postcard, and a challenge to come up with a story that would fit it."

"Did you?"

"I sat down at supper and wrote the start. I wrote a snatch at a cocktail party, another at breakfast. And yes, twenty-four hours later I stood up to read to a convention full of people from a rather densely written postcard. Used a micropoint." I look out at changed stars and remember a smallish meeting hall, in Columbia, Missouri, and an audience the members of which had had about as much sleep as I had. "Two hours' sleep. Two thousand words."

"Did it work?"

"I read it the close way you have to read letters that small—never dared look at my audience; I just hoped to get through it without faltering, blind tired as I was. The time went in that kind of fog time gets to when you're in a story; and it was over, and I looked up. Nobody moved. I was kind of disappointed, I mean, when you write what you think is a nice little story and you don't get any reaction at all, you feel worse than if people walked out. I thought they were asleep.

"Then the audience stirred and some wiped eyes and others, I think, got to their feet and cheered, and I just stood there in one of those moments that come to a storyteller a few times in a lifetime—I don't know, maybe we all were tired." I smile, seeing those faces reflected out of nowhere in the glass. "But spare me that. I wrote it to read aloud. It was a special moment. That's all. It doesn't come twice."

The Last Tower

THE OLD MAN climbed the stairs slowly, stopping sometimes to let his heart recover and the teapot settle on the tray, while the dormouse would pop out of his sleeve or his beard and steal a nibble at the teacakes he brought up from the kitchen. It was an old tower on the edge of faery, on the edge of the Empire of Man. Between. Uncertain who had built it—men or elves. It was long before the old man's time, at least, and before the empire in the east. There was magic in its making . . . so they used to say. Now there was only the old man and the dormouse and a sleepy hedgehog, and a bird or two or three, which came for the grain at the windows. That was his real talent, the wild things, the gentle things. A real magician now, would not be making tea himself, in the kitchen, and wasting his breath on stairs. A real magician would have been more—awesome. Kept some state. Inspired some fear.

He stopped at the halfway turning. Pushed his sliding spectacles up his nose and balanced tray, tea, cakes and dormouse against the window-ledge. The land was black in the east. Black all about the tower. Burned. On some days he could see the glitter of arms in the distance where men fought. He could see the flutter of banners on the horizon as they rode. Could hear the sound of the horses and the horns.

Now the dust and soot of a group of riders showed against the darkening east. He waited there, not to have the weary stairs again—waited while the dormouse nibbled a cake, and in his pocket the hedgehog squirmed about, comfortable in the stillness.

The riders came. The prince—it was he—sent the herald forward to ring at the gate. "Open in the king's name," the herald cried, and spying him in the window: "Old man—open your gates. Surrender the tower. No more warnings."

"Tell him no," the old man said. "Just tell him—no."

"Tomorrow," the herald said, "we come with siege."

The old man pushed his spectacles up again. Blinked sadly, his old heart beating hard. "Why?" he asked. "What importance, to have so much bother?"

"Old meddler." The prince himself rode forward, curvetted his black horse under the window. "Old fraud. Come down and live. Give us the tower intact—to use . . . and live. Tomorrow morning—we come with fire and iron. And the stones fall—*old man.*"

The old man said nothing. The men rode away.

The old man climbed the stairs, the teaset clattering in his palsied hands. His heart hurt. When he looked out on the land, his heart hurt him terribly. The elves no longer came. The birds and the beasts had all fled the burning. There was only the mouse and the hedgehog and the few doves who had lived all their lives in the loft. And the few sparrows who came. Only them now.

He set the tray down, absent-mindedly took the hedgehog from his pocket and set it by the dor-mouse on the tray, took a cake and crumbled it on the window-ledge for the birds. A tear ran down into his beard.

Old fraud. He was. He had only little magics, forest magics. But they'd burned all his forest and scattered the elves, and he failed even these last few creatures. They would overthrow the tower. They would spread over all the land, and there would be no more magic in the world. He should have done something long ago—but he had never done a great magic. He should have raised whirlwinds and ele-mentals—but he could not so much as summon the legged teapot up the stairs. And his heart hurt, and his courage failed. The birds failed to come—fore-knowing, perhaps. The hedgehog and the dormouse looked at him with eyes small and solemn in the firelight, last of all.

No. He stirred himself, hastened to the musty books—his master's books, dusty and a thousand times failed. *You've not the heart*, his master would say. *You've not the desire for the great magics. You'll call* nothing— *because you want nothing.*

Now he tried. He drew his symbols on the floor—

scattered his powders, blinking through the ever-shifting spectacles, panting with his exertions. He would do it this time—would hold the tower on the edge of faery, between the Empire of Man and the kingdom of the elves. He believed, this time. He conjured powers. He called on the great ones. The winds sighed and roared inside the tower.

And died.

His arms fell. He wept, great tears sliding down into his beard. He picked up the dormouse and the hedgehog and held them to his breast, having no more hope.

Then she came. The light grew, white and pure. The scent of lilies filled the air—and she was there, naked, and white, hands empty—beautiful.

"I've come," she said.

His heart hurt him all the more. "Forgive me," he said. "I was trying for something—fiercer."

"Oh," she said, dark eyes sad.

"I make only—small magics," he said. "I was trying for—a dragon, maybe. A basilisk. An elemental. To stop the king. But I do flowers best. And smokes and maybe a little fireworks. And it's not enough. Goodbye. Please go. Please do go. Whichever you are. You're the wrong kind. You're *beautiful*. And he's going to come tomorrow—the king—and the armies . . . it's not a place for a gentle spirit. Only—could you take *them* . . . please? Mouse and Hedgehog—they'd not be so much. I'd not like to bother you. But could you? And then you can go."

"Of course," she said. It was the whisper of wind, her voice. The moving of snow crystals on frozen crust. She took them to her breast. Kissed them in turn, and jewels clothed them in white. "Old man," she said, and on his brow too planted a kiss, and jewels followed, frosty white. White dusted all the room, all the books and the clutter and the cobwebs. She walked down the stairs and out the gate, and jeweled it all in her wake. She walked the land, and the snow fell, and fell, and the winds blew—till only the banners were left, here and there, stiffened with ice, above drifts and humps of snow which marked the tents. The land was all white, horizon to horizon. Nothing stirred—but the wolves that hunted the deer, and the birds that hunted the last summer's berries.

Death drifted back to the tower, and settled there, in the frost and the lasting snows, where the old man and magic slept their lasting sleep.

She breathed kisses on him, on the little ones, and kept watch—faithful to her calling, while the snows deepened, and even the wolves slept, their fur white and sparkling with the frost.

VI

WE SHARE THE lounge with passengers now. A young couple holds hands under a table over to the corner. Some things never change.

There is crisis aboard. One of the passengers has locked himself in his cabin and the steward and a doctor have been back and forth down the hall trying to get the door open. Jump and transit does this to some people.

I don't think he ever went near a window. He would always sit with his back to them. He talked through all the status advisories.

"You wonder why some people come out here," you say.

"I suppose he has to. Business, maybe."

There is a certain amount of to-ing and fro-ing, up and down the halls. Some passengers delight in the drama. And sip their drinks and hug their own superiority in their boredom.

"It's a terrible thing for that man," I say. "Perceptions again. The first time you know you're not anywhere near where you were, not anywhere near where your whole world is—then you have to know that you're somewhere else. That man has just learned something. His safe world is shattered."

"Look at the rest of these people. *They* don't lock themselves in their rooms. And I don't think they ever think about the universe. They just have their drinks. And their canned music. And when they look out the windows they don't see the stars. They just see lights."

"That's the tragedy of the man in his room, isn't it? He can almost see the universe. He's so much closer to the truth than he ever was in all his life." I sip my own drink. "And he's locked his door."

"Couldn't they open it from the main board?"

"They could. Or just use the master key. They will if they have to."

More to-ing and fro-ing.

"Perceptions," you say.

"Perceptions. Taste, scent, touch, hearing, sense of balance, sight—of course, sight. And the systems we make and the systems others make for us. The orders and the logic. It's so easy to take what others give us. Gifts are so hard to say no to."

"We want so much to believe we know. That's the trouble."

"Even to believe we can't know is a system. Maybe we can know the universe. Maybe there is an answer. It's dangerous to assume there isn't."

"There. I thought you'd gotten sane."

"It's dangerous to assume anything and stop looking."

"You can't guarantee it isn't dangerous to look, either."

"No," I say. "I can't." We have gotten to that stage of renewed honesty. The potential for friendship, it may be. And we know nothing at all of each other.

It is so hard even to know ourselves.

The Brothers

I

THE WIND CAME from the west out of the rocky throat of the Sianail, even while the morning sun was shining in the glen, and there was something singing on it. Perhaps unGifted men could not hear it yet, that faint, far wail, but it echoed clearly off the mountain walls of Gleann Gleatharan, down to Dun Gorm, and it gave the king no peace.

There was storm in that wind as it came, scouring hills the stones of which were old and dread, hills which remembered darker things than storms and hid things at their hearts—the bones of warriors and kings, and even, men said, spirits older than the gods.

*   *   *

HIGH WITHIN the hills was also bright green, even on this murky, misty day, grass green as life and peace; but whenever this mood came on the mountains that hove up northward, souls keened on the gray wind and black crows flew on it, and it was well to think of shelter.

The traveler never did. He came down from the rocky heights, taking chances with stones turned slick with mist. He went gray-cloaked in wool, his feet in scarred brown leather that had seen many a league and many a fording and many a soaking before the one that threatened. He had hanging about his neck, did this gray traveler, a flat stone that a stream had worn through in its center; if a man looked through this opening, then he would see things as they were and glamors had no power on him. But the traveler had limited faith in this magic, putting more trust in the iron of his plain sword, which he had gotten on Skean Eirran off a dead man, on that narrow spit of sand, when they raided up by Skye. This he carried and no other weapon but a dagger for his meat; and no armor but his gray oiled-wool cloak to keep the cold mist from his skin. His name he did not have. He had not been using that since he passed into the southland; and perhaps they were hunting him by now; perhaps they had sent men ahead of him so there would be men to meet him when he came. When he looked over his shoulder he saw nothing but bare old stones and lawless gorse besides the mist-damp green, but now and again from hillsides he heard dogs baying that might be shepherds' dogs disturbed by his passage or might not; they might be pursuit from his enemies and they might not, in this fey, foul day that wrapped itself in storm.

Then with the passing of a hill he found all of a broad glen dropping away at his feet, himself in storm-shadow and the most of the glen still in sunlight that speared down through gray-bottomed cloud and turned the dark green to dazzling emerald. It was a land of neat hedgerows and careful fields and pasturages well cared-for. The very hills surrounding this valley had a tamer look, as if here kinder powers blessed the hedges and fenced out the hazards of the wild hills.

Amid it all, surely the reason and center of this tranquility—a Dun sat on a hill above a pleasant stream, in the face of low hills where its cottages clung as faint dots against the green.

He knew where he had come. It was no great dun. It was built of the wreckage time had made of its hill, so that one melded with the other—Dun Gorm it was, the Blue Keep, and it took its name from those stones as well, that deep gray stone that mimicked the sky and turned strange colors, one thing in storm and another when the sun was shining as it did now in spears across the glen, between the clouds, while the mist on the hills sent freshets down.

It held peace, and luck, this land where he had come. He had known neither in his life, and seeing this before him, he went to it.

THERE WAS a window of Dun Gorm that looked out above the stableyard fences, up toward the hills, and dread brought the king to it constantly this day. Cinnfhail was this king's name; and he was feyer than all his line, all of whom had been on speaking terms with the Sidhe, the Fair Folk who had known and held this valley before men came.

There had been a time that men and Fair Folk had lived closer than they did now: the Sidhe, the dwellers under bough and the dwellers under stone, had lived close beside the hewers of both, at peace. From most places in the world nowadays the Sidhe had indeed gone, leaving the hills and the glens to man. But in Gleann Gleatharan the Sidhe still pursued their own furtive business in the hills and woods while men built of stone and wood in the valley. And so long as a man took his wood and stone from the lonely heights of Gleann Gleatharan northward and far from the forest at the south of the valley he got on with the Sidhe well enough—if he were born to Dun Gorm, whose first king had been their friend.

Sometimes even in these days, Cinnfhail had heard their singing, oftenest in the evenings, fair as dream and haunting his mind for days; or sometimes in his riding he had heard a whisper which gave him good advice, and he came back from his riding wiser than he had gone out to it. Cinnfhail King had always cherished such encounters and longed for more meetings than he had had in his long life.

But today—today he heard a song he did not wish to hear. It was the bain sidhe wailing, not the singing of the fair glas sidhe; it was the White Singer, the harbinger of death. She sang along the heights thus far, that sawtoothed, gorse-grown ridge that walled them from the world; or from down the glen where the brook vanished into woods the Sidhe-folk still owned.

Stay away, he wished her. *Come no nearer to my land.*

But the singing kept on, rising and falling on the wind.

"It will be a storm tonight," his wife said, queen Samhadh, finding king Cinnfhail watching there alone. He held her close a while and murmured agreement, glad that Samhadh was deaf to any worse things.

All the day, coming and going from that window, Cinnfhail could not help thinking on dangers to those he loved. He considered his son Raghallach, a youth handsome enough to break the heart of any maid in Eirran, him the bravest and fairest of all the youth of Gleann Gleatharan. The love Cinnfhail had for his fair-haired son, the pride he took in Raghallach, was such that he could never tell it, especially to Raghallach—but he went to Raghallach and tried, this day, and that attempt set a glow in Raghallach's eyes, and afterward, set a wondering in Raghallach's heart, just what strange mood was on his father.

In the same way Cinnfhail King looked on Deirdre his daughter, who was not yet fourteen: so small, so high-hearted, the very image of what his Samhadh had been in the glory of her youth, as if time turned back again and laughed through the halls in Deirdre's steps. He had so much in his family; in all this land; he had wife and children and faithful friends and he thought the Sidhe might be jealous of such luck as he had: there were Sidhe reputed for such spite. So while he listened to that singing on the wind he contrived excuses that would keep all he loved indoors.

"Lord," said Conn his shieldman, coming on him

at this window-vigil, together with Tuathal his Harper, "some worry is on you."

"Nothing," Cinnhfail King said to Conn, and searched Conn's eyes too for any signs of ill-luck and death, this man so long his friend: his shieldman, who had stood with him in his youth and drunk with him at his board. There were no more wars for them. They had settled Gleann Gleatharan at peace, and now they grew old together, breeding fine horses and red cattle and laughing over their children's antics. His shieldman was clad farmer-wise, like any crofter that held the heights. Of treasures he held dear, this man was one of the chiefest, in his loyalty and courage; and hardly less, Tuathal the harper, the teacher of his children in riddlery and wit. "It's nothing," Cinnfhail said. "A little melancholy. Perhaps I'm growing old."

"Never, lord," Conn said.

"Not by my will, at least. But an old wound aches, that's all."

"Cursed weather," Conn said.

One should never curse the Sidhe. The impiety chilled the king. But Conn was deaf to what he cursed. "Go," Cinnfhail said, "have cook put on something to warm the bones; there'll be cold men coming from the fields early today; and have the fire lit in hall; and have the lads give the horses extra and one of them to sleep there in the stable tonight. Athas will be kicking the stall down again."

"Aye, lord," said Conn, and went.

"Lord," said the harper Tuathal then, lingering after Conn had gone, "there's something in this wind."

Of course his harper heard it. A harper would,

and Tuathal was a good one, whose songs sometimes echoed Sidhe dreams that Cinnfhail King had had. Tuathal had indeed heard. There was worry in the harper's gray eyes.

"It comes no nearer," said Cinnfhail. "Perhaps it will not." He was suddenly wishing the bain sidhe to go along the ridge, among his people, to any other house in the glen, and he felt a stinging guilt for this moment's selfishness. So he was not altogether virtuous as a king, not selfless. He knew this in himself. It was his weakness, that he desired a little peace in his fading years; and time, time, the one thing his life had less and less of.

Is it myself it sings for? he wondered. *O gods.*

2

CINNFHAIL WAS BY the window again as the clouds came down, as the last few rays of westering sun walked the green of his valley within its mountain walls. The sun touched a moment on the heights and for a while the song seemed fainter, overwhelmed by this last green brilliance.

In the fields nearby the horses raced, tails lifting, as horses will who play tag with ghosts before such storms; the boys had the gate open and the horses knew where they should go, but horses and young folk both loving to make chaos of any scheme, it was all being done with as much disorder as either side could muster. Sheep were tending home on their own like small rainclouds across the earth: their fleeces would be wet and scattering the mist in waterdrops— the old ewe was wise as a sheep was ever likely to be, selfishly thinking of her own comfort, and she brought the others by example, her bell ringing across the meadows. From their own pastures came the cattle, not hurrying unseemly, but not lingering either, home for byre and straw, needing no herdboy to tell them. This was the way of the beasts in Gleann Gleatharan, that they would not stray (excepting the horses, and them not far); it was the nature of the crops that few weeds would grow in them and of the folk that they grew up straight and tall and laughing much. And Cinnfhail King had a moment's ease thinking on his luck; but the clouds took back the sky then, and the mist came down.

The hills were everywhere laced with skeins of sky-white streams that only existed when the mist and the rain were on the mountaintops. They joined in waterfalls that merged with the tumbling Gley and ran right beneath their walls, in their green pastures.

And down beside the Gley-brook a red-haired man came walking.

He might have been one of their own, wrapped in an oiled-wool mantle, in dull brown clothes else, his head bowed against the wind. But the singing was louder, filling the very air. And this man walked like none of theirs returning, but with the weight of miles on him and a shadow of ill about him that the king's Sight knew. Knowledge closed like ice about Cinnfhail's heart.

This is what I have feared all day, Cinnfhail thought. *It is in this man.*

* * *

"LORD," SAID Conn, meeting Cinnfhail soon after on the stairs, "there is a traveler at the gate."

A mean thought touched Cinnfhail in that moment, that he should simply order this traveler away. But fate could not be turned. And never had any traveler been turned from Dun Gorm's gate, not in Cinnfhail's reign, and not in all the reigns of the Sidhe-blessed kings before him. It was part of the luck of the place and he dared not break it. "Bid him to table," said Cinnfhail.

"Lord," said Conn, doubtfully, "I don't like the look of him."

"Bid him," said Cinnfhail.

Why? he should have asked Conn, *why do you not like his look?* Conn was a wise judge of men. But it seemed pointless, something there was no helping, as if this man had to be here tonight and they had to let him in. Cinnfhail had felt it all the day. The singer had fallen silent now. She was content, perhaps. The wind brought them only rain, and this stranger at their door, toward suppertime, as the sun went down in murk.

CINNFHAIL'S WIFE Samhadh came and kissed him as he went down to the hall; Deirdre came, with her hair dewed with mist as she had crossed the yard, her green and blue Gleann Gleatharan plaid wrapped about her still and all dewed on its fibers in the lamplight; Raghallach came in all wet-haired and ruddy-cheeked from putting the horses to stable, and Conn came and Tuathal joined them, with others of the hold. The common-hall echoed with steps on stone and wood, with the busy scrape of benches, the rattle of plates: there was the smell of mutton stew in the pot, of hot bread, of good ale queen Samhadh brewed herself, none better in the land.

Cinnfhail saw the stranger then, who had come into the warm hall still all muffled with his oiled-wool cloak; a page tried to take it, but the man refused and sat down at the end of the table in the place of least honor.

"My lord," said Samhadh, slipping her arm within Cinnhfail's, "is something still amiss?"

He saw blood within his vision, a bright sword. The dark Sight passed with a shiver. He thought of bundling his family elsewhere, of contriving some excuse to take them out of hall tonight, but it all seemed futile. He did not sense danger to them; it was something far more vague.

So he sat down, his family about him. The harper Tuathal leaned near Conn the shieldman and whispered something. Conn looked sharp and frowning down the table, toward their guest, then got up and went here and there to men about the hall and to some of the women. Cinnfhail did not miss this, and caught the harper's fey, Sighted eye as the servants poured the ale. So Tuathal had also Seen, and Conn had seen, after his own fashion, as he judged men; and quietly these two faithful men took their own precautions.

"Look to it," said Cinnfhail to the servant nearest, "that the visitor's cup is never dry a moment,"—for it seemed prudent to ply this visitor with strong ale, to muddle him, to keep him well-pleased, propitiation, perhaps, or at least, should swords be drawn—to make him drunk. Cinnfhail's own men would not be.

Conn had surely seen to that. Cinnfhail's own shield was on the wall, his sword hung beside it years unused; a door was nearby. All these things were not by chance, in the years he and his fathers before him had ruled in Dun Gorm, in years when other folk had coveted this fair green land. The danger seemed quiet for the moment, biding; he determined he would be wary with this guest about what he said, and send his family as early as possible from the hall.

The thunder broke above the hold, and rain pattered on the straw above, but the thatch was tight and snug; and below was warmth and good food and plenty of it. It was a rowdy hall; it had always been, with hounds that came and went and children who ate at the hearthside or filled and carried their bowls to some favored corner to laugh and giggle together; and a few youngsters old enough to take their places at the long table with men and women. About them all were the implements mostly not of war at all, but of their craft—old plowshares, a horseshoe or two, a great deal of rope and bits of harness and poles and such; it might have been any farmer's cottage, Dun Gorm, but for its sprawling size. It smelled of peace and plenty and the earth beneath its floors.

When bellies were full, Tuathal the harper took up his harp and sang the sort of song that set the children clapping; and then he sang a quiet song, after which the young ones must to bed in their lofts and nooks and some few must take them. Afterward the place was quieter while the harper meddled with his strings, a bright soft rippling of notes.

"Deirdre," said the king, taking the chance that he had planned, "be off to your own bed. Samhadh—"

"But there's the traveler," said Deirdre. "He hasn't told his tale."

Her young voice carried. There was stillness in the hall. It was truth. There was something owed Dun Gorm for the meal, news to share, purposes to tell. It was the custom in any civil hall—that gates were open and hearts ought to be, to honest folk; and honest folk returned something, be it news or a tale, for their supper.

And when the eyes of everyone in hall turned in anticipation to the traveler, their visitor lifted his head. He was a young man, with pale red hair and beard, the hair straggling about his shoulders and his eyes hard and bleak and colorless. "I come from over hills and by streams," he said in a hoarse dull voice. "And I have no harper's skill. I came here to ask the way ahead—how the road goes and how things sit up ahead."

It was rudely said; a countryman's bluntness, perhaps, lacking courtesy, but there was just enough grace to the voice to remind one it was rude. And that discourtesy slid like ice over Cinnfhail's skin, advisement this man was dangerous.

"As to that," said Cinnfhail, "ahead lies Gleann Fiach."

"What sort of place is this Gleann Fiach?"

"Not a happy place, visitor."

"Perhaps you will tell me."

Conn stirred in his place like a watchful dog, a dangerous one himself in his youth. His hall was a place of peace. Its own folk took merry liberties with their king; but this stranger took too much and had no grace in his taking, no courteous word, no tale, no peace.

"Dun Mhor is the name," Cinnfhail began, "of the dun that holds Gleann Fiach." He lifted two fingers of his right hand, a motion for Conn's sake, and others saw it who knew him well, that he was wary. "Fill my cup," Cinnfhail said, as if that had been the nature of the signal. A servant came and poured. Cinnfhail drank, and looked at the stranger in his hall. "And between here and Dun Mhor, traveler, lies a woods that has gotten wider through my reign. For its sake I counsel you to go some other way. Sidhe own it. But if you do go that way, walk softly; bruise no leaf. Speak nothing lightly to anyone you meet.

"Beyond that wood—" Cinnfhail drew another breath and the ale and old habit and Sidhe-gift cast his voice into the rhythm of the tale-teller, so that his heart grew quieter and the power of it came on him. It was the teller's spell, and while it lasted no harm could come. It brought peace again on the hall, and calmed hearts and quieted angers, being itself one of the greater magics: even the anger of the teller himself fell under its spell, and he saw good sense and quiet come to the eyes of the stranger who listened. "Beyond that wood lies Gleann Fiach; and there is no luck there. Gaelan was its king. His brother set on him and killed him. Have you not heard before now of Dun Mhor?"

"Tell me," said the stranger softly, and finding his manners, for it was a ritual question, "if you would, lord king."

"Fratricide." Cinnfhail drew a deeper breath. "And

more general murder. Here in Gleann Gleatharan we hear the rumors that come over the hills—but there is the Sidhe-wood between us, and we will not trespass that, nor will they of Gleann Fiach from their side. To spill blood there has no luck in it, be you right or wrong. So we cannot mend affairs in that sorrowing land, even if we would break our own peace for it. Gleann Fiach has had no end of miseries, and today they are worse. My tale is two brothers; and the Sidhe—they are part of it: two brothers, Gaelan and Sliabhin—Gaelan the elder and Sliabhin the younger. Gaelan was a good man, traveler, proper heir to Dun Mhor after his father Brian; he was fair-spoken and fair in judgment and respecting the gods and the Sidhe-lands though Brian his father had not always done it. Once king Brian chased a deer and killed it, and it ran into the Sidhe-wood and bled there. That was the ill luck on him. And Brian's queen lay in childbed that very hour: she gave him Sliabhin, as foul a boy in his youth as Gaelan was fair, poaching to the very edge of the Sidhe-forest when he had the chance, fouling everything that was good—this was Sliabhin, a man eaten up with spite that he was not firstborn, that he had not been given Dun Mhor. There was no luck in such a man, and after king Brian died and Gaelan had the kingdom, Sliabhin was greatly afraid, imagining that his brother Gaelan would do him hurt. So Sliabhin rode away to the hills in fear. This is the kind of man Sliabhin was: it never occurred to him that Gaelan would not think immediately of his harm, because that is what he would have done to Gaelan himself if he had gotten the kingship.

"Now kindred-love can be blind and perhaps it was fey as well. Gaelan entreated his brother home and they fell on one another's neck and reconciled themselves; this oath was good in Gaelan's mouth but never in Sliabhin's. For a little time there was peace, but after that little time Sliabhin began to think how he could cause mischief. And he found men like himself and he hunted the land for his amusement, taking every chance to be apart from the dun and to plan and plot with these greedy men. They took delight in hunting near the forest edge, and though they would not go into it they mocked the Sidhe, trampling its edge and harrying the game up to it. They ranged the hills and one day they grew weary of the sport they had had and caught a poor herdboy, making him their quarry, and made it seem wolves had torn him, and not their dogs. But the boy's sister had seen. Her brother had hidden her in the rocks when he saw the men come, and the poor maid ran with all her might, all through the night she ran. Drucht was her name, and she was a wise young girl, knowing her brother beyond help and her father like to be killed if she should go first to him and tell him what was done: she went to the dun and poured out her tale to king Gaelan himself.

"Then Gaelan believed what he should have believed before; and he was hot after his brother to bring his justice on him. But one of Sliabhin's ilk was at hand, who took horse and rode ahead to warn Sliabhin not to go back to the dun that day.

"That was the parting of the ways finally between the brothers, Sliabhin banished, but late, far too late. The Sidhe set misfortune on the land. Crops failed.

Gaelan's queen, Moralach, was with child; and it came stillborn. She lost others after; until one she had alive, and that one stole her health.

"Now from the day Sliabhin was cast out, he had been laying plans. Twenty years he bided, causing trouble where he could, and in a land with no luck on it there will always be discontent, and among young folk there will always be those who do not believe the truth of things that their elders were alive to witness.

"Now this next that I tell you is no long-ago tale. It came about a year ago, when Gaelan rode out of Dun Mhor to tend to his land, after the damages of a flooding of the Gley. There was murder done at home. Every servant that was loyal was killed; every man who could not be corrupted. So we in Gleann Gleatharan surmise. No one knows. Gaelan rode back within his own gates that day and never out again, nor any loyal man with him. Sliabhin is king in Dun Mhor now, over all Gleann Fiach. He took Gaelan's queen Moralach to his bed, holding her young son to hostage against her willingness to please him; his brother's corpse was not cold yet in the hall below. He spared the boy, that one grants; but the queen died after. They say she hanged herself from the rooftree. Whatever passes in Dun Mhor these days, it is no hall I would guest in. A man walking down the glen and through the Sidhe-wood should know that, and go some other way if he could."

There was silence for a space. It was a tale everyone in Dun Gorm knew, if not all parts of it. And all of a sudden Cinnfhail was thinking of that grim hold beyond the woods, how such a wicked king as Sliabhin might well draw others of his ilk to come and live at his board. The thunder cracked and shook the very posts of the hall. The wind wailed and set the hairs to lifting at the back of Cinnfhail's neck as he stared at the traveler.

"So you have no love for Sliabhin," the stranger said.

"None," said Cinnfhail.

The traveler stood up, hurled a sword clattering onto the table to the dismay of those nearest. Conn's sword ripped from its sheath in his startlement; benches were overset as swords came out and men and women came to their feet all around the room. But the stranger did no more than let fall his mantle.

"Gods help us," said Samhadh, pulling Deirdre to shelter behind her, and Raghallach was on his feet with a naked sword as Conn moved between the stranger and Cinnfhail, for about his shoulders was the red tartan of Dun Mhor.

"It is a ghost," said someone.

"No," said Cinnfhail, and waved the swords away, feeling a weakness in his knees and a tightness in his chest, for the price of the Sight was sometimes blindness to fated things; and now that badge of Dun Mhor made him see, at the same time that Conn saw, and the rest. Others remained on their feet, but Cinnfhail sought his chair again, feeling suddenly the years of his life upon him. "Man, what is your name?"

"Caith is my name," the traveler said, "mac Gaelan. First born. Gaelan's true heir and Moralach's own son."

There was silence for a space in which Cinnfhail's

heart beat very hard. Raghallach moved close to him; Conn stood between this intruder and all the family.

"My father fostered me north," said mac Gaelan, never stirring from where he stood. "To Dun na nGall for safety. And he gave out his first son was stillborn. He knew that Sliabhin would strike at him. He wished me safe. And we got the news up there not three months gone, that I had delayed my homecoming—overlong."

"We have things to speak of," said Cinnfhail. He moved aside and touched Samhadh's hand, wishing her to be prudent and to take Deirdre away from this, out of danger of this man and the things that he could say. "Go," he said softly, "go up, go upstairs, now, Samhadh."

"There is no need," said the traveler, coming forward of the table's end, heedless of hands on swords all about him. There was a weariness about him, but he moved with grace all the same. He was a man that could walk soft-footed through a hall of enemies and bemaze them all, as he ensorcelled them.

"My sword is back there. I left it, did I not? And you were my father king Gaelan's friend. And never were you Sliabhin's."

"Father," said Raghallach. "Can it be truth?"

"It might be," Cinnfhail said heavily. "I did hear more to the story. I heard it long ago. So tell me— Caith mac Gaelan. Why have you come here?"

"To hunt out my father's killers. To take Dun Mhor. You were his neighbor, lord. His friend. I'd think you would be weary of Sliabhin by now."

"We'll speak of it."

"*Speak* of it. Lord, I have a young brother in that man's hands. I did not come here to *speak* of it."

There was a stillness then, in which the stranger stood among them with the ring of anguish dying in the air. And with justice on his side.

"What are you asking?" asked Raghallach. "That we go to war for your sake?"

"No," said Caith mac Gaelan. "That would do my brother no good. Sliabhin would kill him at the end of any siege, and do other things before. I want my brother safe before I take Dun Mhor, whatever the cost."

So there was honor in this young man; it touched that honor that was in Raghallach, like a fire to straw, in their valley that had had its peace, and Cinnfhail felt a chill raise gooseflesh on his neck.

"We will talk of it," Cinnfhail said again. "A night for sleep. A night for thinking. Then we will talk."

"Father," said Raghallach. "We have suffered Sliabhin far too long, the way I reckon it."

"We will take time to think about it, I said." The cold was about Cinnfhail's heart, a sense of doom, of change. And he remembered the singer on the wind. "To bed! We've said all tonight that wants saying. Morning and sober heads are what's needed, not ale-thoughts and ale-talk."

"Lord," Raghallach said. There was fire in his glance. He longed for honor, did Raghallach, here in this glen Cinnfhail had made quiet and at peace with all his deeds and all his striving. Raghallach heard Tuathal harp the ballads; Raghallach dreamed, in his innocence, of undoing it all and doing it over again. Cinnfhail knew.

"Off with you." Cinnfhail kissed Samhadh, and Deirdre, who looked past him at the stranger with wonder in her eyes. She had also heard the hero-songs, the sad, fair ballads; and Deirdre dreamed her own dreams of adventures. Both Cinnfhail's children then were snared; and Cinnfhail turned to his son smiling gently, though his heart hurt him; he clapped a hand to Raghallach's shoulder. "In the morning, hear? Quietly, as such things should be thought out. Obey me. To bed, all, *to beds*! And no rumor-mongering, no speaking of this beyond the gates. I have said it. Hear?"

He rarely spoke as king. It was not his way. When he did so now, folk moved, and bowed their heads and scurried in haste.

"Leave it!" he bade the servants, to have them gone; and to Conn, catching him by the arm, he spoke certain words which grieved and shamed him to speak.

But he had the Sight, and what he Saw now gave him no peace.

3

CAITH GATHERED HIS sword from the table and sheathed it, having no desire in his mind now but rest, being well-fed and easier in the finding of friends than he had been in the long weeks since leaving Dun na nGall.

But: "Come with me," the king's harper said now, plucking at his sleeve. "The king will speak with you privately. He has more to tell to you. You'll want your cloak."

Caith considered it and weighed the risks of treachery; but he had eaten this man's bread and judged him as he sat, that the lord of Dun Gorm was what he had heard, a king worth listening to and a man to be trusted.

So he gathered his cloak about him and went where the harper led him, nothing questioning, down the stairs and, as the harper took up a torch from the bracket there, out a lower door into the dark and the retreating thunder. They stood beneath the smithy shed, with the rain dripping off the wooden roof and standing in puddles in the yard beyond. Cattle lowed; horses were restless in their pen nearby, a solitary dog barked in the dying of the storm, but it knew the harper and it was silent at his word.

"What is this?" Caith said. "What is this skulking about?" He suddenly doubted everything in this lonely place, and his hand was on his sword in the concealment of his cloak.

"My lord will speak to you," the harper repeated. And truth, from around the side of the yard came the king of Gleatharan with his shieldman by him, all muffled up in cloaks themselves.

Caith waited, his hand still on his sword, scowling at the two coming toward him and still uneasy. He had trusted few men in his life. Nameless, nothing, he had no teaching in things he needed to become what he was born to be. *Stay here in Dun na nGall,* his foster-father had said. *Don't meddle. There's nothing in Gleann Fiach for you.* And again: *If you go there, then plan to keep going. You defy me, boy—you'll not be coming back here.*

That was well enough. There was nothing that

man who fostered him had ever given him but whipmarks on his back, and worse within his soul: *You take what's given you*, this man had said, Hagan, his father's cousin. And: *Keep your mouth shut, boy, whose son you are. Mind my words. So they name you foundling bastard. Maybe that's what you really are.*

A girl-child had looked up at him, flower-fair tonight; a man he wished had been his father had smiled at him; a man he would had been his brother had offered him help; a grave-eyed queen had looked on him with amazement— It was the way he would have seen Dun Mhor at his homecoming if he could have dreamed that dun clean and fair again. In this place he had had at least one homecoming such as an exile might dream of.

But the king of Gleatharan asked him out into the rain, into the dark to speak with him; and this was not part of his dream, this was not the welcome he had expected. Rather it held something of connivances and tricks—and this kind of thing he had dealt in often enough in his life.

The king came to him, squelching up in the mud, in the falling mist, till he passed beneath the roof of the shed and into the torchlight the harper held. The shieldman stood behind his king, his hands both out of sight beneath his oiled-wool cloak.

"Mac Gaelan," said Cinnfhail King, "forgive me. I ask that first."

"For what, then? Can we get to that?"

"Go back to Dun na nGall. Tonight. There's no gain here for you."

Caith drew in his breath. It wanted a moment to know what to say to such a warning from a king so two-faced. "Well, lord," he said, "gods requite you for it."

"I'll give you provisions," the king said, "and a horse—the pick of all I have."

Keep your gifts, Caith would have said then. But he was too much in need for pride. "We may be neighbors yet," he said in his anger. "I will return the horse."

"Mac Gaelan."

"You were my father's friend. So the price of your friendship is a meal and a horse. That's well. A man should know his friends."

"Mind your tongue," the shieldman muttered.

"He has cause," the king said. "Mac Gaelan—" He stayed Caith with a hand against his shoulder. "Go back to Dun na nGall. I have the Sight, mac Gaelan. And there is no luck for you. For the gods' own sake go home."

"In Dun Mhor is my home. My brother is still in their hands. I will tell you something, lord of Dun Gorm: I had something of that kind from my foster father. I know what a whip feels like, *my lord.* No, I'll not leave my brother to Sliabhin. And for my father's murder—where on the gods' own earth should I go, tell me that, until I have killed that man?"

"A kinslayer has no rest in the world. Whatever his cause."

"Sliabhin's no kin of mine. I'll not own him mine. He murdered my father, lord! His own brother. If any man could have come and set matters right, it *might* have been my father's friend, but I see how things sit here at Dun Gorm, how eager you are to set things right. You leave me no choice. No. I'll kill Sliabhin myself, without a qualm."

There was terror in the old king's eyes and something hard at the same time. "Stay," Cinnfhail said, stopping him a second time, this time with a biting grip of a hand still powerful. "I cannot let you go—mac Gaelan! stop and listen to me."

Caith turned, then, flinched from under the king's hard hand, his own upon his sword. "I'll need the horse," Caith said.

"You'll have the horse. And whatever else you need. Go back to Dun na nGall; or go ahead to Gleann Fiach and rue it, rue it all your life. I don't think you know; you don't want to know more than I said in hall. Listen to me: I have a selfish cause. If you take my son with you, he'll die there. I see it. I see it in the moon. There'll be blood, blood—no hope for you—*For the gods' sake, lad, listen. You don't know who you are!*"

The cold went to Caith's bones. *Bastard,* his foster father had hurled at him. "Old man," he said, "it was no grand place my father sent me to be fostered. Maybe he had little choice in his relatives. Sure enough he had little luck in his brother. And maybe a lord would send his son to the likes of Hagan mac Dealbhan if he had no choice of other kin—Or is it another kind of tale? Whose bastard am I? Yours?"

"Sliabhin's."

Caith whirled and lashed out with his bare right hand, but the king's man brought his arm in the way and seized him about the neck. The breath stifled in him, not alone from the strangling hold on him. "Liar," he said. "O gods, you whoreson liar—"

"Stay!" the king said to his man. "Let him go."

"Lord," the shieldman protested.

"Let him go, I say." And to Caith: "Lad, Sliabhin had his way with Gaelan's wife, with Moralach, the queen. *That* Gaelan discovered when the herder-girl came to the hall and told her tale: Moralach confessed to him Sliabhin's other betrayal and her own shame. And that was the second cause of Sliabhin's exile. Gaelan forgave queen Moralach: she claimed it was rape and her fearing to tell him because of his blind love of Sliabhin and hoping the child in her was her husband's after all. But the child grew in her like guilt; and she feared it; and now that she heard the herder-girl tell her tale, she believed it might be a murderer's child in her belly. So she confessed. Four days Gaelan shut her away and she lived in dread of him; but on the fifth he wept and forgave her and this was a thing few knew, but Moralach confessed it to my queen when she rode there to be with her in the birthing. And at the last, lad, my lady was not in the room; they said Moralach commanded it, wanting only her nurse and the midwife with her; but it was a living child they carried from that room that night: my lady was there, close by, and saw it moving in the blanket. With her own eyes she saw it. And afterward when my lady came to Moralach, Moralach wept and clung to her and raved until they gave her a potion to make her sleep. Of the babe they gave out that it was stillborn. And my queen came home and carried that in her heart for two days before she told it me. After that I went no more to Gaelan's hold and my queen did not: it was worse than fostering we feared, for in queen

Moralach's raving she told still another tale." From harsh the king's voice had become pitying, from anger had gone to shame, and still Caith stood there, shivering in the rain. Somewhere nearby a horse snorted and stamped, splashing a puddle. "Do you understand, lad? Need I say it? It was never rape. She let Sliabhin in, this vain woman, and paid for it all her life. When her other babes died she was crazed and thought it her punishment; when she bore the last alive she was no more mother to it—she gave it to a nurse to care for. Perhaps she let her old lover in; perhaps they had met before. Whispers said as much. To do her mercy, likeliest it was some other hand let Sliabhin's men into Dun Mhor. And it is true Moralach hanged herself; so surely she repented. *That* is the tale they tell, of servants who were there to see and fled to the high hills when they had the chance. There is more to it: before she was with child the last time, Moralach went out riding. And she rode often that season, and always toward the hills. Do you understand me? The younger boy— may be Sliabhin's son. Hence the whispers who it was let those gates open. And Gaelan either fey or fool, he refused to credit rumors. So they say. Perhaps Gaelan knew and counted it all one with the curse on his land, the curse on his bed. Maybe he only wanted peace in his life. He was a sick man and his heart was broken and he became a fool. So he died. And by what they whisper, the younger boy is safe in Sliabhin's hands if anyone is."

Caith no more than stood there. It all fitted then, all the pieces of his life. He set them all in order, his hand upon his sword.

"Is that the truth?" he asked, because the silence waited to be filled.

"I will give you the best help that I can give. Only go from here, back to Dun na nGall. You are Sliabhin's true son. The Sidhe have set a curse on him, on all his line, and I have the Sight: I *tell* you whose son you are. Go back. This is not a place for you; and gods know a patricide is damned."

"My foster father said that I should not come back to him," Caith said in a voice that failed him. "So he believed it too. All these years. And you've known. *How many others?*"

"Does it matter? Nothing can mend what is."

"You forget. I have a brother in Dun Mhor."

"A brother you've never seen. Sliabhin's son."

"Why, then, my true brother still, would he not be?"

"Don't be a fool! Sliabhin's likely son and in Sliabhin's keeping. You can do nothing to him but harm."

"I can get him out of there."

"For the gods' sake, lad—"

"You promised me a horse."

The old king considered him sadly. "O lad, and what good do you bring? See, brother, will you say, I've killed our father to set you free? It goes on. It won't stop. It will never stop."

"The horse. That's all I want."

King Cinnfhail nodded toward the pen. Caith walked that way, in the dying rain, with the mist against his face. The horses, let from their stable in the dying of the storm, stared back at him, with the torchlight in their eyes and shining on their coats, more wealth of fine horses than any king had in Eirran, horses to heal the heart with the looking on them and the touching of them. On such horses a man could ride and ride, leaving everything behind. Men would envy such horses, would fight a war over any one such horse as he saw to choose from.

But a man who wanted to go quietly, who wanted no attention on himself when he came into Dun Mhor— "That one," Caith said, choosing a shaggy white horse which stood within the shadow near the stable, raw-boned and ungainly beside the rest.

"Not that one," said the king. "Choose another. That one is mine."

"It is the one I will have," Caith said harshly. "Everything else of your hospitality turned false. So I will take that one or walk. No other will serve me."

"Be it as you will," the old king said, and stayed his shieldman with a shake of his head. "Be kind to my horse then. Dathuil is his name. And he will serve you."

Fair, it meant. It was an ugly horse. The king leaned against the fence and held out his hands to him and he trotted over like a child's pet. "Get his bridle," king Cinnfhail said to his shieldman, "and his saddle."

And when the shieldman had gone in and come out with the stable lad and the gear, the king would none of their help, but stepped under the rail and took the bridle and saddle, and saddled the raw-boned horse himself, all with such touches that said the old man loved this beast, he who had so many stronger and finer.

"I will not use him ill," Caith said sullenly when he

saw that it was not all a lie, that he had chosen a horse which the old man truly loved above the others, "and I will send him home again if I can. But truth, no other would serve me. I'll come into Dun Mhor as I came here, a wanderer—unless you intend to betray me, unless you have already sent a messenger out tonight. And then, my lord—" He looked king Cinnfhail full in the eyes. "—I'll trust you and Sliabhin have your own compacts: in that case he'll return your horse himself to you, I'm sure, and keep as much of me as pleases him."

"Take Dathuil," said the king. "I will not wish you anything."

Caith climbed up to the horse's back, and took the sack of provisions that the shieldman gave him. Need compelled, and rankled in Caith's soul. Quietly he began to ride away, then drove in his heels and sped off through the open gate, a white ghost flying into the dark and mist.

"Dathuil," said Conn. "O gods, my lord—"

"There is a doom on him," said Cinnfhail, staring after the retreating rider. Tears spilled down his cheeks though his face remained composed. "He chose Dathuil. It was his fate to choose; and not mine to stop him. I know it. Gods help us. Gods save us from Dun Mhor."

The harper Tuathal was there, somber in the rain, holding aloft his torch. "Come inside, my lord."

Cinnfhail walked over the trampled yard. A horse whinnied long and forlornly; others did, distressed. And a cold was in Cinnfhail's bones that not all the warmth of his hall and cheer of his friends and house could assuage.

4

THE UGLY HORSE ran on, down the glen, beside the Gley, never checking his pace and never breaking stride. Smooth as the wind Dathuil ran, and the cold mist stung Caith's cheeks, stung his eyes which pain had already stung. There was power in this horse, as in no horse he had ever ridden; its ugliness masked both strength and unlikely speed. So the king had had reason in his affection for this beast; Caith laid no heel to it and hardly used the reins at all, finding something true-hearted at least, this brute that bore him on its back and gave him its strength, when it was beyond his own power to have traveled far this night.

He reined it back at last, having fear for it breaking its heart in this running, but it threw its head and settled easily into a tireless rack. Its power hammered at him, kept him on his way, and while he rode, while its hooves struck the wet earth in tireless rhythm he had no need to think, no need to reckon what he was or where he went.

Bastard. Far more than that, he was. He recalled the rage in his foster-father's face when he knew where he would go. *Kinslayer. Patricide.*

He had a brother he had never seen. Brian was his name. He had built a fantasy around the boy, this innocence, this one kinsman he might recover who would be grateful to an elder, wiser brother, a quasi-son who should be the staying point of his pivotless life. He needed someone. He had loyalty to give and none would have it. He had made himself by ceaseless work and striving—everything a father could respect and love, in hopes his father would come to him at Dun na nGall and claim him.

Now he was going home, world-scarred and bereft of all innocent dreams but one. He had fought at Skye, a pirate no less than the man he was fostered to.

O father, come and get me. I am better than this man. Better than these pirates— When I am a man I will come to you instead and you will be glad that I am your son. Do you know where I am, or what we did at Skye? I have had my first battle, father.

Done my first murder. . . .

I have got a sword. I took it off this dead man—
O father!

"GONE?" asked Raghallach.

The narrow stairs flowed with shadows in the torch-light. Samhadh was waiting there as he came in from the cold, Samhadh and Deirdre in their shifts, wrapped in blankets from their chambers; and Raghallach was there, still dressed, while servants put their heads about the corner and ducked back again, sensing no welcome for themselves.

"He left," said Cinnfhail, uneasy in his half-truths. He was cold. He was drenched from the rain. He had thought only to come upstairs and warm himself in his bed at Samhadh's side, but sounds and steps carried in Dun Gorm, in its wooden halls, and so there was this ambush of him at the upper stairs. "We talked a time. He asked a horse and provisions. Stealth is best for what he plans. He's going on to Dun Mhor against all my advice."

"Gods, they'll butcher him."

"And where would you be going?" Cinnfhail cried, for Raghallach went past him, downward bound on the stairs. "No! You'll not be helping him, young lad; you'll be putting both your heads under Sliabhin's bloody axe. No. I'll not have it. Let be."

Raghallach stopped. There was a terrible look in his eyes as he stood on the steps below Cinnfhail and looked up at him in the torchlight. "It's raining," Raghallach said. "For the gods' sake, it's raining out; what sane man goes riding off on such a night with choice of a bed— 'Talk in the morning,' you said, father. In the morning. But he's to be gone by then, isn't he?"

"Watch your tongue, boy!"

"You've shamed me," Raghallach said all quietly. "In the hall tonight. This man told the truth. We've let Dun Mhor alone all these years for fear of that truth. And now you've sent him off. You've sent him out of here to add another to Sliabhin's crimes."

"Raghallach—"

"It's been on you all the day, hasn't it, this dread, this fear of yours? This blackguard in Dun Mhor— gods, father, how did we seem tonight? 'Talk in the morning,' you said. 'Take counsel in the morning.' "

"Be still," said Samhadh. Deirdre only stared, her young face struck with shock and shame.

"I love you," said Raghallach. There were tears on his face. "I love you too much, father, to let you do a thing like this. You have the Sight; and having it you wrap me in and keep me close and what am I to think? We were fronted in our own hall by a man who wanted justice. Gaelan was your friend; but if he was your friend, father—then where *were* we in those days?"

"Sliabhin's son," said Cinnfhail, going down to catch him on the steps, for Raghallach turned to go. He seized Raghallach by the arm and turned him by force to face him. "Raghallach, that is Sliabhin's own son. You know what they whisper about Moralach. It's true."

His son's face grew pale in the torchlight. "O gods."

"It's *patricide* will be done at Dun Mhor," said Cinnfhail. "And by the gods this house will not aid it."

Raghallach gnawed his lip. "And do we sit with our hands in our laps? All the hall heard. All the house will know you sent this man away. And all Dun Mhor will know he guested here—and take revenge if he fails. Or this Caith may be our enemy for long years if he rules Gleann Fiach instead. No. This house is going to do something, father. I'm taking twenty men as far as the border. And if need or trouble falls back to threaten the Sidhe-wood, at least we will have some chance to tell Dun Mhor where our border is, and that we won't have trespassers. If he fails—if he fails, father, we have a stake in it, do we not? Sliabhin will be sending us his threats again. He'll be finding his excuse. And if so happen this Caith comes back in haste with Sliabhin's throat uncut, and we be there the other side of the Sidhe-wood, well, there is help we *can* give then and have our hands clean. It's no kinslaying *we* intend."

Cinnfhail thought a moment. His face burned with

shame and his heart widened with pride in Raghallach, for his goodheartedness and wit. "I will go myself," he said. "It's a good plan."

"No," said Raghallach. His eyes glittered damply in the light. His jaw was set in that way he had that nothing would dissuade. And suddenly, passionately, he embraced Cinnfhail and thrust him back at arm's length, his young face earnest and keen. "All my life you have kept me from any hazard, wrapped me in wool. No mother, father. I'm not a boy and you're not a young man to be dealing with Sliabhin's hired bandits. This one, this time, is mine."

THERE WAS a time Caith had no remembrance of, how he had gotten into the woods, for he was weary and the shaggy horse's tireless gait had never varied. He might have slept, might have been dreaming when he first passed beneath the trees that were all about him now, whispering in the wind.

He rode slowly, the horse treading lightly on the leaves, and Caith rubbed at his eyes and wondered had he slept a second time, for he remembered the horse running and could not remember stopping, nor account for where he was. And rubbing his eyes and blinking them clear again he saw a light before him in the dark, a fitful light like a candlegleam, jogging with the course the shaggy horse followed on this winding track among the trees. The wind blew and scattered droplets from the leaves; made the light wink and vanish and reappear with the shifting of branches and limbs between him and the source. The pitch of the land was generally downward, and there was a noise of moving water nearby, so he knew they were coming to a stream, perhaps the wandering Gley itself, or one of the countless other brooks that lived and died with the rains. Someone must be camped on this streamside up ahead, and Caith gathered his wits and rode with care, fully awake and searching the trees and the brush on this side and that for some way to avoid this meeting.

But the ugly horse kept on, patient and steady. Sooner than Caith had looked for (had he somehow drowsed again?) he was passing the last curtain of black branches that screened him from that light.

It was one man camped on the trailside, a ragged-looking fellow the like of which one might find along the roads and between the hills, a wanderer, an outlaw, more than likely. Such men Caith knew. He had met them and sometimes shared a fire and sometimes come to blows with such wolves; and he was alive and some of them were not. This much he had learned of his foster-father and the king of Dun na nGall: the use of that sword he wore. He had no overwhelming fear in the meeting, but he had far rather have avoided it altogether.

"Good night to you," Caith said perforce, reining in. The man no more than looked up at him over the fire, a mature man and lean and haggard. Then with the wave of a thin hand the man beckoned him to the fireside.

"Here is courtesy," Caith muttered, still ahorse, and considering how Dun Gorm had cast him out into the night and the rain. There was a pannikin by the fireside. Caith smelled meat cooking; he had provisions on him he was willing to trade a bit of in turn. By now he ached with traveling, he longed for rest in all his bones, and more, he saw a harpcase on a limb near the man, the instrument protected against the weather.

So it was a wandering harper he had met, which was another kind of man altogether than bandits. Such a man might walk through bandit lairs untouched and stand equally secure in the halls of kings. That harp was his passage, wherever he wished to go; his person was more sacred than a king's, and his fireside, wherever set, was safer than any hall.

A second time the harper beckoned. Caith stepped down from the shaggy horse though he did not pause to slip its bit or loosen its girth. He was not that trusting in any new meeting. He crouched warily before the fire, warming his numb hands and studying the harper close at hand.

"Looking for some hall?" he asked the man.

"Not I," the harper said. "I prefer the road."

"Where bound?" Caith felt still uneasy, wishing still in a vague way he had no need to have stopped and yet too proud to leap up and run from a harper. "Gleann Fiach?"

"I might go that way," said the harper.

"I might keep you company on the way," said Caith, with devious thoughts of passing Dun Mhor's gates in such company.

But suddenly he became aware of another watcher in the bushes, a man—a youth, all in dark. Between seeing him and springing to his feet with his hand on his sword was only the intake of a breath; but the youth stepped out into the open, holding his hands wide and empty, and grinning in mockery.

"My apprentice," said the harper. "Is there some

dread on you, man? Something on your mind? Sit and share the fire. Peace."

"I've thought again," said Caith. "My business takes me on."

"But I think," said the square-jawed youth, whose eyes peered from a wild tangle of black bangs, "I think it is the horse—O aye, it would be that fine horse, wouldn't it? He has got something doesn't belong to him."

"The horse was lent," Caith said shortly. Harper or no, he had made up his mind and retreated a pace: when he drew his sword he had the habit of using it at once and never threatening, but it was part of its length drawn. "Teach your apprentice manners, harper. He will bring you grief."

"But that horse *is* stolen," said the harper. "His name is Dathuil. And he is mine." The harper unfolded upward, tall and slim and not so ragged as before. Beside him the youth took on another aspect, with mad and ruby eyes, and the harper was fair now, pale and terrible to see.

Caith drew the sword, for all that it could do. They were Sidhe, that was clear to him now. And he was in their woods. He stood there with only iron between himself and them and all their ancient power.

"I will be going," he said, "and I'll be taking the horse. He was lent to me. He's not mine to give, one way or the other." He backed farther, and saw the horse not ugly but fair, a white steed so beautiful it touched the heart and numbed it, and Caith knew then what blessing he had taken from Dun Gorm.

"He is Dathuil," said the Sidhe again. "We gave him to a friend. You must give him back to us."

"Must I?" Caith said, turning from his bedazzlement, discovering them nearer than before. He had his sword in his hand and remembered it. "And what if not?"

"That horse is not for anyone's taking. He must be freely given. And better if you should do that now, man, and give him to me—far better for you."

A Sidhe horse could not be for his keeping. Caith knew that. But he kept the blade up, reckoning that his life was the prize now, and them needing only a single mistake from him to gain it. "If you have to have it given," Caith said, "then keep your hands from me."

"That horse was lent to the kings of Dun Gorm," said the youth. "Cinnfhail has cast him away, giving him to you—with whom we have no peace. So we will take him back again."

Caith backed still farther, seeking Dathuil's reins with his left hand behind him; but the horse eluded his reaching hand once and again, and the two Sidhe stalked him, the tall one to his left now, the dark youth going to his right.

"So," Caith said, seeing how things stood. "But if I give you what you want, you have everything and I have nothing. That seems hardly fair. They say the Sidhe will bargain."

"What do you ask?"

"Help me take Dun Mhor."

The dark one laughed. The bright one shone cold as ice.

"Why, let us do that!" the dark one said.

"Be still," said the taller; and to Caith, with chill amusement: "Phookas love such jokes. And those who bargain with the Sidhe come off always to the worse. You have not said the manner of the help, leaving that to us; and leaving the outcome of it to us too. Things are far more tangled than you think they are. So I shall take your bargain and choose the manner of my help to you, which is to tell you your futures and the three ways you have before you. First: you might go back over the hills the way you came. Second: you might go back to Dun Gorm; Raghallach would help you. He would be your friend. Third: you might enter Dun Mhor alone. All of these have consequence."

"What consequence?"

"A second bargain. What will you give to know that, of things that you have left?"

"My forbearance, Sidhe."

"For that I trade only my own. What more have you left?"

Caith hurled the amulet from his neck. It vanished as it hit the ground.

"A fair trade then. You have made yourself blind to our workings, and in return I shall show you truth. This is the consequence if you go back where you came from: that you will die obscure, knifed in a quarrel not of your making in a land not of your choosing. Second: if you go back now to to Dun Gorm: that Cinnfhail's son will die in your cause; you will win Dun Mhor; you will take Cinnfhail's daughter to your wife and rule both Dun Gorm and Dun Mhor, king over both within three years."

"And if I go alone to Dun Mhor?"

"Sliabhin will kill you. It will take seven days for you to die."

Caith let the swordpoint waver. He thought of Dun Gorm, that he had wanted, the faces, Deirdre's young face. But there were traps in every Sidhe prophecy; this he sensed. "And gaining Dun Gorm," he said, "what would I have there but sorrow and women's hate?"

"For a son of Sliabhin," said the Sidhe, stepping closer to him, "you are marvelous quick of wit. And now I must have the horse you have given me."

"Curse you!" he cried. He struck, not to kill, but to gain himself space to run. The Sidhe's blade—he had not seen it drawn—rang instant against his own; and back and back he staggered, fighting for his life.

A black body hurtled against him, trampling him beneath its hooves, flinging his sword from his hand; Caith staggered up to one knee and lunged after the fallen sword.

"Rash," said the Sidhe, and light struck him in the face and a blow flung him back short of it. "The horse is mine. For the rest—"

"*Sidhe!*" Caith cried, for he was blinded in the light, as if the moon had burned out his eyes. All the world swam in tears and pain. He groped still after his sword among the leaves and as the hilt met his fingers, he seized it and staggered to his feet. "Sidhe!" he shouted, and swung the blade about him in his blindness.

He heard the beat of hooves. A horse's shoulder struck him and flung him down again; this time he held to the sword and rolled to his feet.

But blind, blind—there was only the shadow of branches before a blur of light in a world gone gray at the mid of the night, a taunting, moving shape like a will-o'-the-wisp before his eyes.

"*Sidhe!*" he cried in his anger and his helplessness.

It drifted on. Laughter pealed like silver bells, faint and far and mocking.

5

THERE WAS NO sight but that fey light, no sound but that chill laughter, pure as winter bells. Caith followed it, sobbing after breath, followed it for hours because it was all the light he had in his gray blindness and if he turned from it he was lost indeed. He tore himself on brush and thorns, slipped down a streambank and sprawled in water, clawed his way up the other side. "Sidhe!" he cried again and again. But the light was always there, just beyond his reach in a world of gray mist, until he went down to his bruised knees and on his face in the leaves and lost all sense of direction.

He got up again in terror, turning this way and that.

"Sidhe!" His voice was a hoarse, wild sound, unlike himself. "*Sidhe!*"

A horse sneezed before him. The will-'o-the-wisp hovered in his sight, near at hand. It became Dathuil and on his back the tall fair Sidhe, against a haze of trees, of moon-silvered trunks.

"Will you ride?" the phooka asked, at his other side, and Caith turned, staggering, and caught his breath in. Red eyes gleamed in the shadow. "Will you ride?" the phooka asked again. "I will bear you on my back."

Caith's eyes cleared. It was a black horse that stood there. Its eyes shone with fire. Suddenly it swept close by him, too quick for his sword, too quick for the thought of a sword.

"If you had kept the white horse," said the will-o'-the-wisp on his other side, "even the phooka could not have caught you. Now any creature can."

"Sliabhin hunted in these woods," said the phooka-voice, from somewhere in the trees. "Now we hunt them too."

"Go back," said the will-o'-the-wisp, and horse and rider shimmered away before him without a sound. Caith caught after breath and stumbled after, exhausted, wincing at the thorns that caught his cloak back and tore his skin.

"Go back," said the voice. "Go back."

But Caith followed through thicker and thicker brush, no longer knowing any other way. His sight had cleared, but in all this woods there was no path, no hope but to lay hands on the Sidhe and compel them or to wander here till he was mad. A pain had begun in his side. It grew and grew, until he walked bent, and sprawled at last on the slick, wet leaves.

"You cannot take us," said the Sidhe, and was there astride Dathuil, paler and brighter than the newborn day. A frown was on the Sidhe's face. "I have given you your answers. Are you so anxious then to die? Or are you looking for another bargain?"

Caith caught his breath, holding his side. It was all that he could do to gain his feet, but stand he did, with his sword in his hand.

"Ah," said the Sidhe. "Proud like your father."

"*Which* father? I've had three."

"You have but one, mac Sliabhin. The house at Dun Mhor has but one lord. And a curse rests on it and all beneath that roof. Hunters in our woods, slayers of our deer—for your line there is neither luck nor hope. But for the gift of Dathuil and for my own pleasure, I will give you once what you ask of me. And pitying mortal wits I will tell you what you should ask—if you ask me that advice."

"That would use up the one request, would it not?"

The Sidhe smiled then as a cat might smile. "Well," he said, "if you are that quick with your wits you may know what you should ask."

"Take the curse off Dun Mhor."

The smile vanished. The Sidhe went cold and dreadful. "It is done. And now it is to bestow again. I give it to *you*."

Caith stared at the Sidhe in bleak defeat, and then took a deeper breath. "Sidhe! One more bargain!"

"And what would that be, mac Sliabhin, and what have you left to trade?"

"It's Dun Mhor you hate. I'll work this out with you. There's a young boy, my brother, inside Dun Mhor. Brian is his name."

"We know this."

"I want to take him out and free of Sliabhin. Help me get him out and safe away and I will kill Sliabhin for you; and take Dun Mhor; and so you can have it all. Me. Dun Mhor. My brother is the price of my killing your enemy."

The Sidhe considered him slowly, from toe to head. "Shall I tell you what you have left out?"

"Have I left something out?"

"Nothing that would matter." The Sidhe reined Dathuil aside. "I take your bargain."

Caith had his sword still in hand. He rammed it into his sheath and felt all his aches and hurts. He looked up again at the Sidhe, cold at heart. "What did I leave out, curse you? What did I forget?"

"You are not apt to such bargaining," said the phooka, there in young man's shape, leaning naked against a tree at his right hand. "I will tell you, mac Sliabhin. You forgot to ask your life."

"Oh," Caith said. "But I didn't forget."

"How is that?" said the fair Sidhe.

"If you want some use out of your curse, you can't kill me too soon, now can you? It would rob you of your revenge."

The phooka laughed, wild laughter, a mirth that stirred the leaves. "O mac Sliabhin, Caith, fosterling of murderers and thieves, I love thee. Come, come with me. I will bear you on my back. We will see this Dun Mhor."

"And drown me, would you? Not I. I know what you are."

But the black horse took shape between blinks of his eyes and stood pawing the ground before him. Its red eyes glowed like balefire beneath its mane.

"Trust the phooka," said the tall Sidhe with the least gleam of mirth in his eyes. "What have you left to risk?"

Caith glowered at the Sidhe and then, shifting his

sword from the way, roughly grasped the phooka's mane and swung up to his bare back.

It was the wind he mounted, a dark and baneful wind. It was power, the night itself in horse-shape; and beside them raced the day, that was Dathuil with the Sidhe upon his back.

Caith heard laughter. Whence it came he guessed.

THE FOREST road stretched before the men from Dun Gorm in the dawning, and the sun searched the trees with fingers of light. It was the green shade before them, the green deep heart of the Sidhe-wood.

"No farther," Conn said, "young lord, no farther."

Raghallach thought on Conn's advice as he rode beside the man. His father had given him into Conn's hands when he was small, and never yet had he put his own judgment ahead of Conn's and profited by it.

But the years turned. It was after all Conn, his father's watchdog, who had tutored him, cracked his head, bruised his bones, taught him what he knew, and Conn, he reckoned, who had orders from his father to protect him now, against all hazard.

"There is one captain over a band," Raghallach said to this man he loved next to his own father. "And it is not lessons today, now, is it, master Conn?"

"Life is lessons," Conn muttered to the moving of the horses. They went not at a gallop; they kept their strength for need. "Some masters are rougher than others, lad, and experience is a very bitch."

"That man you sent to scout ahead of us; Feargal. We're of an age, he and I—do you always call him *lad*, Conn?"

"Ah," said Conn, and cast a wary look back, to see whether the men were in earshot of it all. The sound of the hooves covered low voices at such distance. "Ah, but, me lad, you are young. Yet. And will not get older by risking honest men who put their lives into your hand. Do not be a fool, son of my old friend; I did not teach a fool."

Anger smouldered in Raghallach. He drove his heels into his horse's sides and then recalled good sense. Raghallach grew a great deal, in that moment; he reined back, confusing the horse which threw its head and jumped.

Arrows flew from ambush. A man cried out; a horse screamed.

Raghallach flung his shield up in thunderstruck alarm. Arrows thumped and shocked against it; he reined aside, knowing nothing now to do but run into the teeth of ambush, not turn his shieldless back to the arrows or delay while some shot found his horse or legs. The good horse leapt beneath his heels, surefooted in the undergrowth, heedless of the breast-high thicket: "Ware," Conn yelled, as the horse's hindquarters sank under a sudden impact: Conn hewed a man from off Raghallach's back that had flung himself down from the trees.

Next was a confusion of blows, of curses howled, of blades and blood, the scream of horses and the crack of brush.

Then came silence, deep silence, after so much din, horses crashing slowly back through brush, blowing and snorting as riders sought the clear road and regrouped, a man fewer than before.

"Feargal," Raghallach said of the body they found

there on the trail. A red-fletched arrow had taken him in the throat. Gleann Fiach marking.

"*Think,*" said Conn, fierce at his side. Conn's brow ran blood. "Think and do it, boy! They have come into the Sidhe-wood. They are forewarned, they've made ambush against us and this Caith mac Sliabhin. Hagan mac Dealbhan has warned them!"

"He's dead," said Feargal's brother Faolan, who had gotten down to see and knelt by his brother. Faolan hovered somewhere lost in the horror, not touching the arrow that had felled his brother, only frozen there.

"*Boy,*" Conn said; the word cursed them all. "*What will you do?*"

"Get him home," Raghallach said gently to Faolan, and jerked his horse's head about in the direction opposite to home, using his heels to send him down the road after the fleeing enemy. Others followed. Conn was one, drawing close beside him.

Raghallach looked at Conn as they rode.

"Not I, boy," said Conn. "I have not a word."

The road opened out before them, obscured in leaves and green.

"It wants answer," said Raghallach. "This death of ours wants an answer."

"On whom," asked Conn. "Gleann Fiach cattle? Where will we stop? We know they hold the woods. Those that ran will regroup; meanwhile they'll have a man sent to Sliabhin to get help up here. It's war, lad; it begins. Blood is on the Sidhe-wood and our own hands have shed it too."

A hollow lay before them, a small clearing in the wood, which was one of their own Gley's fords. It was a place for ambushes; the air here all was wrong, sang with unease, in the leaves, the water-song.

They thundered into it. The newborn light grew strange, the beats of the hooves dimmer and dimmer.

The peace, a voice said, *the peace is broken, son of Dun Gorm. No farther, come no farther.*

Panic took Raghallach suddenly, a fear not of arrows. He was Cinnfhail's son: he Saw, for the first time in his life, he Saw. "Conn!" he cried. "Stop!" He reined in his horse. His face was hot with shame and self-reproach, that even to this moment he had led from fear and pride, not sense. He had ridden on for pride's sake, blown this way and that by what everyone would think instead of regarding what was wise. *Fool,* Conn had said. A shadow came on them, and about them, and into them, horse and rider, all, darkening their sight.

It was the forest, managing its own defense.

6

THE PHOOKA STOPPED, having leapt the stream, and Caith went sprawling over his neck, rolling in the leaves, bruised and battered.

The phooka stood in man-form on the bank, naked and laughing at him, grinning from ear to ear and leaning on his knees.

"You bastard," Caith said, gathering himself up.

"I thought," said the phooka, "that it was yourself were the bastard, Caith mac Sliabhin."

Caigh caught up his sheathed sword and all but hurled it; mastered his temper instead. "Of course it is," he said, at which the phooka laughed the more, and overtook him as he went stamping up the bank. The phooka clapped him on the shoulder and hooted with laughter. Caith hurled off the hand, whirled and looked at the Sidhe, the sword still in his hand.

"O come," said the phooka, grinning. His teeth were white and the frontmost were uncommon square and sturdy, in a long beardless jaw. His eyes were black and merry, and red lights danced in them even by daylight. "Do you not like a joke?"

"It will be a great joke when you drown me. Of that I'm sure."

The phooka grinned. "O I like you well, mac Sliabhin. I missed the water with you, did I not?"

Caith said nothing. He limped onward, flung off the hand again as they walked along the streamside, picking up the road. The phooka walked by him as if he had only started out a moment ago, fresh and easy as youth itself.

"Where is the other?" Caith asked, after some little walking. "Where has he gotten to?" For the bright Sidhe had been with them until that leap across the stream.

"Oh, well, that one. He's not far. Never far."

"Watching us."

"He might be." The phooka kicked a stone. "He has no liking for roads, that one. Nuallan is his name. He's one of the Fair Folk." An engaging, square-toothed grin. "I'm the other kind."

"What do you call yourself?"

The phooka laughed again. "Call myself indeed. Now you know we'd not hand you *all* our names. Dubhain. Dubhain am I. Would you ride again?"

"Not yet, phooka."

"Dubhain," the phooka reminded him. It was the wickedest laugh ever Caith had heard. There were dark nights in it, and cold depths where phookas lived, deep in rivers, haunting fords and luring travelers to die beneath the waters. *Darkness,* his name was. "So we walk together." The phooka looked up. His eyes gleamed like live coals beneath the mop of black hair. "We are in Gleann Fiach now, mac Sliabhin. Do you not find it fair?"

The road took them farther and farther from the woods. The deep glen showed itself bright with sun, its hilly walls different from Gleann Gleatharan, untilled, unhedged. Gorse grew wild up the hillsides, from what had once been hedges, and grass grew uncropped. It was a fair land, but there was something wrong in that fairness, for it was empty. Untenanted. Waste, even in its green pastures.

And coming over a gentle rise, Caith could see the dun itself at this great distance, a towered mass, a threat lowering amid its few tilled fields. Now indeed Caith saw pasturages up on the hillsides; but they were few for so great a place, and all near the dun. The most of the tillage closely surrounded the dun itself, gathered to its skirts like some pathwork order struggling to exist in the chaos of the land. Gleann Fiach was wide. There was promise in the land, but it was all blighted promise.

Caith had stopped walking. "Come on," the phooka said with a sidelong glance that mocked all Caith's fears and doubts. Caith set out again with Dubhain at his side, the two of them no more than a pair of dusty travelers, himself fair, his companion dark.

Caith was weary of the miles, the flight, the restless night; his companion had strength to spare. Like some lawless bare-skinned boy Dubhain gathered stones as he came on them and skipped them down the road.

"There," he would say, "did you see that one, man?"

"Oh, aye," Caith would answer, angry at the first, and then bemazed, that a thing so wicked could be so blithe, whether it was utterest evil or blindest innocence, like storm, like destroying flood. The phooka grinned up at him, less than his stature, and for a moment the eyes were like coals again, reminding him of death.

"A wager, man?"

"Not with you," he said.

"What have you to lose?" And the phooka laughed, all wickedness.

"You would find something," he said.

The grin widened. The phooka hurled another stone. No man could match that cast, that sped and sped far beyond any natural limit.

"I thought so," said Caith, and the phooka looked smug and pleased.

"Cannot match it."

"No."

The phooka shape-shifted, became again the horse, again the youth, and broke a stem of grass, sucking on it as he went, like any country lad. Dubhain winked. He was more disreputable than he had been, a ragged wayfarer. A moment ago he had been bare as he was born, dusky-skinned. Now he went in clothes, ragged and dusty, ruined finery with a bordering of tinsel gold.

"It is a glamor," the phooka said. "Can you see through it?"

"No."

"If you had the amulet you might."

"I don't."

Another grin.

"You will help me," asked Caith, "inside the walls—or just stand by?"

"Oh, assuredly I shall help."

"—me."

"O Caith, o merry friend, of course, how could you doubt?"

Caith looked askance at Dubhain, uneasy in all his thoughts now. The Sidhe would both trick him if they could, if he gave them the least chance. He thought through the compact he had made a hundred times as they walked the sunlit dust, as they came down farther and farther into the glen. Of what lay before him in Dun Mhor he wished not to think at all, but his thoughts drifted that way constantly, darker and more terrible, and the phooka beside him was constant in his gibes.

Sliabhin's son. And Moralach's. All his life seemed lived beneath some deceiving glamor. He had conjured loyalty to Gaelan, to a dream that never was. He came to avenge Gaelan, and his own father was the murderer.

But the stones before them were real and no illusion. There was truth about to happen. It must be truth, finally, after a life of lies and falseness.

*   *   *

THE DAY and distance dwindled in the crossing of the glen. Caith rested little, except at the last, taking the chance to sleep a bit, in the cover of a thicket, at the edge of the dun's few tilled fields and scant pastures, before he should commit himself to all that he had come to do.

And quickly there was a nightmare, a dream of murder, of Moralach the queen hanging from the rooftree of Dun Mhor.

"You," Caith said to the phooka when he waked sweating and trembling to find him crouching near. "Is it some prank of yours, to give me bad dreams?"

"Conscience," said the phooka. "I'm told you mortals have it. It seems nuisanceful to me."

And then Dubhain reached out and touched Caith's face with callused fingertips, and there came to him a strength running up from the earth like summer heat, something dark and healing at once, that took his breath.

"Keep your hands from me!" Caith cried, striking the Sidhe-touch away.

"Ah," said Dubhain, "scruples even yet. There is that left to trade."

"That I will not." Caith scrambled to his feet, shuddering at the wellness and the unhuman strength in himself.

"You've dropped your sword," the phooka said, handing it up to him with a grin on his face and the least hint of red glow within his eyes.

Caith snatched it, hooked the sheath to his belt and caught his oiled-wool cloak about him and his tartan as he hit out upon the road.

Dubhain was quickly with him, striding lightly at his side.

And Dun Mhor rose ever nearer as they came past the wild hedges onto the road. The dun lowered as a dark mass of stone in the evening that had fallen while Caith slept in his thicket.

No lights showed from Dun Mhor in this twilight time, not from this side, though some gleamed about the hills. Cattle were home; sheep in their folds; the folk behind the walls of their cottages and of the great keep that was many times the size of rustic Dun Gorm.

I am mad, Caith thought, having seen the size of the place. *As well walk into Dun na nGall and try to take it.*

But he kept walking with Dubhain beside him. The phooka whistled, as if he had not a care in all the world, and a wind skirled a tiny cloud up in the sky right over Dun Mhor, a blackness in the twilight.

"I think," said the phooka, "it looks like rain. Doesn't it to you?"

"You might do this all," Caith said in anger. "If you can do all these things, why could you not come at this man you hate?"

"Not our way," said Dubhain.

"What is your way—to torment all the land, the innocent with the guilty?"

The eyes glowed in the darkness. "Men seem best at that."

"A curse on you too, my friend."

The phooka laughed. Dun Mhor loomed above them now, and the cloud had grown apace as they walked. Dubhain's hand was on Caith's shoulder, like some old acquaintance as they passed down the last hedgerow on the road, as they left the last field and came up the hill of the dun to the gate. Lightning flashed. The cloud widened still.

"Hello," Caith shouted, "hello the gatekeep. Travelers want in!"

There was a long silence. "Who are you?" a man shouted from up in the darkened tower to the left of the gate. "What business in Dun Mhor?"

"Business with your lord!" Caith shouted back. "Word from Dun na nGall!"

"Wait here," the gatekeep said, and after was silence.

"Perchance they'll let you in," the phooka said.

"Oh, aye, like the raincloud is chance." Caith did not look at Dubhain. He knew how Dubhain would seem—quite common to the eye, whatever shape suited the moment and Dubhain's dark whims. The cloud still built above them. Thunder muttered. "I will tell you, phooka. Hagan—the man who fostered me—might have sent word south when I left him. He knew where I might go and what I might do. He hated me; I know that. Gods know what side of this he serves, but it was never my side. He might well betray me to curry favor with Sliabhin, since Sliabhin is king. I reckon that he might." He had begun to say it only to bait the phooka and diminish Dubhain's arrogance. But the pieces settled in his mind, in sudden jagged array of further questions. "I know nothing. Who fostered me out, how I was gotten from here—the king of Gleatharan never told me. Was it Gaelan or was it Sliabhin, phooka?"

The mad eyes looked up at him, for once seeming sober. "Would you pity Sliabhin if you knew that?"

"Gods, phooka—"

"Perhaps it was." The red gleam was back. "Perhaps was not. They are coming, mac Sliabhin, to open the gates."

"Why have you done this? Why do you need my hands to wield the knife?"

"Why, mac Sliabthin—should *we* take on our own curse?"

The lesser gate groaned on its hinge. Torchlight fluttered in the wind, in the first cold spats of rain. "Gods, this weather," the gatekeeper cried against the skirling gusts as he led them through a courtyard and to a second door. "Come in, there. What would be your name?"

"Foul, foul," Dubhain chortled, pulling Caith along, beside, beyond, "Huusht, hey!" The lightning cracked. The sky opened in torrents. "O *gods*, we're soaked."

"A plague on you!" cried Caith, but Dubhain's hand gripped his arm, stronger than any grip ever he had felt. The creature of rivers fled the rain, called on gods younger than himself, jested with the guards. "Curse you, *let me go!*"

"Never that," the phooka said as they came within the doors of the dun itself. Dubhain stamped his booted feet, shed water in a circle in the torchlight in the hall, as the guards did, Dubhain did and Caith did, made fellows by the storm.

They were in. The stones about them, warm-colored in the light, were the nature, the solidity of his home, the very color and texture that he had imagined

them; or the reality drove out the dream in the blink
of an eye and deceived him as reality will do with
imaginings. Here was the house he had longed for,
dreamed of, in the grim walls of his fostering; but
here also were rough, scarred men, the smell of oil
and stale straw as womenless men had managed things
in Hagan's hold up by Dun na nGall. There seemed
no happiness in this dim place either, only foreboding, the noise of shouts, of heavyfooted guards, the
dull flash of metal in the light and the surety these
men would kill and lose no sleep over it.

*O father, Sliabhin!—are we not a house that deserves its
death?*

"One will tell the lord you are in," a guard said.
"Bide here, whether he will see you. You are not the
first to come tonight."

Caith looked sharply at the guard, whose brute
broad face held nothing but raw power and the habit
of connivance in the eyes. No, not dull, this one.
Huge, and not dull. "Some other messenger?" Caith
asked with a sinking of his heart, thinking on Dun
na nGall, on his foster-father Hagan, and treachery.
"From where?"

"Messenger. Aye." The voice was low, the guard's
face kept its secrets. Caith looked round on Dubhain
with a touch of fey desperation in the move, even
defiance. *Save me now*, he challenged the Sidhe, meeting Dubhain's eyes, and had the joy of seeing a
phooka worried. The thought elated him in a wild,
hopeless abandon. He looked upward at the stairs
that would lead up, he reckoned, to the king's hall: a
man had gone stumping up the steps to a doorway
above. *I am the Sidhe's own difficulty*, Caith thought

again, sorry for himself and at the same time sure that his revenge was at hand, whether he would kill or be killed and likely both. Time stretched out like a spill of honey, cloying sweet and golden with light and promising him satiety.

Enough of living. For this I was born, my father's son.

And my mother's.

7

THE GUARD WHO had gone up came out again from a room near the head of the stair and beckoned to them.

"Come," said the guard by Caith's side.

Caith was very meek going up the steps. He made no protest as they began to prevent Dubhain from going up with him. In truth, he had no great desire of the company, trusting more to his sword. But he heard a commotion behind him, and the phooka joined him at the mid of the stairs, eluding the guards below. Caith heard the grate of drawn steel above and below them at once as Dubhain clutched his arm. "Master," Dubhain said, "I'll not leave ye here."

"Fall to heel," Caith said in humor the match of the phooka's own. "Mind your manners, lad." He looked up at the guard above them. "My servant is frightened of you," he said, holding out his hand in appeal till the guard, satisfied of his own dreadfulness and well-pleased with it, made a show of threat and waved them both on with his sword drawn.

It might have been a boy outright terrified, this

old and evil thing that clutched Caith's arm, that went with him miming terror and staring round-eyed as they passed the guard and his naked blade. But the phooka's fingers numbed Caith's hand, re-minding him as they went. *You cannot shake me, never be rid of me.* The touch felt like ice, as if something had set its talons into his heart as well as into the flesh of his arm, so that Caith recovered his good sense, remembering that he was going deeper into this mesh of his own will, and that he still under-stood less of it than he ought. Doors closed some-where below, echoing in the depths under the stairs. There were a man's shouts from that direction, sharp and short.

"What's that?" Caith asked, delaying at the door of the corridor, and looking back down the stairs.

It was not his business to know, only the anxious-ness of a man entering where there was no retreat, hearing things amiss behind him. The faces of the guards below stared up at him—distant kin of his, perhaps; or Sliabhin's hirelings: they were nothing he wanted for family: wolf-sharp, both of them, cruel as weasels. "Never you mind," one of them called up, and that one was uglier than all the rest. "There's those will care for that. Keep going."

"Lord," Dubhain said, a shiver in his voice, "lord—"

"Be still," Caith said. There was humor in it all, a fine Sidhe joke in this frightened phooka by his side, grand comedy. Caith played it too, with his life, with the phooka's grip numbing him, owning him and making mock of all Dun Mhor. Caith turned toward the door as they wished him to and came into the hall where they wished him to go, into warmth and firelight and a gathering of men the likeness of the rest, as likely a den of bandits as he had seen anywhere along the road he had traveled to come here.

And one sat among them, on a carven chair over by the fire; the light was on his face, and it was a face without the roughness of the others, a mouth much like Caith's own if bitter years had touched it; and this man's hair and beard were his own pale red, faded with years; and the tartan was Dun Mhor.

This man looked at him, thinking, measuring, so that Caith felt himself stripped naked. The resemblance—in this hall—would surely not elude Sliabhin mac Brian. Or riders from Dun na nGall might have outpaced him down the coast, on a longer road but a swifter. Quite likely his murder was in preparation even now; and his only chance was to move before the man believed he would. But he had got inside. He still had his sword. This much of his plan he had worked, feigning simplicity within deviousness: this was all his plan, to stand this close.

Sliabhin will kill you, he suddenly heard the Sidhe promise him. But never that he might kill Sliabhin. *Sliabhin will kill you. It will take seven days for you to die.*

"King Sliabhin?" Caith asked, all still and quiet. He weighed all his life in this moment, reckoning how long he had, whether the nearest man would draw and cut at him with steel or simply fall on him barehanded to overpower him: worse for him, if they got him alive. Before that happened he must spring and kill Sliabhin at once, face the others down with their king dead and give these bandits time to think how things had changed. There was Dubhain to reckon with, at his back—if they turned swords on *him*—

If I come alone— That was how he had made his question to the Sidhe. *If I come alone to Dun Mhor.* It was as if his hearing and his memory had been dulled in that hour as his eyes had been, glamored and spellbound. He was *not* alone. He had brought Dubhain. The question was altered; at least one thing in his futures would have changed.

But this man, this man who looked at him with a kinsman's face, in this bandit hall—

"Who are you?" Sliabhin asked.

"Hagan sends," Caith said, "for Caith's sake: he wants the other boy."

Sliabhin got to his feet and stared at him. Caith's heart was pounding in his chest, the cloak about him weighing like a great burden, covering the red tartan that would kill him and the sword that would kill Sliabhin, both beneath its gray roughness. There was no way out. Not from the moment he had passed the door. He felt the phooka's presence against his arm, biding like a curse.

Dubhain. *Darkness.*

He is one of the Fair Folk. I am the other kind.

"So," said Sliabhin, and walked aside, a halfstep out of reach; looked back at Caith—*My father,* Caith thought, seeing that resemblance to himself at every angle; and his throat felt tighter, the sweat gathering on his palms. *This is what I am heir to, this bandit den, these companions.* Beside him the phooka. There would be no gleam in Dubhain's eyes at this moment, nothing to betray what he was.

Sliabhin moved farther to his side. Caith turned to keep him in view as he stood before the door, and an object came into his sight, nailed there above the doorway, dried sprigs of herb; elfshot on a thong; a horseshoe, all wards against the Sidhe.

To make them powerless.

"Hagan wants the boy sent?" Sliabhin said, and Caith set his gaze on Sliabhin and tried to gather his wits back. "I find that passing strange."

"Will you hear the rest," Caith asked, with a motion of his eyes about the room, toward the guards, "—here?"

"Speak on."

"It's the elder son, lord; Caith. So Hagan said to me. Caith has heard rumors—" He let his voice trail off in intimidated silence, playing the messenger of ill news. "Lord—they've had to lock him away for fear he'll break for the south, or do himself some harm. He mourns his brother. He's set some strange idea into his head that he has to see the boy or die. I'm to bring the lad, by your leave, lord, to bring his brother out of his fey mood and set reason in him."

A long time Sliabhin stood staring at him, this elder image of himself, gazing at the truth.

He knows me, he knows me, he knows me, now what will he do? Can he kill his own son?

And if he will not—have I all the truth I think I have?

There was a silence in the room so great the crash of a log in the fireplace was like the crumbling of some wall. Sparks showered and snapped. Caith stood still.

"How does he fare?" Sliabhin asked, in a tone Caith had not expected could come from a mouth so hard and bitter. A soft question. Tender. As if it mattered; and it became like some evil dream—this man, this his true father asking the question he had wanted for all his days to hear a father ask. "Who?" Caith returned, "Hagan?"—missing the point deliberately.

"Caith."

"Sorrowing. I hear." There was a knot in Caith's throat; he fought it. He went on in this oblique argument. "If Caith could see the lad, lord, that he's well—I think it would mend much. It might bring him around to a better way of thinking."

"Would it?" Sliabhin walked away from him. Caith let him go, his wits sorting this way and that, between hope and grief. Then he felt the phooka's hand clench on his arm through the cloak, reminding him of oaths, and he was blinder than he had been when the Sidhe-light dazed him.

This place, this hall, this villainous crew—Was I lied to? Was it Gaelan the villain from the beginning, and this my father—innocent? Confession hovered on his lips, not to strike, to betray the Sidhe beside him for very spite and see what Dubhain would do. *But—father—*

"It's a long journey," said Sliabhin, "and dangerous, to send a young lad off in the dark with a man I don't know. You'll pardon me—" Sliabhin walked farther still, safe again among his men. "Tell me—messenger. What color Hagan's beard?"

"Bright red, lord. A scar grays it."

Sliabhin nodded slowly. "And how fares my neighbor?"

"Lord?"

"Cinnfhail." Sliabhin's brow darkened. His voice roughened. "You'll have passed through Gleann Gleatharan. *How fares Cinnfhail?*"

"Well, enough, lord."

Sliabhin snapped his fingers. "Fetch the other," Sliabhin said.

Men left, but not all. Caith and Sliabhin waited there, frozen in their places, and Dubhain waited. *Other, other*—Caith's mind raced on that refrain. The meshes drew about him and he saw the cords moving, but he did not know the truth yet, not the most basic truth of himself, and his hand would not move to the sword.

There was noise of the guards going down the steps outside; there was shouting that echoed up from the depths; and then the noise began to come louder and nearer—Someone cursed from the echoing lower hall, kept cursing as that someone was brought with loud resistance up the stairs. Caith slid his eyes to a point between Sliabhin and that doorway, most to Sliabhin, to the men that stood with him, all confessions stayed upon his lips, his heart beating hard. Dubhain was at his back, laughing inwardly, he thought, at mortal men; at father and son so meshed in must and would not.

Resistance carried into the room, a fair-haired man in a tartan green and blue, a red-blond youth who flung back his head and stared madly at Sliabhin, all bloody that he was.

It was Raghallach in their hands.

*   *   *

"IF," SAID Sliabhin, "you had denied being with Cinnfhail I would have take it ill. You know this boy—do you not?"

"Yes," said Caith. The warmth had left his hands, the blood had surely left his face. Raghallach strove to look his way and twisted helplessly in the grip of two well-grown and armored men. "Cinnfhail's son. I guested there last night. They sent me on my way in the rain, but they gave me provisions and a horse. He broke his leg in the forest. Lord, let this man go."

"He rode right up to our doors, messenger. He tells a pretty tale—do you not, boy?"

They had hurt Raghallach already. They hurt him more, the wrench of a wounded arm; Raghallach fought, such as he could, and cried out, half-fainting then, for the sweat broke out and runneled down his waxen face; and Caith thrust himself half a pace forward, Dubhain catching at his arm. "No, lord," Dubhain said, "no, be not rash."

"How you guested there with Cinnfhail, how you were received, what tale you told," said Sliabhin, "all of this he's sung for us."

Raghallach lifted his head. His weeping eyes spoke worlds, denying what Sliabhin said with a desperate move. *No*. Only that. *No*.

"There was nothing to tell," said Caith, "but I see that I was followed. Lord, this man—"

"—offends me. What do you say to that?"

The air seemed close. He felt pinned between will and dare not—Sliabhin out of reach behind a hedge of swords. He needed caution, wit, something of answers in this place, and the Sidhe was still holding his arm. *Be not rash, be not rash,* he heard Dubhain's wicked voice in his mind. And Raghallach bleeding and tortured before him—*He will die,* Cinnfhail had prophesied of his son; so the Sidhe had said also, that Raghallach would die if he came with him to Dun Mhor. *O gods. Raghallach—who spoke for me to Cinnfhail—*

"Why did you come?" Caith asked in a thin, hoarse voice. "Why did you follow me, Raghallach?"

"Revenge," said Raghallach, and gave another heave in the hands of those that held him. Tears ran down his face and mingled with the sweat and the streaks of blood and dirt. "For my *sister,* man—"

Caith's heart turned over in him. *Well played, O gods, man—brave and well played.*

Caith turned his shoulder as a man accused of villainy might do, walked a space frowning as the phooka let him go. He looked back at wider vantage, Dubhain in the tail of his eye as he glared at Raghallach mac Cinnfhail.

"He's mad."

"He calls you thief as well," Sliabhin said. "He says you stole a horse."

"So, well." Caith turned away, disdaining all accusation.

"*Caith* he calls you."

Caith drew his sword, flinging back his cloak; and all about him men moved—but Sliabhin stopped everything with a move of his hand.

"You never learned that from him," Caith said. "You've known me from the moment I walked in here."

"I've waited for you." Sliabhin's voice was soft. "I was sure you would come someday, somehow."

"I came to kill you—for Gaelan's sake. But I heard another tale, there in Dun Gorm. And which is true—*father*? Who sent me to that whoreson Hagan? Was it Gaelan—or yourself?"

"Who is your companion?" Sliabhin asked, turning his shoulder from the menace of his sword. There were guards; they never moved. "Some other of Gleatharan's fine young lads?"

"Oh, that." Caith kept the blade point between them at their distance, but he took a lighter tone, an easier stance. "Dubhain is his name. One of Hagan's whores' sons. I've gotten used to such comrades—I get on well with them, *father*. Any sort of cutthroat. That's a skill they taught me well—your cousin Hagan and his crew. Why not? We breed such merry sorts—*father*." He gained a step on Sliabhin, but sideways, as a man moved to block him; it all stopped again. "Pirates. Brigands. Are these my brothers? How many did you beget—*and on what, when you tired of my mother*?"

"Enough!" Sliabhin's face congested. He lifted a shaking hand, empty. "It was Gaelan—Gaelan tormented her. She and I loved, boy—*loved*—you'd not know that. Oh, yes, whelp, I saved your life. I rode—myself—and bestowed you where I could or Gaelan'd have given you up for wolfbait that night. He gave out you were stillborn. He beat her—hear me?"

Caith faltered. More of truths and half-truths shuttled back and forth in this tapestry of lies. His mind chased after them, sorting one and the other, and he darted a glance from Sliabhin to Raghallach, to

Sliabhin again. Raghallach lied for him, risked his own sister's name in his defense and tried nothing for himself. But Sliabhin's voice had the ring of true outrage. And the Sidhe was there beside him, doubtless laughing at his plight.

The sword sank in Caith's hand, extended again to Raghallach. "What of him?"

"What *of* him?"

"I don't know. Someone's lied. I don't know who. Where's Brian? Where's my brother?"

"You'll not be taking your brother anywhere tonight, my lad," Sliabhin said.

"I want to see him."

"What's he to you?"

"A whim. Father. Like you."

"Put up the sword. *Put it up.*"

Caith laughed, a faint, strained laugh, and his own fey mind surprised him. The look in Sliabhin's eyes surprised him, that they were lost together in this sea and clinging desperately one to the other still unmurdered.

"Put it up."

Caith thought on it a long moment, with another look at Raghallach, at Dubhain; then there were only Sliabhin's eyes, bewitching as the Sidhe's, to cast a glamor on things. There was Sliabhin's voice, promising nothing at all. There was death here; the room was full of it.

I am the curse, Caith thought. *The Sidhe send their curse back to Dun Mhor—in me. And I cannot be rid of it.* He slid the sword back into its sheath, a neat quick move, never quite taking his eyes from the guards, who kept their swords drawn. *But if it is in me I can delay it, I can take it away again—if I will. If Sliabhin wills it.*

And what if I am wrong?

"You'll rest here," said Sliabhin, "as my guest."

"And this one?" He meant Raghallach. He gestured that way, where Raghallach hung in the guard's cruel grip. *O gods, he accused me—how can I defend him, how save him, what can I do to save his life but win my father and turn his mind from killing him—*

"He'll tell us tales. By morning—he'll have a many of them. You'll hear them all."

"My brother—where is he?"

"Oh, the boy's well. Quite well enough. Go. They'll take you to chambers, these men of mine. Leave this other to me."

Shame burned Caith's face, betraying shame; he looked at Raghallach, and for a moment then his heart stopped, for Raghallach smiled unexpectedly in a way only he could see, a cat's smile, that chilled him through.

Dubhain tugged at him. "Come, lord, come—do what he says."

Caith cast a wild glance at Dubhain and covered it. The phooka took his arm in a grip fit to break it as Sliabhin's men closed in about them.

"Trust," said Sliabhin, "or have no safety here." Caith looked back at him. Not yet had Sliabhin's men tried to disarm him—and this omission and their likeness, their crying likeness to each other, together with *that* which hung in the hands of the guards— robbed him of volition, of any last hope of understanding what happened around him.

It was not Raghallach they had taken, but the Sidhe Nuallan—*Nuallan* they dragged struggling away in the other direction, past the door with its wards, its diminishments of Sidhe power.

They passed the door with Nuallan-Raghallach. Directly a shout rang out, a blow, a cry of pain that jarred his nerves as it echoed in the hall.

Then one man took Caith by the arm and drew him aside to another door. A guard opened it on more stairs, a dark and musty ascent higher into the hold.

"*Sliabhin!*" Caith jerked about to turn back again, halfway, but no one was prepared to listen. Dubhain came perforce, at sword-point. Caith tried to break from them; and there in the doorway they held a sword to his throat and disarmed him of sword and dagger both.

"*Sliabhin!* Damn you!" He fought once they took the sword away from his throat, and he hoped for the phooka's help, but three men got Caith's arms behind him and began to force him up the stairs. He braced his feet against the steps and struggled. "*Sliabhin!*" His voice echoed in the halls, in the heights and depths of the place. "*Sliabhin!*" And despairing: "*Brian!*"

One struck him, bringing him stunned to his knees on the stone steps.

And no one listened.

8

THERE WAS A hall beyond the stairs, a room at the side of it; a dank darkness, masonry built into Dun Mhor's very hill, dirt floored in stone. Rough hands hurled them both in, and quickly slammed the door.

The phooka's eyes glowed, company in the dark, and a light grew about them both, until Caith could see Dubhain plainly. The phooka sat on the floor of this stonewalled chamber—he was the country lad again, all dusty. And Dubhain brushed himself off as if he had taken some easy spill, as merry as before, and got to his feet.

Caith sat, bruised and sullen, winded. He bowed his aching head against his hands.

"Welcome home," the phooka said.

Caith looked up and glowered. For a long time there was silence.

A scream shuddered through the thick door, a man's voice and not yet a man's—Caith flinched at hearing it and then he hardened his heart to it, thinking on the Sidhe Nuallan. "You knew," he said to Dubhain, shuddering when it came again, more horrid than before. "It's all a sham. Isn't it?"

"Of course it is." Yet another cry rang through the halls at some distance, a man in deepest agony. Dubhain looked that way, uncommon sobriety on his face.

"Dubhain. Dubhain—for the gods' sake, what's in Nuallan's mind, to come here like this?"

Silence.

"He's in trouble, isn't he? Dubhain?"

"Oh, never." Dubhain dusted his hands and, blithe as he had begun, his voice quavered as the cry rang out again.

"Can you do something?" It was not love that made Caith ask. It was humanity, all unwise and simple-minded; he knew it, and yet the sound— It came again, and they both winced. *"For the gods' sake, phooka, can you do something?"*

"The wards—" The phooka fretted and paced back and forth, dark within the light he himself cast. He was naked now, dusky-skinned, his hair falling black and thick about his shoulders, his eyes glowing murky red. "Oh, Nuallan loves a joke, he does, and this one is quite rich, is it not? He's come to see the revenge. To keep his word to you."

"Get us out of this."

Dubhain stopped his pacing. Another scream shuddered through the air and Dubhain wrung his hands. "The wards—the wards—they—muddle things."

"You mean they work? Nuallan *can't get out?*"

The phooka said nothing.

"He's testing me, Sliabhin is." Caith got to his feet, staggering as he did. "Using Raghallach—*Nuallan.* It's for my benefit, all this—O *gods.*" There was another scream. Caith tried the door again and again, at last turned his shoulders against the rough wood and stared at the twin red gleams that glared at him. Still another cry echoed beyond their dark. "Maybe he's laughing at them all the while. But I don't care for your jokes, phooka. Do something. I've got a brother in this place, remember? Where is he? Listening to *that?*" He laughed, a brief, strained laughter. "O gods, you do love a joke. But this is enough, phooka, enough!"

"Be still, man," Dubhain hissed, sinking down on his haunches and hugging his arms about himself. The red eyes gleamed, feral and terrible, glowing alternately brighter and dimmer as scream after scream echoed up the dark. "Be still. He'll give up soon, Nuallan will. Even his humor doesn't carry to this."

It went on, all the same, and on, and on.

"The wards—" Caith said.

"Fair Folk," said Dubhain.

"What does that mean?"

"Nuallan's of the Fair Folk. He says wards aren't that much against him."

Caith crouched down in like position, facing the boy-shape in the dark. "He says."

The phooka said nothing. Dubhain's face was not good to look on, nor his eyes good to look into.

"My *brother*, phooka. You bargained. Do something. Find him. Where is he?"

"Patience," the phooka whispered at last, a voice so still it seemed to chill the air. "Patience, mac Sliabhin."

It was long that Caith waited, crouched there with his arms clasped about his knees and shivering. The wailing died and began again. "Phooka," Caith said.

"Hssst." The look that fixed on him was dire and distraught. "What will you pay for it?"

"*Pay* for it? It's your friend down there!"

"There's the boy," the whisper came back; the red eyes looked into his with sudden keenness as if

Dubhain had been somewhere and now came back to him. "I know where your brother is. What will you pay?"

"Curse you, you've already bargained for that answer, for all I've got!"

"Your scruples, man. I told you you had that left to trade."

"What do you want?"

"I'll tell you. If we survive this. When I go, hold to me." Dubhain shut his eyes till only the merest slits gleamed fire.

Suddenly it was the black horse rising to its feet, a scrape of hooves on the stone, the surge of a large equine body. Caith scrambled to his feet and in the scattering and gathering of his wits seized it by the mane and swung up to mount it in that low-ceilinged room.

The door was like mist about them as they passed, like nothing at all; and abruptly it was not the horse-shape, but the boy, and himself tumbling to land on his feet with his hand on Dubhain's naked shoulder, fingers still tangled in Dubhain's hair. "Let go," the phooka said. "Follow me."

They padded along the hall, down the dark stairs, quiet and quick. Quietly and quickly they pushed open the door on the hall and the guards there turned suddenly to see what had broken among them, a desperate man and an improbable black horse that swept to the far door scattering men like leaves before its rush of wind and storm-sound.

A sword fell loose. Caith seized it up and hewed his way in Dubhain's wake, turned with his back to

the doorway and the phooka and at once found
himself beset by five of Sliabhin's guards.

He swept a furious stroke in the doorway, taking
one in return, beating blades aside—ducked under
one and thrust for a belly. A sword came down at
him while his was bound and he sprawled aside
against the door frame, in worse and worse trouble,
but he got that man's knees as he fell in the doorway
and stabbed up at the next guard as the rest of him
fell in reach, expecting a blade down on him in the
next moment.

A black sudden shape swept him over, as the
phooka sent the surviving pair screaming in retreat
up the inside stairs.

Then the horse-shape turned and changed as it
twisted like black smoke into the boy-shape, into
Dubhain who reached for him and drew him to his
feet.

Caith caught his balance against the wall and turned
for the door and the second, downward stairs. There
was no time for thought, no time for anything. He
ran the stairs down into the hold as a black shape
drifted past him straight down the drop off the
landing, a dire thing with burning eyes and the
rush of wind and cold about it. Down and down it
went, showing him the way as it coursed the hall
below.

Other guards came at them in the lower hall. Thunder cracked outside, shaking the stones. The phooka
laughed like a damned soul and flickered out of
man-shape and in again about one luckless guard;
and that man wailed and gibbered and fell down,
eyes open and staring. Caith battered down the guard

in his own path, not troubling to know whether that one or the other lived or no. He broke clear. Dubhain was by him, running now, having settled on human shape after all.

"Take us there," Caith breathed, seizing Dubhain by the hair.

"You're heavy," Dubhain complained. "Heavy—" The phooka was panting now, even running on bare human feet. "This way—" It was Dubhain that faltered, the red light in his eyes dimmed as he caught his balance against the wall. "The wards, man—I cannot—much farther, much oftener. Haste—be quick."

Stairs gaped ahead of them, going downward yet again. Caith turned then, with a wild suspicion of betrayal. "My *brother*," he said. "Not Nuallan—*hang* Nuallan: he can save himself."

"Go on," said Dubhain. "We keep our bargains."

Caith spun about and went, trusting the phooka to guard his back. Light showed below as he made a second turning of the narrow stone stairs, and yet no one barred his way. He descended in haste, turned suddenly, feeling his back naked.

Dubhain was gone. Caith cursed and wiped his face, shaking; then taking a fresh grip on the bloody sword, drew a whole breath and kept going the only way he knew now to go.

The tumult above had died. There were no more screams from below. He heard thunder rumble, distant from these cellars, above him. A torch at a landing was the only light, and that was scant and guttering in a sough of wind down the stairwell.

But beyond that lighted corner the stairs took another bend, onto a wider scene, onto a hell of torchlight and torment in the cellars of Dun Mhor.

9

THEY SAW HIM as he saw them—a dozen men, Sliabhin. . . . Swords were out, waiting for what should come on them from the commotion above.

Motion stopped then—all frozen. There was a wooden cage, and in that a smallish, half-starved dark-haired boy; there were chains, and in those chains Nuallan hung in Raghallach's red-haired likeness, next a reeking brazier and its irons. Nuallan had burns on his naked body, burns and bleeding wounds and no sense within his eyes.

"Sliabhin," Caith said ever so quietly, with everything in ruins—his last and furtive hope of home, of wholeness for himself. He felt sick and fouled, forever fouled, from his origins to this hour, this bloody, dreadful truth beneath the floors of Dun Mhor. "*Father* mine. . . . You know I'd have believed you? You should have spoken me fair, you know. Is this my brother? Brian—is it you?"

There was silence from the boy in the cage. Whether the waif heard at all he could not tell from the tail of his eye. Swords were poised all about the room, his, theirs, every sword but Sliabhin's own, that stayed within its sheath. An oilpot bubbled softly and sent up its acrid, stinging reek. An ember snapped. The air stank of burned flesh and dust and sweat.

"I've killed your men upstairs," Caith said, baiting them all. Such a crime as he had come to do wanted anger, not horror, not blood as cold as his ran now. "I've killed every one I could reach and I've driven off the rest. There are no women here. None I've seen. No small ones. Nothing. It's a fortress of bandits, father, this house of ours. . . . How did my mother die? A suicide, I've heard."

Sliabhin's face twisted. "Shut your mouth."

"After she found out what she let in. After she saw what you did. She had some scruples left. Even I had scruples left. But you have none, and I've given mine away. Why didn't you call me home long ago—to your loving care? Hagan—was nothing to what you've done here. *Nothing.*"

"Listen to me, Caith." Sliabhin took on a tone of reason. He moved closer, among the swords. "This whelp's no son of mine—not this one. Hers and his—not mine. I'd still have taken him in, for her sake. But young Brian-lad wouldn't have it. Gaelan taught him to hate me—his son. Hers. He hates like Gaelan. He has Gaelan's look about him—"

"Take your sword. I'm no murderer by choice. Not like you. But I'll kill you one way or the other. I swear I will."

"*He's not my son!* You are."

"Are you sure? Could we *ever* be sure?"

That touched home in Sliabhin. Caith saw it, the long, long hate, the madness. "Boy," said Sliabhin, "I kept you up there—safe in Dun na nGall. Safe, all these years. Gaelan would have killed you, do you know that?"

"The way you're killing his son? No. I don't know that. I don't know anything you say. Ever. —*Boy.* Brian—" Caith moved near the cage, shifting ever so carefully. "I'm your brother, Brian, hear me? I've come for you. I'll try to get you out of here."

There was no response. Perhaps the boy had passed beyond all wit. Caith reached with his left hand through the bars without looking, the sword in his right hand, his eyes upon Sliabhin and his men. He felt a hand grip his then, a small hand all thin and weak and desperate. In the same moment Sliabhin's men shifted like so many wolves in a pack.

"You face me," Caith said softly, looking Sliabhin in the eyes. "Come on, man, draw your sword. What's one killing more?"

A small shake of the head. "I'd not kill you."

"Why not? I'll wager you were never sure—*never* sure which of us was yours; or if either was. Or ever will be. Isn't that what eats at you? Oh, aye, you loved my mother. You wanted her to yourself, even more than you loved her—and still you'll never know."

Steel hissed its way to light. Sliabhin drew, quietly.

"That's what I wanted," Caith said. He disengaged his left hand with a gentle tug. The boy clutched at it a second time, hampering him. But beyond Sliabhin the Sidhe Nuallan had lifted his head, and watched it all unfold with a gaze bright and perilous as fire.

Nuallan's chains suddenly fell, still locked, and clinked against the stone as Nuallan-Raghallach stood free and unfettered, as he burned like daylight in the murk of the cellar. Panic broke among the men.

Some turned toward one of them, some toward the other, in utter confusion; but Caith stood his ground, whirled when he had won a scant moment and slashed and kicked at the cage the bars of which had begun to bud and leaf inexplicably and to swell and burst their bindings. "Come out!" Caith shouted at Brian, turning to hold the rest at dubious swords' point, having now to circle to keep stalkers from his flank and from the boy. What the boy did then he could not know. His eyes were all for Sliabhin, for his purpose, for what he had come to do.

"Nuallan," Caith said hoarsely, desperately, "the boy. *Dubhain promised.*"

Light burst. The Sidhe was not where or what he had been; Nuallan was beside him like a glare of light while men flinched and shielded their eyes. There came a boy's faint sob. "I have him," Nuallan said. "I leave you—to solve it all—mac Sliabhin."

Then was darkness, or the parting of the light, as if light had gone out in his soul as well and left him only the horror, the men, his father closing on him, having one hate now and one focus of their malice.

Caith seized the brazier one-handed, overturned it across their path, hurling red coals and irons across the planks. He kicked a bubbling oilpot and its tripod after it and fled, up the stairs.

"Dubhain!" Caith cried, desperate, half-prayer, half-curse. Steps rang close behind him—he whirled, spitted the man that came at him in the torchlight, and gazed on Sliabhin's dying face.

"Patricide," said Sliabhin, holding to Caith, clutching at his clothes, at the tartan of Dun Mhor, "*patricide*, twice as damned as I."

Caith freed himself, hearing the shrieks of burning men below, seeing the whole stairwell flared up from beneath, aleap with flame and horror. A burning man raced up toward him, mad with pain: that man he killed over Sliabhin's corpse, and turned, gasping for breath, to race stumbling up the stairs, sword in hand.

Other guards were coming down. Caith met them in the hellish light, hewed past them, one and the other, while they were still amazed at what came at them, dark amid the glare of fire. He trod on their bodies and ran, up into the hall, toward the door, where two more guards made their rush at him.

One he killed, and rushed past the other out into the drizzle and the glare of shielded torches. All about him the alarm dinned—*help, fire, assault!*

"Kill him," someone shouted. "Watch the gate!" another.

Caith ran; that was all he knew to do. He ran splashing through the rain-soaked yard with his side aching and blood binding his hand to the hilt of his sword. Before him he saw the gates were sealed; and in front of those gates a shining rider sat a horse whose mane itself was light. The boy Brian was a shadow in that rider's arms.

"Nuallan!" Caith cried.

He did not expect help. He stumbled forward and caught himself as the horse leapt into motion away from him and passed through the sealed gates as if they had been no more than air.

"Brian! *Brother!*" It was all his hope fleeing him, in Sidhe hands—in their hands, who could bargain a man's soul out of his body. The Sidhe had no pity in them.

"There he is!" someone shouted behind him. Caith gave only half a look and ran along the wall, trapped, whirling to kill a man as he went, still dealing murder with the tears mingling with the rain on his face and blinding him. He loathed all that he had done, loathed all that he was, all his bargains with fate and the Sidhe; and still he went on killing those who wished to end him. He ran, and they hunted him along the wall by the stables.

"Alive!" someone screamed, full of hate. "Take him alive!" That put a last burst of speed into him, rawest desperation to evade the corner they drove him for.

The beat of hooves sounded at his right as if it were coming from somewhere far, and a cold wind blew on him, and a black horse crossed his path, moving slowly like a dream, its eyes gleaming red within the darkness. It offered him its back; it wanted him.

That was the bargain, then. It was better than Dun Mhor offered, the phooka-ride, that should end in numbing cold water, some lightless riverbottom, to drift among the reeds. Caith clenched the black thick mane in his fists and flung himself astride the phooka, felt it stretch itself to run in earnest and saw the wall coming up before them—but it was only mist about them when they met it.

They were away then, with the wind rushing past them. He heard the phooka hoofbeats like the beat-

ing of his heart, felt the spatter of the mist like ice
against his face and his neck and his arms. On and
on they ran, and the cold went to his bones. When
he looked over his shoulder he saw an orange glow,
a jagged ruin, that was Dun Mhor, which was all his
hope and his hate and every reason that had ever
driven him. It sank in ashes now.

He laid his head against the phooka's neck, buried
his face in the darkness of Dubhain's mane and let
the black Sidhe bear him where he would, having
had enough of blood, of fire, and of life. The rain
washed him, soaked him through till he was numb;
leaves and branches began at last to sweep over him,
passing like the touch of hands and the memory of
rain as wet leaves brushed his hands and head.

Abruptly he was falling, falling; but as before it
was not a stream that met him, but solid ground, an
impact that drove the wind from him.

Caith sprawled, dazed, and it was a moment before he could get his arms beneath him and lever
himself to his knees, expecting phooka-laughter and
phooka-humor and all the wickedness they could do.

Sidhe-light broke about him, a pale glow. Sidhe
stood all about him, bright and terrible Fair Folk.
One was Nuallan; and there were a score of others.
Their horses waited beyond the circle, themselves an
unbearable light in the darkness.

A small boy lay among them, sprawled unconscious on the grass at their feet and, seeing that,
Caith found his strength again and tried to get up
and go to Brian; but he could not. Nuallan moved
between and a chill came on Caith's limbs that took

the strength from his legs. He got to the Sidhe all the same, and grasped at his shining cloak: but it passed through his fingers and he fell to his knees.

"I'd not do that," Dubhain said, squatting nearby, his eyes aglow and wicked.

"Let him go," Caith shouted at the chill and mocking faces above, about him. "Let my brother go. I never rescued him to give him to you."

"But you didn't save him," Nuallan said. "Safe and sound, you said. Was that not the bargain, mac Sliabhin? Would you ask more now?"

Dubhain drew back his lips in a half-grin, half-grimace. "Listen," the phooka said, "don't be reckless. You have the curse on you. It's all yours now. Didn't we help you? We've more than kept our bargain. What else have you to give up, beyond your scruples? Think, man."

Caith managed a laugh, despairing as it was; then the laugh died in his throat, for the Sidhe glow brightened, showing him where he was, in a small clearing at a ford, where a sleeping company sat sleeping horses, heads bowed, bodies slumped, and the rain on them like jewels, as if time had stopped here and all the world were wrapped in nightmares.

"They should not have come here," said one of the Sidhe.

"No man should," said another.

"Now, mac Sliabhan, what will you pay," asked Nuallan, "to free the boy from *us*?"

Caith turned a bleak look on him, blinking in the rain. "Why, whatever I have, curse you. Take me. Let the rest go. All of them. I'm worth it. Isn't that what you've most wanted—to have one of Sliabhin's blood in your reach? And I'm far more guilty than the boy."

"You've not asked what the curse is," said Nuallan.

"You'll tell me when it suits you."

"Torment," said Nuallan, "to suffer torment all your days, mac Sliabhin—the boy, oh, aye, he's free. We accept your offering; he's no matter to us. The curse is yours alone."

"Then let him go!"

"I shall do more than that," Nuallan said; and bent, the tallest and fairest of all his fellows, and gathered the boy into his arms ever so gently, as if he had been no weight at all. He bore him to the sleeping riders; and the light about him fell on their faces. It was Raghallach foremost among them; and Cinnfhail's shieldman; and others of Gleatharan. And Nuallan set Brian in Raghallach's arms on the saddlebow, sleeping child in the keeping of the sleeping rider, whose face was bruised and battered with wounds from Dun Mhor's cellars.

"What have you done?" Caith asked in horror. "Sidhe, what have you done?"

"Ah," said Nuallan, looking at him, "but they will get on well, don't you think?—Raghallach will remember a thing he never did; but it will seem to him he was a great hero. And so the boy will remember the brave warrior who bore him away and took him safe to Gleatharan. Oh, aye, they'll wake at dawn, and think themselves all heroes; and so men will say of them forever. Is that not generous of me?"

Caith let out a breath, having gotten to his feet. He clenched his fists. But it looked apt, the tired small boy, asleep in safety, the honest man who sheltered him. "You could make him forget the rest," he said.

"You've nothing left to trade."

"For your own kindness' sake—if it exists."

"I've done that—already." The Sidhe all were fading, leaving dark about, and the gleam of phooka eyes. But Nuallan took Caith's arm. "Come with me," he said.

10

CAITH WAS ALONE then, left utterly alone in a place where the sun blinded him, and when his eyes had forgotten the dark the light seemed soft. There were fields and hills—fair and green, spangled with gold flowers. Herds of horses, each the equal of Dathuil, ran free, and trees grew straight and fair on the hillsides.

No one hindered him. Caith wandered this beautiful place waiting to die; and then taking comfort in it, for it seemed no heart could grieve here long except for greater causes than he possessed. He felt thirst; he slaked it at a stream over which trees bent under the weight of their fruit.

The water washed the pain from him. It healed his heart and when he washed his face in it he felt stronger than he had ever been.

He considered the fruit and risked it, growing reckless and fey and calm all at once, as if no death could touch him here, nor any grievous thing. Only then he felt afraid, for he felt a presence before he saw it, and looked up.

"It gives the Sight," said Nuallan . . . for Nuallan

was suddenly there, astride Dathuil, bright as the
setting sun. Dathuil dipped his head to drink, and
the Sidhe slid lightly down to stand on the grassy
margin.

"And what will you ask for that, Sidhe?"

"Nothing here has price."

Caith thought on that, taking what leisure he
had to think. Every saying of the Sidhe seemed tangled, full of riddles, and he felt unequal to them,
and small. "I've been waiting for you," he said.

"For the curse. Oh, aye, that matter. But it is
settled. Or will be." The Sidhe looked less terrible
than before. There was pity in his eyes. "I like you
well, man. You bargain well—for a man. Would you
know the truth—whose son you are?"

"Sliabhin's."

"The boy is Gaelan's. Half brother to you. And
innocent. Come." The tall Sidhe knelt beside the
brook. "Look. Look into the stream."

Caith looked, kneeling cautiously on the margin—
and his heart turned in him, so that he almost fell,
for it was the night sky he was looking into with
the day still above him. "Ah!" he said and lost his
balance.

Nuallan caught his arm and drew him back safe
on the margin. "Nay, nay, that were a death neither
man nor Sidhe should wish. An endless one. Look.
Is there a thing you would wish to see? These waters
show you anything dear to your heart. Would you
see your brother?"

"Aye," Caith murmured, foreknowing a wound-
ing. The Fair Folk were terrible even in their
kindness.

The stars gave way to green hills, to Dun Gorm in the sunlight. A boy raced on a fine white horse, the wind in his hair, untrammeled joy in his eyes—

"Is that Brian? But he's *older*—"

"He's fourteen—Ah, you're thinking of others now—oh, aye, Raghallach—Brian follows him about; and Deirdre—she's grown very fair, has she not? Like Cinnfhail's own son, Brian is; and his queen's, the darling of their fading years, he is. The lad remembers very little of that year, only that it was terrible; he remembers fire and the long ride, and Raghallach bringing him away—it's thorough hero-worship. He doesn't remember you at all, save as one of Raghallach's men."

Caith bit his lip. "Good."

"Would you have it? Would you have what Brian has?"

"There's cost."

"In their world, always."

"His cost."

"Aye."

"No. I won't." Caith kept looking, until the image faded, until the abyss was back. He stood up as Nuallan did, there upon the brink. The gulf was below him again, the fall so easy from this place. He turned his back to it, there on the very edge, waiting as Nuallan set his hand lightly on his arm.

"Go your way," said Nuallan.

"Go?"

"Just go. You're free."

Nuallan let fall his hand. Caith turned away from the void, walked a little distance in disbelief, and then the rage got through. He turned back again, shaking with his anger. "Curse you, *curse* you to play games with me! You're no different than *his* sort, Sliabhin's, Hagan's. I've known that sort all my life. Is it your revenge—to laugh at me?"

"Oh, not to laugh, mac Sliabhin. Not to laugh." Nuallan's voice was full of pity and vast sorrow. "Torment is your curse; and I know none worse nor gentler than to have drunk and eaten here—and to know it forever irrecoverable. I have spared you what I could, my friend. . . ."

"Nuallan—" Caith began.

But the dark of the Sidhe-woods of Gleann Gleatharan was about him again, and the cold, and mortality, in which he shivered. He had the ache of his wounds back; and the gnawing of hunger and remorse in his belly.

"A curse on you!" he cried in the night of his own stained world.

He heard only a moving in the brush, and saw there the gleam of two eyes like coals. Dubhain was there, in boy's shape, a naked ruffian again.

"I am still with you," the phooka said. "This is *my* place."

Caith turned his shoulder to Dubhain and walked on, lost in this mortal woods and knowing it. He walked, until he knew that he was alone.

THE VISIONS crowded in on him, too vivid for a while: the vision of Dun Gorm that he had seen; and his brother growing up—but never must he go there, nor to the ruins of Dun Mhor, where he was a murderer and worse. His new Sight told him this, not acute, but dull, like a wound that hurt when he touched it, when he thought of the things he wanted and knew them lost.

There was no life for him but banditry, and regret, and remembering forever, remembering a land where everything was fair and clean.

"I'll give you a ride," the phooka offered in his dreams, on the next dark night when Caith slept fitfully, his belly gnawed with hunger. "O man, you need not be stubborn about it. I like you well. So does Nuallan. He did let you go—"

—the phooka took more solid shape, seated on a stump as Caith dreamed he waked. "—O man, don't you know Nuallan could have done far worse? He repented the curse. He wished it unsaid. But a Sidhe's word binds him. Especially his kind."

But there was no comfort in Caith's dreams, when he dreamed of the beauty he had seen, and of ease of pain; and when he rose up in the morning and had the miles always before him.

"I'll bear ye," the phooka offered wistfully.

"No," Caith said, and walked on, stubborn in his loss. Where he was going next he had no idea. He looked down from the height of the green hills and saw Gleann Gleatharan, and Dun Gorm with its herds fair and its fields wide; but he came no nearer to it than this, to stand on its hills and want it as he wanted that land he saw only in his dreams.

"I am your friend," the phooka said, whispering from behind him.

It was well a man should have one friend. Caith

held his cloak about him against the wind and kept walking, passing by Dun Gorm and all it had of peace.

"Come," he whispered to the wind. "Come with me, phooka, if you like."

VII

THE SHIP APPROACHES dock. The star glows in the window, red and so dim they do not need the visual shielding. We can look on its spotted face directly, if not for long. Its light momentarily dyes the table, the ice in our glasses, the crystal liquid, the bubbles that rise and burst. Then the ship's gentle rotation carries the view away.

There are no planets in this system. Only ice and iron. And a starstation.

Bags are packed. Most of the passengers are leaving. Soon the take-hold will sound.

"Packed?" I ask.

"Yes," you say. And gaze at the unfamiliar stars, thinking what thoughts I do not guess. "They're going to have to ship that poor fellow home. Next ship back. He just can't take it out here."

"His world always traveled the universe," I say. "He thinks it's abandoned him. Maybe it has. He thinks he'd be safe there. I'm not sure he'll ever feel quite so safe again."

"You're immune?"

I think about it. I see miniature worlds in the bubbles amid the ice in my glass. Microcosm in crystal. "I haven't left home," I say. "I don't know what it is to leave home. And I'm as safe here as most places."

"You mean the universe."

"That, yes."

The alarm sounds then. I down my drink quickly, we both do. I rise and toss glass and ice into the disposal. Yours goes after it.

We stare at each other then, at the point of farewells.

There is no choice, of course. This is a transfer-point. Our separate ships are already waiting at the station.

And they keep their own schedules.

Science Fiction and Fantasy from Methuen Paperbacks

While every effort is made to keep prices low, it is sometimes necessary to increase prices at short notice. Methuen Paperbacks reserves the right to show new retail prices on covers which may differ from those previously advertised in the text or elsewhere.

The prices shown below were correct at the time of going to press.

☐	413 55450 3	**Half-Past Human**	T J Bass	£1.95
☐	413 58160 8	**Rod of Light**	Barrington J Bayley	£2.50
☐	417 04130 6	**Colony**	Ben Bova	£2.50
☐	413 57910 7	**Orion**	Ben Bova	£2.95
☐	417 07280 5	**Voyagers**	Ben Bova	£1.95
☐	417 06760 7	**Hawk of May**	Gillian Bradshaw	£1.95
☐	413 56290 5	**Chronicles of Morgaine**	C J Cherryh	£2.95
☐	413 51310 6	**Downbelow Station**	C J Cherryh	£1.95
☐	413 51350 5	**Little Big**	John Crowley	£3.95
☐	417 06200 1	**The Golden Man**	Philip K Dick	£1.75
☐	413 58860 2	**Wasp**	Eric Frank Russell	£2.50
☐	413 59770 9	**The Alchemical Marriage of Alistair Crompton**	Robert Sheckley	£2.25
☐	413 41920 7	**Eclipse**	John Shirley	£2.50
☐	413 59990 6	**All Flesh is Grass**	Clifford D Simak	£2.50
☐	413 58800 9	**A Heritage of Stars**	Clifford D Simak	£2.50
☐	413 55590 9	**The Werewolf Principle**	Clifford D Simak	£1.95
☐	413 58640 5	**Where the Evil Dwells**	Clifford D Simak	£2.50
☐	413 54600 4	**Raven of Destiny**	Peter Tremayne	£1.95
☐	413 56840 7	**This Immortal**	Roger Zelazny	£1.95
☐	413 56850 4	**The Dream Master**	Roger Zelazny	£1.95
☐	413 41550 3	**Isle of the Dead**	Roger Zelazny	£2.50

All these books are available at your bookshop or newsagent, or can be ordered direct from the publisher. Just tick the titles you want and fill in the form below.

Methuen Paperbacks, Cash Sales Department,
PO Box 11, Falmouth,
Cornwall TR10 109EN.

Please send cheque or postal order, no currency, for purchase price quoted and allow the following for postage and packing:

UK	60p for the first book, 25p for the second book and 15p for each additional book ordered to a maximum charge of £1.90.
BFPO and Eire	60p for the first book, 25p for the second book and 15p for each next seven books, thereafter 9p per book.
Overseas Customers	£1.25 for the first book, 75p for the second book and 28p for each subsequent title ordered.

NAME (Block Letters) ....

ADDRESS...

....